THE MYSTERIOUS TONGUE
OF DR. VERMILION

ROBERT ISENBERG

backpackmedia

Phoenix, Arizon

Backpack Media, LLC
615 E. Portland St., Unit 130,
Phoenix, AZ 85004

Printed in the United States of America.

For you.

CONTENTS

"I will have no locked cupboards in my life."

— *Gertrude Bell*

THE INCIDENT OF THE CUBAN AIRSHIP

January, 1921

I
T WAS NEARLY MIDNIGHT WHEN ROYCE ABBOTT saw
himself in the mirror and decided he wanted to die.

He felt silly, leaning against the oak bar, his forehead
glistening with sweat, as the barman set another tumbler of
spiced rum before him. His head wobbled downward, and his
brain acknowledged the ice cubes floating in bilgy liquid. It
took him a moment to remember the cigarette burning between
his lips, and he slowly removed the butt and stubbed it into a
chipped white ashtray.

Silly, yes, because Havana was the last place on earth
anyone should want to die. The room vibrated with bongos,
trumpets, and the stamping feet of dancers. Women in tissue
dresses whirled around the floor, smiling their infectious Latin
smiles, while fat American men tottered to the rhythm,
laughing gutturally.

Royce had not yet considered the mechanics of his death.
He knew so little of Havana, only its boozy clubs and hotels,
and any tools of self-destruction seemed blunt. Should he
throw himself into the calm Caribbean? Leap from a three-
story building? Step into slow-moving traffic? Pay an unmet
mobster to rub him out? All these plots felt intangible.

1

"Order one for me?" shouted a voice, and Royce winced as Albert appeared, slapping hands on Royce's shoulders. "Can you believe this place? What a madhouse! I think I could live here forever!"

Royce hung his head, thinking of something to say.

"Come on, old sport, don't leave me out to dry!" chided Albert. "Tomorrow it's back to Prohibition! Let's drink up while we can, shall we?"

Royce felt cloudy as he waved a finger, trying to catch the barman's attention. The people around him were only a flurry of movement. He wanted to leave so badly that his stomach ached, but he had nowhere else to go.

"Hey, *amigo!*" shouted Albert. At first Royce didn't realize Albert was talking to him, but then his friend grabbed his face in both hands and pulled him close. Albert stared at him, smiling wildly, squeezing Royce's cheeks together like an anxious grandmother. "What's with the long face? We've had a *time*, haven't we?"

Royce summoned only enough enthusiasm to nod his head, which satisfied his friend. Albert released his hands, then smacked Royce playfully across the jaw.

"Snap out of it, will you? She's only a girl. You'll find another one! How about one of these Cuban dames? Have you even noticed the scenery?"

Royce turned toward the barman again, who was only a blur among blurs.

"You're a crackup, you know that?" said Albert. "How about that girl over there? I'd swear she's making eyes at you."

The statement gave Royce vertigo. A girl? Noticing *him?* He scanned the room, finding only whirling dancers and waiters in cream-colored suits. But then he spotted her, and his eyes cleared up, as if waking from a dream. He couldn't believe what he beheld.

"I'll be jiggered..." Royce whispered.

"You'll be *what?*" Albert shouted.

"I... I know that girl."

"What do you mean, you *know* her?"

Royce took only a second to make his decision. He slammed back his rum, wiped the icy rivulets from his lips, and sauntered forward.

It was her. In all these years, the girl had barely changed. She was still youthful and slim, her skin papery beneath the light of the chandeliers. The profile of her face looked drawn in Indian ink—slivers of eyes, a jotted mouth, the subtlest point of a nose. She looked demure and pensive, the curve of her dark bob pressed beneath a black cloche hat. The lack of color was funereal, but Royce adored her mordant presence—just as he had always adored it.

Royce approached, and then, just when he had nearly arrived, the girl turned her head and grinned wryly, as if she'd been expecting him all along.

"Why, hello, stranger," she said. Her alto was as acerbic as ever. The way she looked up at him through her eyelashes stopped him dead.

Royce swelled with a joy he hadn't felt since time immemorial, and a smile burst across his face.

"*Elizabeth Crowne!*" he declared.

"The one and only," she said, and reached for her martini glass. She lifted it to her lips, but then paused to adjust the olives with a finger. "Last I checked, this stool was free."

"Hmm?" Royce then spotted the empty stool beside Elizabeth and exclaimed, "Oh!" He seated himself quickly, like a schoolboy late for class.

Elizabeth swiveled her shoulders toward him and set the glass down, then rested a hand on her palm. The movement was so ineffably graceful, the way a cat arranges itself on a chaise longue.

"I left my abacus at home," she said. "You'll have to tell me how long it's been."

Royce snorted a laugh, and the sound embarrassed him. He covered his nose with a fist. "Um… well… when did we graduate?" He spread his fingers and examined his robust brass ring, where the name ST. LUKE'S MEDICAL ACADEMY was etched around a green stone. "According to this, it was 1913. So I suppose it's been… eight years, now."

"Eight years," echoed Elizabeth. She sat up straight and examined a distant point. "At least it *would* have been eight years, had I graduated."

"Oh, yes!" said Royce. "I'd forgotten!"

"A fact worth forgetting," said Elizabeth. "So—what brings you to Havana?"

Royce thought for a moment. What *had* brought him here? Albert, obviously. It had been his idea to get away from the hospital, spend some time among swaying Caribbean palm trees, far from the January sleet of Manhattan. Royce had gone along with it, though the sunshine was blinding and the heat tormented him day and night. He had spent the boat ride to Havana staving off seasickness, and his nights with Albert were so soaked in hooch that he could barely discern one event from another. A week in Havana had produced few memories, only cerebral snapshots of their hotel room, promenades in the wide streets, then music, dancing, liquor, women—mostly observed from the safety of a wicker chair. He might as well have seen a picture show.

"I don't remember," he blurted. "And isn't that a relief to say? To be quite honest… I haven't any idea why I'm here."

Elizabeth smirked, but not unkindly, as if she were in on the same unspoken joke.

"You know," she said. "I wouldn't kill for fresh air. But I'd consider manslaughter."

Royce felt himself knitting his brow, trying to decode her words.

"That's your cue to escort me outside," said Elizabeth. She hopped down from her stool, smoothed her dress, and then, as an afterthought, waved her hand toward the bar. "And pay my tab, of course."

As they strolled down the cobblestone streets, the corners lit with pools of orange streetlamps, Royce felt swollen with excitement. A moment ago he prayed for oblivion, but the very sight of Elizabeth filled him with fond remembrance. As they now walked abreast through the din of Havana, every sound seemed enhanced—the Spanish voices in the alleys, the clop of horses, the revving of a motorcycle engine. Cars and foot traffic circled slowly around them as they walked, a tunnel of sensations.

"I feel like such a fool," said Royce. "I haven't asked you why *you're* here."

"Business," said Elizabeth.

"Not the usual place for a woman to find herself alone."

"Who says I'm alone?" Elizabeth abruptly changed trajectory and headed across the street, careless to passing traffic, until she arrived at a bold white statue hovering above a circular fountain. The figure had an androgynous face but a full and naked bosom; she was draped in robes, topped with a headdress, and she clutched a round shield at her side. She was slouched but powerful, a regal presence. "Fuente de la India," said Elizabeth reverentially.

"And who might she be?"

"Habana," said Elizabeth. "An Indian queen. The namesake of the city."

"Is she now?" Royce examined the statue's dragon-like dolphins that spat arcs of water into the fountain, which was in turn shaped like interlocked half-shells. He saw the dark plumes of palm trees wafting above, the imperious buildings beyond. This was the Parque Central, he surmised, the heart of the city he had failed to truly explore. "Are you an art dealer, then?"

Elizabeth leaned against the edge of the fountain and sniffed. "I should be so lucky. Sublime life, those art dealers."

Royce felt a surge of inspiration. He placed a shoe on the edge of the fountain and leaned against his knee. It was a debonair pose, but he aimed to live up to it. "May I ask a question?"

"I never like that preamble," Elizabeth said.

"Why should an intelligent girl—like yourself—leave medical school, anyhow? Doesn't make a lick of sense, does it?"

Elizabeth smiled humorlessly, then leaned back, her eyes trained on the violet-black sky. The way she arched, so confident and carefree, stuck thorns in Royce's throat, but he maintained his stance.

"There was a professor," said Elizabeth slowly, "I didn't agree with." She took a purging breath. "Let's leave it at that, shall we?"

"Let's do that," said Royce, and he forced a grin, as if willing himself to be handsome. "Then what have you been up to all this time?"

"I traveled," said Elizabeth.

"The European tour, I presume?"

"Europe," she said thoughtfully. "Egypt. China. India. Indochina. A stint in the Congo, if you'd believe it. A good bit of the Eastern Hemisphere, really. But if you ask me, Pittsburgh still takes the cake."

Royce felt his jaw go slack. He removed his shoe from the fountain and stepped back, then slowly enveloped his hands in his jacket pockets. He was suddenly aware of his perspiring brow.

"Egypt, you say? *And* China?"

"Not at the same time," said Elizabeth. "There were certainly some months in between."

"And you were—nursing?"

"No," said Elizabeth. "Not exactly. But what about you? Didn't you marry that one gal—the curly-haired one? What was her name?"

"Prudy," murmured Royce, feeling himself deflate.

"Prudy, of course! Where is she? You didn't leave her in New York?"

"Leave her, no," said Royce. "Rather, she left me."

"Oh, dear," said Elizabeth. "Well, every silver lining has a raincloud."

Royce smiled at this, then tapped his toe against a maverick stone. "It's terribly funny," he blurted. "I've delivered two hundred newborns. All shapes and sizes. Every kind of mother. I've coached scores of women through their pregnancies. But somehow, for whatever reason, Prudy and I couldn't conceive our own. She couldn't stand it. Month after month, she yearned for a child. She saw children in the park and burst into tears. She—" Royce faltered. "After a while, she couldn't take it anymore. She left. And I won't deny it, Elizabeth, I've felt like half a man ever since."

Elizabeth nodded, then shrugged her shoulders. "Well, every man deserves to drown his sorrows now and then. Even half-men."

Royce snickered at this as he gazed at the pavement. "When do you head back?"

"Tomorrow," said Elizabeth.

"What a coincidence!" exclaimed Royce, perhaps too boisterously. "So do we!"

"Which liner?"

"Oh, no liner. Albert—oh, for goodness sakes! You remember Albert! He was in our chemistry class!"

If Elizabeth felt any excitement, she did not betray it.

"Albert," she said. "Well, how about that."

"Yes, this whole trip was his idea. I would never have thought of it myself, but he's a good friend, and he said, 'You should take a holiday.' And he was right, of course. But Albert, he has a thing for aviation. He seems to think the future is in aircraft. I think he's lost his marbles, but when he booked the tickets, I thought, 'That's a splendid idea—'"

Elizabeth was standing now. The dry gaiety had drained from her face. She stared at him, stonily, as he continued to ramble. At last she interrupted. "You're not *flying*, are you?"

"I am indeed!" burst Royce. "I mean, *we* are, Albert and I. First thing tomorrow morning. And you'll never believe it— we're flying in a *dirigible*."

"Oh, Royce," said Elizabeth in a dark tone. "You really mustn't do that."

"Come now, Elizabeth, nothing to fear. It's just a big balloon, is all."

"Yes, I know what a dirigible is," Elizabeth snapped. "But you really ought to take a boat."

"It's an adventure!" exclaimed Royce. "It's the perfect cure, don't you think? See the world from a thousand feet in the air. Get some perspective. Honestly, I think it's the best medication there is—"

"Royce," said Elizabeth grimly. "Listen to me. I understand, but I think you'd better take a boat. You can fly in a blimp whenever you like. Just don't take *this* one."

"Elizabeth, you're talking crazy. Why not *this* one? They're all the same, aren't they?"

"It's not the—" Elizabeth stopped herself and waved away the sentence. "You're flying the Líneas Aéreas de Corazón, I presume?"

"That's right. How'd you know?"

"They're the only airship service between Cuba and the States."

Royce grimaced. "I suppose that narrows it down."

"I just think you should reconsider," said Elizabeth.

"But it's already arranged," protested Royce. "We fly to Miami, then take the sleeper to New York. It's our last hurrah, you see. And I've only flown in a single airplane in my entire life. I think it'll be splendid. Think of it—the Caribbean from the air! The height of luxury!"

In the following silence, Royce registered Elizabeth's disappointment, but he couldn't understand the cause. Why shouldn't he fly? And why should Elizabeth object? Wasn't it just like a woman to ruin a happy moment? When did Elizabeth become such a killjoy?

"Well, at least think about it," said Elizabeth, and she turned toward the street. It took Royce a moment to realize she was walking away.

"But Elizabeth, are you leaving?"

"I'm giving myself a curfew," she called over her shoulder.

"But when will I see you again?"

She had nearly vanished into the shadows when Royce heard Elizabeth say, "Probably tomorrow. I've booked the same flight."

Royce and Albert stepped out of the taxi and tossed the driver 20 centavos. The moment Royce's shoes struck gravel, he stood stock-still, enthralled by the sight before him: The dirigible was larger than he could have imagined, like an overturned skyscraper dominating the sky. It blocked the rising sun and cloaked the vast greensward in shadow. The city of Havana stood far from here, and the scattered whitewashed houses glowed cheerfully in the morning sun.

Albert adjusted his shaded round spectacles and belched into his gloved hand. "I say, that sunlight is a bear." The cabbie opened the car's trunk and pulled out their four suitcases, which Albert and Royce then toted across the well-mowed field, toward the titanic spheroid.

"I didn't even hear you come back last night," said Royce. "How late were you out?"

"I haven't the foggiest," confessed Albert. "Someone nabbed my pocket watch."

"They didn't!"

"They did. And it's a damn shame. It was a gift from a girl I used to go with. Amy Sue. That watch was the only good thing about that courtship." He paused in mid-step and lowered his glasses. "And I'll have you know I blame you entirely."

"Me?"

"Who else? You abandoned me in that place. You know I can't be trusted."

"Well, I do know *that*," admitted Royce. "You have the restraint of a starving hyena."

"I'm glad you agree," said Albert, smugly smiling. "Now tell me you have some spare aspirin. I'm all out."

But Royce didn't catch this last part, because he caught Elizabeth in his field of vision, and suddenly nothing else mattered. There she stood, beneath the bulbous zeppelin, clasping a large carpetbag in both hands. Upon spotting Royce, she smiled dryly, and he could barely stifle his blush. He had so many questions—why had she discouraged him from flying, if she herself had booked the same passage? Indeed, what business did she even have in Cuba? For that matter, how had such an attractive woman evaded marriage all these years, for surely she wouldn't come here without her husband?

"Howdy," she said. "Going my way?"

"So it seems," said Royce.

"Nowhere to go but up," Elizabeth added. "And is that Albert I see?"

Albert slowly removed his glasses. "I say, is that—Elizabeth

Crowne? As I live and breathe!" He extended a hand, but Elizabeth merely grimaced until Albert retracted it.

"If you wouldn't mind breathing a little less, I'm sure we'd all appreciate it," said Elizabeth. "From the smell of you, I'm surprised there's a bottle of rum left in the Caribbean."

Albert looked amused by this. "Not *much* rum, I'm sure. Royce and I had a time, didn't we?" He clapped Royce on the shoulder, so roughly that his friend let out a sputter. "Was that you sitting at the bar last night? I thought it was the light playing tricks on me."

"It must be kismet," Elizabeth muttered.

"You're traveling lighter than we are," observed Albert cheerily.

"I checked a bag. Too heavy to carry, I'm afraid."

Royce smiled sheepishly, now embarrassed by his circumstances. Divorce, hooch, and a boorish friend—how could he make a worse impression on a woman he had once so thoroughly admired? He had been younger, back at St. Luke's. He had been free and full of spirit. Elizabeth had been a fond acquaintance, yet hardly a friend. He would have described her as *a lovely girl*, a phrase meaning nothing at all. But now he appreciated her so much better—her plain prettiness, her youthful face punctuated by cunning eyes. She was a woman who could seem ageless and sage at the same time. In hindsight, calling her a lovely girl was like calling the Queen of Sheba congenial.

"Shall we?" Elizabeth swiveled on her heel toward the waiting staircase, which led into the bowels of the airship. She was just beyond earshot when Albert leaned in and whispered.

"She's a minx, isn't she? If I had a girl like that, I'd never leave the boudoir."

Royce glared at him, feeling a flash of temper.

"Don't deny it, old boy," said Albert, adjusting his bowtie. "Surely it crossed your mind."

As they stepped aboard, Royce took in the novel scenery: The floor was tiled black and white, and the commons area was roomier than he'd expected, half the size of a tennis court, with plush chairs evenly spaced around circular tables. The rails were polished wood, as was the matching trim, and the place felt both streamlined and homey.

His trance was broken when a porter said, *"May I take your bags, sir?"*

The voice startled Royce, and when he saw the face that spoke, he couldn't help but pause. The young man was not Cuban, nor any Spanish race, but a figure cast in porcelain white. His lips were thin and pink. He had a narrow head and golden, wiry hair that seemed sculpted into a perfect wave. He wore a double-breasted coat and bellhop's cap, but his expression was also coy. Royce could barely tear his eyes away, but he couldn't tell why. The porter was slender as a girl and his voice was serpentine, yet he emanated a palpable charisma. Royce felt himself weak in the knees, tingling unexpectedly in his arms; his heart raced, as if meeting a lover for the first time.

"Yes... please," he said, his voice cracking. "Cabin number seven."

"Lucky number seven," said the porter, who stepped forward and clasped the bags' handles. Their knuckles brushed together, and a refreshing coolness seeped into Royce's skin.

Royce was still swooning when he found his cabin. The room was small and quaint—a pair of small beds, a reading lamp, and framed posters advertising Havana nightclubs.

The porter set down the bags and turned to Royce, who dug a coin out of his pocket and pressed it into the young man's palm. But the porter crossed his thumb over Royce's hand, preserving contact.

"If you should need anything," whispered the porter, *"my name*

is Corwin."

Before Royce could summon a single breath, Corwin turned and quit the room.

Royce fully expected to turn around and see Albert gawking at him. He felt drunker than ever before, as if he'd imbibed a full bottle of wine. Yet Royce was surprised by Albert's expression; he looked thoughtful, even a little dazed. He still held his bags' handles, as if forgetting to release them.

"Very..." Albert's head cocked sideways. "Very *pleasant* service."

The way Albert spoke, so distant and preoccupied, Royce sensed that his friend felt the same strange feeling. They were both heady and lost. They stood in silence for long minutes, having no idea what to do next.

In the common room, Royce and Albert gazed through the broad, slanted windows. The ground shrank below them; the fields receded, distant hills flattened, and the roads became mere veins through the gray splotches of towns. Royce relished the perception of climbing higher, even as his eardrums crackled and popped.

"Divine," said Albert. "This must be what angels feel like."

Once the ribbon of beaches slipped away beyond the expanse of blue ocean, and the white outlines of waves were too far-off to distinguish, Albert turned to Royce and said, "Well, I say it's time for a drink."

"Are you serious?" Royce blurted.

"Haven't you heard? There's no Prohibition at five thousand feet."

"There's hardly Prohibition at sea level, if you know where to look," snapped Royce. "But after a night like yours, how can you even think of it?"

"That's the trick," said Albert, snapping his fingers. "You

mustn't think at all."

They found a corner by the window and seated themselves, crossing legs over knees. Albert drew a cigar from his breast pocket and sniffed it.

"It's such a waste," said Albert smugly. "No man should visit Cuba without smoking a decent cigar."

"You know I'm allergic," said Royce.

"I know you *say* you're allergic."

"It's the type of tobacco. Or the way it's rolled. Anyhow, they smell like a campfire."

Albert rolled his eyes, raised a lit match to his cigar, and puffed decadently.

Royce surveyed the room, where a handful of passengers were scattered about. The airship only contained about twenty cabins, and from the looks of things, they were well below capacity: A bearded man sat in the corner, smoking a stout pipe. Two graying women in floppy hats occupied a center table, one sipping tea and reading a splayed book while the other knitted. A particularly large woman sat on the opposite side of the room, clutching a Chihuahua in her arms and murmuring into its triangular ears.

"So much for decent company," said Albert. "There isn't a cocktail in the world that could make this bunch interesting."

A waiter appeared. Again, Royce was taken aback. The waiter was dressed identically to the porter, but this man looked slightly older. He had chestnut hair slicked back, a trim mustache, and penetrating gray eyes. Royce swallowed deeply, as if tasting water in a time of drought. He felt himself sinking deeper in the upholstery of his chair. But now Royce's reaction was more familiar to him; he felt strangely comforted.

"*Gentleman, may I offer you a drink,*" said the waiter.

Never in his long history of nightclubs and hotels had Royce heard such a voice. The man nearly sang his words. His voice was a crooner's baritone; his diction was precise. Royce felt that he could ask this man for anything, and he felt a surging desire to do so.

"Do you…" Albert tried to speak, but he struggled. "Do you… that is… might you have a signature cocktail? Something…" He waved the cigar in the air, then laughed self-consciously. "I'm sorry. I'm a little off today."

"*Our signature cocktail,*" sang the waiter, "*is called the Blood Meridian—a mix of scotch, grenadine, and lemon. I heartily recommend it, myself.*"

Albert nodded sluggishly but said nothing. He looked as tranquilized as Royce's hospital patients.

"Two, please," said Royce quickly.

"*As you wish,*" said the waiter. Then, in mid-turn, he added, "*My name is Benoît. Should you need anything.*"

When Benoît vanished through a swishing door, Royce felt himself return slowly to normal. But the feeling didn't please him, for normalcy did not compare to that delectable feeling. Every part of him was titillated, alight, the way opium was said to flood the body with euphoria. Now it drained away, and he resented the loss of that sensation. The memory of the waiter now seemed vague, as if witnessed in a dream only moments before waking. Royce's mouth was numb, as was his ability to conjure words. When Albert finally spoke, it might have been a thunderclap.

"What unusual names," he murmured.

"What was that?" rejoined Royce, whose tongue now moved like granite.

"Benoît. Corwin. Not exactly Tom, Dick, or Harry, you know. And not a Spaniard among them. I wonder where this thing is registered?" He gazed dreamily at the ceiling, as if the answer might be printed there. "Quite the feat of engineering, wouldn't you say? I'd say we're damn well living in the future."

The sound of Albert's banter eased Royce back into a proper mindset, and he sat up. He rubbed his face, and when he returned his hands to his knees, he looked up and saw Elizabeth, striding toward them. Royce nearly balked.

Elizabeth had donned a riding outfit, the type worn by equestrians—puffy pantaloons and a jacket over a ruffled blouse. Her boots were high and tightly fastened.

"I say," scoffed Albert. "Not exactly dressed for the opera, I see."

"Luckily," said Elizabeth, "I have no one to impress."

She set down a large leather medicine bag, then plopped into a half-moon chair. "I trust you gentlemen have already ordered something."

"Just now," said Albert. "Although I wish I'd known you were coming."

"Quite all right, Albert. After all, you don't know my tastes." She smiled to herself, then turned her attention to Royce. "So how is the world of medicine, these days?"

"Oh," mumbled Royce, shaking his head. "It's treating me well, overall. It's a decent hospital. Nearly two hundred beds. Low morbidity. Every day is different." He shrugged. "Just work as usual, really. How about you? Are you—"

Royce searched for a question, but he didn't know where to begin. Despite his earlier curiosity, no phrasing felt right. Now he remembered the dark side of Elizabeth, the way she grinned in that superior way, sizing up the people around her. Her wit had always been sharp, even malicious. No one had seemed to know much about her, and he didn't expect much reward for his efforts.

Then he felt a spark of inspiration. "Are you back in— Pittsburgh, was it?"

"Pittsburgh *was* it," said Elizabeth. "And yes, in fact, I'm living there now."

"What are you up to, then?"

She took a long breath, as if devising a way to respond. "I'm living in my family house. Alone, it turns out."

"Oh. Did your parents—pass on?"

"Well, they passed on to new real estate," said Elizabeth. "They've separated, sadly. My parents decided, after thirty-five years, that they get along better when they never see or hear from each other. They couldn't decide who should have the house, so they gave it to me."

"Do I remember you had a brother?"

"One brother, one sister," said Elizabeth. "Also far-flung, these days. It seems even close-knit families can still unravel."

"I'm sorry to hear that," said Royce.

"I'm sorry to say it," Elizabeth said. "Let's talk about something cheerier, shall we? Don't you boys have a baseball game you can argue about?"

"Come on, Liz," uttered Albert suddenly. "We all know you dropped out of school. Inquiring minds want to know! What happened to the great protégée? There isn't one graduate of St. Luke's who doesn't wonder what happened to you. Have some decency and tell us what you're up to."

Elizabeth's smile stretched wide—a crafty visage. "Would you believe I married young? Bore twins? Spend my days on a loveseat, waiting for my hubby to get back from the office?"

Albert leaned forward and jabbed a finger toward her. "I *wouldn't* believe it. Not for a second. The first woman to study at St. Luke's would be the last to live such drudgery. I don't care if the Pope says otherwise. Husbands and twins? For Liz Crowne? That's the tallest tale I ever heard."

Elizabeth looked pleased by this. She reached into her medicine bag and drew a slender white stick, which at first Royce took to be a cigarette, but then he saw the twisted paper, the tapered edges.

"Is that—?" he said.

Elizabeth looked askance at him, the cigarette pressed between her lips. "Ah och?" she said, then removed it to speak more clearly. "A roach, you mean? Why, yes it is. We all have

17

ROBERT ISENBERG

our poison."

"I've... I've just never seen one before," said Royce, trying to dampen his astonishment.

"Airships and cannabis. You *are* having a red-letter day. Does one of you gentleman have a light?"

A second later, Albert struck a match and held it toward Elizabeth. As she inhaled, Albert whipped the match through the air, dousing it among streamers of smoke. He said grimly, "Speaking of poison, I'd love to know where those drinks got off to. You can keep these, by the way. I have another packet." Albert slapped the matches on the table.

Elizabeth nodded her thanks, then exhaled a perfect stream of pungent smoke. Royce was compelled to wave it away from his face, but his old schoolmates seemed unperturbed. She only stared straight ahead, as if flipping backward through the book of her life.

"I'm an uncannologist," she said.

"A what?" said Royce.

"An uncan... uncann..." Albert gave up.

"Don't bother. I made it up. But I specialize in *the uncanny*."

"The uncanny," said Albert dully. "As in?"

Elizabeth puffed her cheeks pensively. "Things that defy traditional wisdom."

"Such as what? Black magic?"

"I don't like to call it magic," said Elizabeth. "But if it seems like magic, I'm interested."

"I don't understand," said Albert. "Do you mean to say you're chasing ghosts and... I can't think what else. Leprechauns?"

"Well, not leprechauns, no."

"Maybe you could give us an example?" said Royce patiently.

"Let's try that," Elizabeth said.

But then the waiter appeared. Benoît, the mustached man.

He cradled a tray in his squarely bent arm. His presence was abrupt—one moment the space was vacant, the next moment he was standing there, beaming.

"*Two Blood Meridians,*" he said, placing the drinks atop cocktail napkins between the two men. "*And for you, Madame?*"

Through the haze of resurging elation, Royce noticed something queer: Elizabeth did not look the man in the eye. She looked away, toward the floor, as if ashamed by his presence. But not ashamed—more *bothered*. But why should she be? Had she met this waiter before? And why should such a charming fellow provoke her? He had half a mind to call her on it, but he felt lethargic, muted. Even if he were moved to speak, he couldn't figure out how to say the words.

"Just a glass of water, thank you," Elizabeth said.

"*As you wish,*" said Benoît, who continued to watch her until he had taken several steps toward the kitchen door. When he was gone, Elizabeth took a moment and tried again.

"Let me give you that example," said Elizabeth. "I'm working on a case now, in fact, which might interest a pair of physicians. You are both familiar with rabies, of course."

"Well, not in the city," said Albert. "Maybe on rare occasion, but it's hardly rampant."

"Still, you know the symptoms."

"Of course!" proclaimed Albert. "Fever, madness, abstention from water..."

"That last one," said Elizabeth. "Isn't that interesting? A virus can make water repulsive to you. The very thing you need to survive, yet you'd rather die than taste it. A disease might change your psychology."

"Well, then, what of it?" Albert said impatiently, slurping his drink and roughly stirring the ice cubes with a straw.

"Now consider elephantiasis," said Elizabeth. "Or leprosy. Notice how they change a man's anatomy. Again, a mere infection, but it transforms the sufferer into—something different."

"Physically, maybe," offered Royce. "But that doesn't make them different *people*."

"Then suppose you found a virus that affects both mind and body," said Elizabeth, drawing on her roach. "You metamorphose. Your scent changes. You modify your diet, to match your changing nutritional needs. Could you imagine such a virus?"

"Well, nothing so extreme," said Royce. "I've never seen such a thing firsthand, I mean."

"Nor anything like it, I should add," said Albert. "Liz, what's all this about? Yes, diseases change our biology, by definition. But whatever parasite lurks in the darkest jungle isn't relevant to modern man. Until we see it, it's meaningless. We might as well imagine ourselves walking on the moon."

Elizabeth leaned back. "Maybe I *have* seen it."

"Well, I'd like to know where. Otherwise, your *uncannology* sounds like a lot of bunk."

Elizabeth smiled, then stubbed her roach into a waiting porcelain ashtray. "I think we should place a bet."

"A bet?"

"Yes. I think I can convince you that uncanny things do exist, and they're as relevant as anything you do in the operating room. I'm so sure of this, in fact, that I think I can persuade you before midnight."

"Now *that's* the Liz Crowne I remember," exclaimed Albert. "You're on. What's the wager?"

"If I win," said Elizabeth, "I'll be content to watch you eat your words."

"Easy enough," replied Albert. "And what will your risk?"

"Anything you like," said Elizabeth huskily. Her smile was so ravishing that Royce could barely stand to look at her. But then she turned blankly to her fingernails, which she examined with disinterest. "After all, I know I'm right."

"Best bet I ever placed," said Albert, raising a glass with satisfaction. "Cheers!"

Elizabeth nodded back, then turned her face away.

Again, Benoît appeared without warning, looming above them handsomely.

"*Your water, Madame,*" he said, setting a tumbler before Elizabeth.

When Benoît had stridden off, Elizabeth drew a small pillbox from her medicine bag and set several tablets on the table. An earthy scent emanated from them, reminding Royce of an herb garden. But it mixed so fluidly with the odor of cannabis that Royce couldn't tell which scent was which.

"Would anyone care for a pill?"

"For?" asked Albert.

"Seasickness. Or airsickness, I suppose. Whatever you'd call it up here."

"I've never had a problem before. Although Royce here might indulge."

"I'm fine," said Royce, feeling woozier than ever.

"Royce," said Elizabeth in a serious tone. "I would strongly recommend it."

Royce huffed and abruptly stood up. "Liz, it's very nice to see you. Genuinely, I'm happy we ran into each other. But you must think me quite stupid."

Elizabeth blinked at him, nonplussed.

"We must seem very funny to you," Royce continued, for tactful speech was now beyond his control. "A pair of bachelors, drinking away our best years. Sure, I can understand that. But I don't know why you'd toy with us. Strange viruses? Uncannology? And *cannabis*, for goodness' sakes…"

Royce caught the other passengers in the corner of his eye. He had forgotten they were there. They also looked glassy-eyed, but they glanced up, conscious of Royce's outburst. The one woman stopped knitting. The man's pipe settled in his lap. Even the puppy glanced his way, seized by curiosity.

"Royce—"

"I'm not a child, you know," spluttered Royce. "I don't get seasick, and I don't need your pills. And if you fancy Albert, by all means, spend some time with him. You two probably deserve each other. But I think I know what I need, and it's about time I figured it out. It's not pills or booze or idle chatter. It's just to be finally left alone." Then, as he stormed away, Royce half-shouted, "*Excuse me.*"

A minute later, he was back in his room, sobbing into a bundle of sheets.

Royce had no reason to wake, and yet his eyes fluttered open. His lashes were crusty and his saliva had moistened the pillow. The walls creaked faintly around him, and the cabin was dark. He squinted, trying to gain his bearings, and saw the outline of the empty bed a few feet away.

That scoundrel, he thought. *I'll bet Albert's necking with Elizabeth this very moment. I'll disown him for life, the cad.*

But why could he see anything at all? The light was dim, but not pitch-black. The cabin had no porthole, so when the lamp switched off, Royce should have seen nothing.

Then he saw the cracked door. It hung open only a few inches, but there was a sliver of space. And in that space, a pair of eyes watched him. Royce could see the black shape of a face, outlined by the silvery corridor beyond.

Yet Royce felt no alarm. The face was familiar—the chiseled countenance of Benoît.

All at once Royce was compelled to slide off his bed and push his feet into his shoes. He wafted across the cabin and touched the door, but when he arrived, Benoît turned around and slipped down the hall.

It was late, Royce could tell. The closed cabin doors offered no signs of life, not even a line of lamplight at their feet. The only illumination was the shine of a three-quarter moon through the windows. Royce was disheveled in the clothes he had failed to remove — but he didn't care. He plodded along the tile, his untied laces flopping, until he reached a final, open door.

Benoît switched on an electric bulb. Royce raised a hand against the blinding yellow glow, but he could see that the space was a storage closet. Shelves were stocked with unlabeled cans and jars. Benoît was silhouetted and featureless before the glowing light.

As he blundered into the closet, Royce felt that aura of cool pleasure. It was like cinnamon; like gelato; like a cold shower on a summer day; like a winter breeze nipping through a cashmere scarf. Royce staggered toward Benoît, and now they stood in the closet together. The two men faced each other, and Benoît's breath was like an alpine breeze on Royce's gooseflesh.

Benoît pushed the door shut. He drifted forward, a glacial movement. His hand rose up, next to Royce's ear. He touched the string that dangled from the ceiling. He yanked it once, and the light went out.

As darkness enveloped them, Royce felt as if he were falling through nothingness. His body existed without borders, blending into that measureless void. He embraced the feeling, both neutral and arousing, as he released his concerns to the empty space around him, the details of his life erased from cognizance.

Then he felt the sting. He heard the breaking skin. He recoiled from the pain, his shoulder slumping beneath the pressure of lips and teeth, but then he let out a long moan. He felt his body lightening, the tingle in his fingers and toes, the airiness in his forearms and legs. He felt relief, as if unloading the burdens that weighed him down, the loathing and the dread, the shame and hopelessness that had metastasized within him. He no longer felt the puncture—no more than a hypodermic needle in mid-injection. He could forfeit the rest of himself, if only to feel so alleviated of his woes. He could live in this moment forever, adrift in the mollifying darkness.

He heard the squeak of hinges. The door opened.

Benoît's head flew back, and a jet of blood spurted from Royce's shoulder.

Royce buckled. His limp body smashed through the wooden shelves. As Royce hit the floor, heavy cans bashed against his folded arm, and the glass jars smashed all around him.

Royce looked up. Benoît was whirling around, facing the open door.

Just beyond, Royce could see a feminine form in a riding outfit, a black cutout against the moonlight.

Elizabeth! his mind shrieked, but his throat only gargled.

Benoît raised his arms, as if to lunge.

But then Benoît lurched backward. His body jolted.

Benoît stumbled, stepped on Royce's outstretched leg, and lost his balance. He tumbled backward, crashing into more jars, the putrid liquid splashing all around them both.

The pallid waiter writhed on the floor, a dark rod jutting from his sternum. In the dim light, Royce could still see black blood blossoming through the white fabric of his double-breasted jacket. His arms flapped back and forth, and his spine arced, fish-like, as dark liquid burst from his mouth.

At last he juddered and exhaled a long groan from deep within himself—low and beastly, like the snarl of a lion.

Now Royce felt cold, as if he had woken in a bath of ice. He wheezed laboriously and pulled himself into a sitting position. His dress shirt was partly unbuttoned and no longer tucked in his trousers. He felt delirious, yet also more cognizant, as if waking from a deep dream. What had happened? Royce shuddered at the body lying next to him, the pools of liquid, the shards of glistening glass. His lower neck burned fiercely, and when he pressed fingers against the pain, the tips were printed with blood.

"Oh, God, Elizabeth!" he whimpered. "What... what *is* this?"

"Let's get to your room," whispered Elizabeth tensely. "Can you walk?"

"I... I... I don't know."

"Give me your arm."

She knelt down beside Royce and threw his arm over his shoulder, then lifted him up. Elizabeth was petite but harbored some strength, and Royce saw stars as he leaned against her. The dark floor looked distant. His legs wobbled beneath him.

"We need to get you some water," said Elizabeth. "That's the first thing."

When they reached his cabin, Royce collapsed into bed. Elizabeth switched on the lamp, and Royce winced, blinded by its illumination.

"God, it *hurts*," he keened.

"Take these," Elizabeth said, slapping a pair of pills on the bed stand, followed by a metal field canteen. "And drink as much as you can."

"What... what happened to me?" Royce said. His body shivered as he dropped the pills into his mouth and guzzled water. The pills tasted savory and strange as they dissolved in his throat.

Elizabeth sat down on the opposite bed. She wrung her hands. She also looked shaken. In the lamplight, Royce could see her jacket and blouse were spritzed with blood. She had jammed that stake into Benoît with great force, he could tell.

And then he realized.

"Do you mean to tell me..." he said, voice quivering. "Was

that… was Benoît…?"

"A vampire," said Elizabeth stoically. "In the flesh."

"But that's… that's…"

"A myth?" Elizabeth frowned. "If only that were true."

Royce felt his eyes widen. For a moment his trembling body seemed to freeze, and a wave of sobriety washed over him. For all his pain and terror, Royce was a scientific man, and the schooled physician inside him struggled for control.

"Elizabeth," he said. "What's going on here?"

Elizabeth took a long breath. "For every myth, there's a grain of truth—and the things we call vampires are among them. They're not demons or ghosts. They're men, just like you. But they're very sick. The virus changes them. And I can't say there's a cure."

"Do you mean… am I…?"

"Don't worry—you're not infected," assured Elizabeth. "These men aren't contagious. But they're everything you'd expect. They can't endure much sunlight. They crave blood. And they'll take a licking."

"You… you used a stake."

"Yes. Because of the blood, you see. Their cardiovascular system is swollen. It makes their hearts vulnerable to rupture, just like a malarial spleen. That's their Achilles' heel. Otherwise they shed their fat, until all that's left is muscle. Their bodies are tough as leather. At least that's what the literature says." She smirked. "Not bad for a dropout, eh?"

Royce said, "Why did I feel…?"

"Lust?" Elizabeth cocked her head sidewalks. "Poor dear, you must be so confused. But it's all chemical. An emission, through their pores. Like the scent of a dog in heat. It stimulates the people around them, no matter what their persuasion. And their eyes—they have a hypnotic power."

"Hypnosis? How?"

Elizabeth sighed. "Now, Royce, I'm not an encyclopedia."

"Right, of course." He struggled to sit up. He touched his puncture wounds, which left only a light film of blood. The wounds were congealing, thank God.

"Lucky for us, they won't bite you again."

"No? Why not?"

"Garlic pills," Elizabeth said. "In a few minutes, they'll avoid you like the plague."

"Then we're safe!" He placed a hand on his heaving chest.

"Not exactly," said Elizabeth. "There'll still want us dead."

"Why?"

"We know too much."

"But—what do we know? I still don't understand."

Elizabeth closed her eyes and nodded. She glanced at the sealed door, waiting for a sound, but they heard only silence. "A few weeks ago, my friend Greta called. She was in a state. She said her brother was missing. He had spent some time in Havana. He had planned to return to Miami by ship, but he wanted to surprise his wife by returning a few days early. He booked passage on an airship—*this* airship. That cable was the last she heard from him."

"But how did you know they were... they were..."

"Vampires? It took some time. I've been in Havana nearly two weeks, asking around. But it all made sense after a while. Passengers board each morning, it takes off by noon, but when the blimp arrives in Miami, it's empty. They forge the manifest, so it seems that no one traveled aboard. Once they feed on the passengers, they dump the bodies in the ocean. The sharks handle the rest."

"You mean..." Royce gagged as hot mucus rose in his throat. "They would—*kill us?*"

"If it weren't for that stake," Elizabeth said, "you'd be fish food by now."

"My God!" he exclaimed. "Where's Albert?"

Elizabeth looked away, then weaved her fingers. "He's

probably gone, I'm afraid."

"Gone? You mean *dead?*"

"If he's not here, they probably seduced him by now."

"But maybe he's alive!" Royce stammered. "Maybe we can do something—"

"There's nothing we can do, Royce," Elizabeth said sternly. "I'd hoped that Albert would take those pills, or at least retire to the cabin with you. I kept him occupied for a while, insisting. I even tried to drop them into his glass, but he wouldn't have it."

"You just *left* him there?"

"There was only so much I could do without rousing suspicion, Royce. And besides, I was busy trying to save your life."

Royce closed his eyes. "Of course, Elizabeth, forgive me. And thank you. I... I didn't realize."

"It's all right," said Elizabeth. "But now we have a delicate task."

"What do you mean?"

"At this moment, the staff of this vessel is probably feasting on the passengers," said Elizabeth, sending a fresh chill down Royce's spine. "They're occupied, which is good for us. But before they land, they'll make a final sweep. They won't want to bite us, but they'll certainly want us dead."

"Then—what do we do?"

"Can you swim?"

"*Swim?*" Royce wheezed. "I hope you're joking!"

"When the airship approaches the Florida coast," said Elizabeth, "we'll start our descent. The airfield is right on the shoreline. For a short time, we'll hover just fifty feet or so over the water before we hit land. That's when we'll jump."

"Jump? Into the ocean? That seems rash, doesn't it?"

"It's all in the timing," said Elizabeth. "We'll have to find exactly the right moment to jump. If we're too high, we'll hit the water like a rock. The impact will certainly do us in. If we wait too long, we'll be flying over land. Either way, we won't be able to stay inside."

"Why not?"

A thumping sound roused them from their conversation, and Elizabeth moved toward the door, pressing her ear against its beveled surface.

Royce's head spun. Everything was happening so fast. Wasn't there another way? Couldn't they hide somewhere until the airship docked, then sneak out and call the authorities? The need for action explained why Elizabeth had exchanged an evening gown for riding gear—the only sporting outfit tailored for a woman—but did she really expect to leap out of an airborne Zeppelin in the middle of the night? Could they really swim through roiling waves in complete darkness?

There was another bump, then a swishing sound in the corridor. Royce could tell that someone was leaning against the wall, raking an elbow along the paneling. Then the sound stopped. The figure rested next to their cabin door.

"Lock the door," whispered Royce.

"Wait," responded Elizabeth.

"Why?"

"If they hear the latch, they'll know we're awake."

"The lamp is already on! Whoever it is probably hears us whispering already!"

Royce shifted, trying to slide off the bed, but before he could move, the latch turned. The door drifted open.

The outline of a large woman stood before them. The first thing Royce noticed was her floppy hat and its lopsided plumage. She wore an evening gown, but the strap on one side had been pulled down, exposing her shoulder and the ample tulip of her breast. Her face was drowsy, her eyes mere slits beneath heavy lids. Her neck was punctured, and blood ran down her shoulder in two clean lines, until they reached her exposed bosom. She had apparently tried to wipe the rivulets away and smudged them across her skin. In her forearm she carried her Chihuahua, though it was evident that the tiny dog was dead, its arms hanging limp, its neck ripped open. She teetered there for a moment, pale as ivory, until one knee bent and she slumped onto the floor, rolled onto her back, and spread her limbs into a perfect X.

"Dear God!" heaved Royce.

But Elizabeth wasted no time with exclamations. She stepped over the fallen body and peered into the corridor.

"It's one of *them*," she shushed. "He's coming!"

Elizabeth grasped the woman's plump ankles and tried to drag her inside the room, and suddenly Royce realized why: The woman's bulky corpse prevented them from shutting the door. As Elizabeth heaved, Royce moved to help her. But the moment he put his feet on the floor, he bent forward, stricken with nausea. He shook, more violently than ever. He couldn't move. Royce raised his head to see Elizabeth struggling with the heavy woman's body. But then she let go. The woman wouldn't budge.

Elizabeth bounded backward, onto the bed, and snatched the bloodstained stake. Just as she did so, a figure appeared in the doorway—pale, dressed like a bellhop.

The porter. Corwin.

"Lucky number seven," frothed Corwin.

But the voice was low and guttural, more like the hiss of a lizard than human speech. Royce had only the energy to shake his head, trying to will Corwin away.

Then Corwin pounced—he sprang forward, tackling Royce and knocking him flat against the mattress. Royce gasped as Corwin pressed into his chest. The young man—the *vampire*—was dense as iron, and Royce could feel his ribs straining beneath the pale creature. Corwin's jaws opened, revealing pearly teeth, a pair of pointed canines as sharp as nails, and the spittle that stretched between his lips —

Elizabeth leapt across the room and rammed the stake into the vampire's back. Corwin screamed — high-pitched, ear-splitting, like a train whistle.

The creature whirled around and hobbled toward the open door, the stake protruding from his right shoulder. He reached around, trying to grasp the weapon half-stabbed into his back, but his fingers only grazed the shaft. Corwin slammed into the doorframe, rounded the corner, and vanished.

Royce grabbed his chest and fought for breath. Again Elizabeth had saved him from certain doom, but he couldn't summon a single word. Terror and pain had reduced him to a stammering invalid.

"Damn it all," cursed Elizabeth. "We'll have to hightail it, now."

She grabbed Royce's wrist and yanked him upward, but the doctor fell to his knees, crawling past the heavy woman's corpse. Elizabeth darted ahead of him, looking both ways to see if the coast was clear. Royce managed to exit the room on all fours, coughing into the carpet. Despite his delirium, he could feel the mild tilt of the floor; he could sense the airship dropping in altitude.

"You have to get up," said Elizabeth brusquely. *"Now."*

Royce wanted to object, but he felt himself rise to his feet. He groped the brass-plated rail for support and slid himself along the wall. Slowly, they made their way down the corridor, toward the bow.

"Where… where are we going?" sputtered Royce.

"The common room."

"But won't *they* be there?"

Elizabeth turned her head just long enough to murmur, "Trust me."

The corridor ended, opening into the main room. When Royce saw what lay within, he doubled over with revulsion.

Royce had seen the gamut of sickness and surgeries in his time, but he had never seen anything like this.

Many of the chairs were overturned. Toppled glasses had splashed liquor everywhere. And throughout the room, a half-dozen crewmen, dressed in their uniforms, were gorging on their passengers. The old man with the pipe was sprawled in his easy chair, a crewman sucking on his neck from behind. The graying women who had been playing cards were trapped in a corner booth, each ravaged by a crewman, while rivers of blood poured down their blouses. The victims' faces were portraits of suffering, but the true grotesquery was the sight of the crewmen themselves, who pressed their mouths ravenously into flesh, the sloppy suction of their lips audible above the drone of the airship's motors. Now and again a crewmen dug his fangs into an especially healthy vein, and a spout of blood squirted past his face.

But as Royce blinked away tears of pain and confusion, his eyes focused on the worst sight of all: *Albert was splayed across a table.* His body was limp as an afghan. Crewmen surrounded him; they bit into his neck, his wrists, even his ankles. Albert's face was granite gray, and his clothes were tousled and torn. His shoes had been tossed away and his socks stripped off. His head rolled forward, and his empty eyes seemed to notice Royce, but soon those pupils drifted upward. He could not summon the energy to blink, much less plead for swift death.

Royce might have fainted. He wanted to resign himself, to donate his exhausted body, to become fodder for their savage banquet.

But Elizabeth sprang forward. She reached under a table, then dragged a heavy canister across the carpet. Royce could barely interpret what he saw—at first he wondered where Elizabeth had found a covered milk pail—until he recognized the canister as a gas can.

Before Royce could wonder how she had smuggled such a

thing aboard, Elizabeth ripped off the lid and kicked the can over. It clunked heavily against the floor, and odiferous liquid splashed out. The gasoline glugged as it saturated the rug, spreading darkly through its fabric. Elizabeth backed away, then reached into the pocket of her riding trousers and drew a packet of matches—the very same box Albert had gifted her.

Over her shoulder Elizabeth called, "Royce, grab one of those!" She pointed to one of the overturned chairs. "Break the window!"

Royce squinted confusedly. *Could she be serious?*

"Royce, *now*," Elizabeth commanded, and she struck a match. The tiny stick flared to life in her shaking fingers.

Royce shuffled to the squat metal chair, and then, with the last of his strength, lifted it above his head. He wobbled for a moment, fearing he might topple. But then he dropped his arms, and the chair fell into the slanted window. The glass exploded into innumerable fragments, a crown of glinting triangles around the single piece of furniture, which receded into the darkness. Engine noise flooded the room, and lukewarm wind burst through, whipping Royce in the face.

When he turned around, he saw Corwin approaching. The boyish face was twisted with ire, his arms were spread wide, and his fingers curled like claws. His mouth and chin were covered with violet film, and the stake still protruded from his spine. He reared, preparing to charge them both.

Elizabeth dropped the match. She retreated, taking big steps, as the floor ignited. Waves of flame washed across the carpet, golden spools of light accented with blue. The fire shot up Corwin's pant legs, engulfing his shins and knees. He looked down in disbelief, then ejected a bird-like shriek—an octave so piercing that Royce thought he might hear it forever.

Then Royce felt a hand clap his shoulder. Unbearable heat singed the exposed skin of his face and hands. His lip curled inward, and he bit down, unable to endure any more. Yet

Elizabeth pushed his shoulder, and Royce turned around, toward the gaping, windy hole where the window had been. He couldn't see the water. There was only darkness, a depthless black void.

"*Jump!*" shrieked Elizabeth.

Royce's arms bumped the sill, but he couldn't lift his leg. His body felt numb and inert. He had nothing left to give, no energy to dedicate to his own survival. His eyes rolled, his shoulders slumped, and then—

—he fell.

Royce flopped forward, headfirst through the window. The movement took no effort. He simply succumbed to gravity. He felt himself flip over into empty space; he briefly saw the airship withdraw into the sky; and he surrendered himself to nothingness. He couldn't tell which way he was falling, for nothing signified up or down. This, he thought, was the peacefulness of afterlife, an existence without sensation. This abyss was the last thing he would ever experience.

Then he struck the water. His shoulder and head hit first, a clumsy, diagonal dive. The roar of bubbles surged around him. His body thrashed in the liquid, and he fought his way to the surface. When his face emerged, he gulped air into his open mouth. He screamed primally into the darkness. His eyes blinked open, and then he saw the vast sky, the steely darkness, and the billions of stars scattered across it. The three-quarter moon burned between a wispy pair of clouds.

"*Oh, God!*" he screamed.

But as he flailed, Royce recognized in himself a long-dormant instinct: *He wanted to live.* Like magma rising to the surface of the Earth, Royce's soul erupted with the desire to survive this moment, and all the languor he had experienced was replaced by sheer vitality. His mad splashing calmed. He started the crawl-stroke he had learned in high school, so many years ago. He pulled himself forward, feeling sober and clear, as if a pall had been removed from his mind, and the crisp beauty of the world was newly unveiled.

His hands brushed something in the water, and he swallowed his momentary panic: The stuff was sea grass, wafting around him, and suddenly his feet sank into spongy muck. The ocean floor swallowed one shoe, then the other, but he didn't care. Royce pressed forward, through the soggy masses of vegetation that tickled his thighs. He had no idea how far he had to slog through the marshes. Yet he had found land, and he was grateful. He was alive, after all, and that was all that mattered.

Then he saw it: a ball of flame.

He had never seen a fire so colossal—a vast cloud of orange light surging skyward, so enormous and powerful that Royce could feel its blaze from nearly a mile away. The outline of the airship's superstructure emerged, its curved black ribs subsumed in streamers of fire.

Almost exactly four seconds later, he heard the sound: a profound boom, followed by the earsplitting noise of billowing fire. That sound reified the airship's fate. Anyone aboard was now immolated in the levitating inferno.

Only then did Royce wonder: *Did Elizabeth also jump?* Was she now floundering in the dark ocean? Again he felt weak, quivering with exhaustion. But he knew that Elizabeth had saved him from certain death. He wanted to see her, to embrace her, to beg her forgiveness. In all his years of surgery, Royce had silently prayed for a hundred souls to outlive the night. But never had he prayed so hard.

It was months later, back in New York, in the hospital, that Royce received a telegram.

Anyone who had met Royce in the past year would not have recognized him. The divorced bachelor was no longer frazzled and slouched. He had taken up exercise at the local gym, and his shoulders looked broader, his posture straighter. His parted hair remained the same, but he now applied grooming cream, and he had decided to grow a mustache, which was filling in nicely. The nurses now smiled at him in a kittenish way he had never noticed before, and he responded with an increasingly flirtatious smile. Royce had abandoned his grim apartment to rent a brownstone in Bedford-Stuyvesant. When he retired there after his shift, he drank a single glass of sherry before bed, never a drop more.

It was a balmy spring day when he entered his office and resolved to admit fresh air. Sun poured through the glass as he lifted each window and set its latch. He took a long breath and closed his eyes, refreshed by the scent of budding leaves and flowers. The moment was so meditative that he did not notice the young man standing behind him.

"Dr. Abbott?" said an adolescent voice.

"Mm-hmm," said Royce, still basking in celestial warmth.

"Telegram for you, sir."

"Just..." He sighed. "Just leave it on the desk, please."

"Will do."

He heard the flap of paper against wood, but he waited a few minutes before turning around and assessing the sealed envelope. He unfolded the paper without fanfare and read the typewritten words.

> Sorry about Al. But I'm glad you're all right.
> And I think I won that bet.

Royce smiled, satisfied to know Elizabeth was alive. He pressed the telegram to his breast. A certain grief washed over him, thinking of Albert, the friend he had known for so many years. Elizabeth had forwarded no address, no phone number that he could ring. She was not a woman to pursue, he knew. She was not a woman who could be tamed or even understood, at least not by a man like him. He must be content to remember her from afar, to appreciate what she had done, and live, and keep living.

THE WARD SEVEN HORROR

March, 1921

MAUDE TIPTOED INTO THE KITCHEN, then stood by the door with her hands folded over her apron. She tried to make herself smaller, to disappear into the yellowed plaster walls.

Flora looked up from her stewpot and scowled. Her oblong face was blemished with rosacea, and her bushy eyebrows narrowed nastily.

"Maude!" she cried. "What are you standing there for? We've got work to do!"

"Y-y-y-y-yes," Maude stuttered, aiming her gaze at the tile floor. "W-w-w-what can I do?"

Flora leaned back, one arm akimbo, the other absently stirring the pot with a wooden spoon.

"You can grab the slop bucket over there," said Flora, "and take it to Ward Seven."

Maude trembled. "But it's…it's…"

"It's what?" Flora spat. "Speak up!"

"It's Thursday, ma'am. Isn't it Helen's turn?"

"Helen didn't start her shift today," grumbled Flora. "She'll be lucky if she's ever let back in. Lazy good-for-nothing. So it's

38

your turn, unless you want to try the breadlines, too."

Maude shook her head vigorously, and her dark hair wobbled beneath a tightly tied headscarf.

"Good then! Now *go*."

As Maude approached the so-called slop bucket, she drew a second kerchief from her apron pocket and wrapped it around her face. Even from a few paces away, the rancid smell was overpowering. She had taken care to soak the fabric in water and baking soda before leaving her dormitory, but the stench still seeped through. The "bucket" was really a metal basin, long and wide enough to bathe a toddler. Maude was instructed not to remove the cloth towel that covered it, but whatever the basin contained had stained the towel a sickly maroon.

Maude was a gangly 25-year-old, barely strong enough to open the sanitarium's heavy doors, so when she grabbed the basin's handle, she struggled to drag it across the floor. She moved in fits and starts, trying to avoid eye contact with Flora, who glared at her menacingly from behind her pots and pans. The room felt more like a dungeon than a kitchen, and the air was thick with steam and the aromas of boiling food. But Maude hated to leave that room, for the corridor beyond bore so much worse.

Inch by inch, Maude pulled her ghastly cargo down the endless hallway, whose brick walls looked like melting wax in the glum electric light. Behind each iron door, Maude heard the moans and shuffling of invisible bodies, the cackles of madmen mixing with the liquidy coughs of tuberculosis. She struggled to ignore the things she heard; the disparate human noises harmonized into an awful din, which echoed in the empty tunnel and followed Maude all the way to the final gate.

She fumbled with the skeleton key, then finally slipped its jagged head into the lock. She opened the door and yanked the slop bucket into Ward Seven.

The chamber was as big as a train station, with high vaulted ceilings and a cul-de-sac of caged openings. Only the common space was lit; each recess was saturated in darkness, invisible beyond their steel bars. But Maude could hear the rustling in the shadows, human clamor that grew exponentially louder, accompanied by a gathering cacophony of grunts and growls.

Maude trembled so severely that she could barely force herself forward, and her bent body was so exhausted from its effort that she wanted only to stop. But still she pulled the basin forward, into the middle of the vast chamber, where the concrete floor was marked with a single, painted X. When she finally positioned the basin, she wanted to curl into a ball and shut her eyes, to pretend that this was not her life, but the sounds of smacking lips and clanging bars roused her from fatigue. She started to walk toward the door, then picked up her pace, until her oversized shoes clouted frantically against the floor.

Then she did as instructed: She flung herself into the corridor and pushed the iron door closed. Her tiny lungs heaved for breath, and she slinked to the rusty lever built into the wall. She grabbed the handle, just as she'd been told to do, and pulled it downward.

She heard the grinding noise within the invisible chamber, a dozen gates sliding open at once. The automated machinery groaned and squealed, and when the doors had synchronously opened, they boomed into place, echoing profoundly. That was the sound to signal Maude's departure. She should return to the kitchen now, to chop overripe cabbage and carrots. She should spend the rest of the night mixing flour into the tasteless porridge the asylum fed its patients. She shouldn't so much as turn around. *Just go back, Maude*, she'd been told. *Be a good girl and don't make a fuss. What happens in Ward Seven is no one's business but mine.*

But she didn't turn around. She stayed there, seized by

curiosity. Maude had always followed orders, had always accommodated the people around her, but tonight she was guided by a unique desire. She inched toward the iron door. She heard the sound of skidding feet and ghastly voices. Maude had seen this door a hundred times before, yet she had never really registered the tiny rectangle in its center. A hatch, only the size of an envelope, which could slide sideways, like a speakeasy grille. She reached out with quivering fingers and grasped the knob on its side. She pulled—but the hatch only jiggled in place. She pulled again, this time with all the force she could muster, and it flew open. Maude was skinny but not tall, and she had to stand on her toes to peer through the rectangular space.

What Maude saw in that moment froze her to the marrow. She could almost feel her thinning blood, the stopping of her hummingbird heart, the contraction of her every organ. Terror stormed through her, and impulsively she groped the knob and yanked, but the hatch didn't budge. Her eyes filled with stars, and her legs wobbled. She knew that she should faint, but then she heard a tiny voice of reason—*Hold on, Maude!* She couldn't faint, or they would see the open hatch, her unconscious body crumpled on the tile, and everyone would know she had broken the rules. She had to fight this sensation. She had to keep herself together.

Maude pulled once more, and the hatch slid reluctantly back into place. The horror vanished from her vision.

Yet the sound persisted: wet, sloppy munching, dozens of maws gnashing all at once, the scrape of rotted teeth, the whine of flesh separating from bone.

Maude backed away, unable to breathe, feeling dizzy and sick, but still she managed to turn round, arms outstretched before her as she sprinted down the corridor, her ears deafened by the wails of madmen in their cells.

It was in the Carnegie Library that Maude first saw Elizabeth Crowne.

Elizabeth stood in the corner, behind a large globe in its compass-stand. She held a leather-bound book high and horizontally, as if she had discovered some strange entrée and wished to scrutinize it from an obscure angle. Elizabeth wore the simple tweed jacket and skirt of a schoolmarm, her hair efficiently pinned up.

Maude approached, her hands clasped at her navel. In the presence of such concentration, Maude could think of nothing to say, and her indecisiveness flirted with panic, so she stared directly at a curl of floor rug.

"I'm trying to decide whether it's a fake," said Elizabeth.

"I'm sorry?" blurted Maude.

"The ink is convincing, and the paper too. But there's something off." She lowered the volume, placed a hand on her hip, and looked squarely at Maude. "What are you in for?"

"I... in for?"

Elizabeth grinned and clamped the book's covers together.

"You're not here to borrow some Proust, I'm guessing."

Maude looked down again. "No."

Elizabeth Crowne beheld this sweet, porcelain stranger. Of all people in the world, none looked more fitting in a public library than Maude. She was skinny and pale, with hazel dots for eyes and freckles on her cheeks that only appeared in certain light. Her pageboy haircut perfectly suited her dark black hair, and Elizabeth had watched, out of the corner of her eye, as Maude had crept along the edges of the broad reading room, as if camouflaging herself against the reference stacks.

And yet Maude seemed a paradox, for she was also *striking* — bookish and shy, yes, and any single part of her might seem plain, but in total Maude was uniquely beautiful. She was the kind of girl who attracted distant gazes, like the statues of angels that adorned the library's rooftop. Maude probably didn't notice this attention, even from the studious young men scattered about the room, but Elizabeth could see them. They sat at carols and in easy chairs, bow-tied and bespectacled, looking up from their texts to steal glances at Maude, who was clearly oblivious. It made Elizabeth smirk.

"Well, then," said Elizabeth. "Out with it."

"I—"

Maude couldn't find the words. She felt distracted, as if she had stared into a light bulb too long.

"I need coffee," said Elizabeth. "Don't you?"

Maude sat breathlessly in the cab as the driver pulled into Forbes Avenue traffic, narrowly missing a pair of builders carrying lumber on their shoulders. Maude hadn't been inside a car for months, and the city seemed to whisk past her—a blur of vehicles, pedestrians, men clutching newspapers, women walking dogs, young boys darting past a parked milk truck, so much excitement that had vanished from her daily life.

Elizabeth seemed so relaxed, reclined against the cushioned seat, one arm thrown over the back, the other pinching the air contemplatively. She looked out the window, blinking at the things that passed, as if memorizing each detail. Elizabeth intimidated Maude, sitting so close that their shoulders abutted, but she also felt a certain excitement.

"Where you go?" called the blubbery driver over his shoulder. "Specific?"

"Cressida Street," said Elizabeth.

He turned onto a narrow side street, and blocks of row houses emerged on either side, the little yards wrapped in picket fence or brick wall, so many dwellings jammed together. Maude knew nothing of Oakland, and the taxi took so many turns down the labyrinthine streets that she could not imagine retracing their route. She had pawned her wristwatch, and the absence of time made her more anxious than ever.

Elizabeth threw open the door before the taxi had properly parked and leapt out, carried forward by the cab's velocity.

"You are here?" said the driver.

"Never been anywhere else," quipped Elizabeth, and she tossed the man a quarter. "Thanks for the lift."

At first Maude saw a row of brick residences, mere variations of the neighborhood's other buildings, and she waited for Elizabeth to move toward one. But then she saw Elizabeth climb some steps, toward a row house that rose above the others. The house's façade was ornately built of red sandstone, the blocks sturdily mortared around broad windows. The domicile was three stories tall, framed with two turrets and topped with a high slate roof. A lukewarm spring breeze nudged the porch swing, whose chain Elizabeth steadied with a hand. Then she dug out her keys and slipped them into the lock of a massive oaken door—an entrance distinguished enough for a church.

Then Elizabeth stopped. "I'm not embarrassed by much," she said. "But let's just say—I'm not a tidy person."

As Maude stepped inside, she swallowed a gasp. Yes, the vestibule was elegantly designed, with wood floors, a beveled ceiling, and a broad staircase. The furnishings were surprisingly old-fashioned, with varnished tables, Persian carpets, and lamps with dangling fringes. The interior might have appeased a shah, were it not for the clutter everywhere. Mounds of books covered the tables, stacks of newspapers moldered on each of the staircase's steps, maps and scrolls and even scroll cases jumbled everywhere, as if purposefully arranged to attract dust. The crown molding along the ceiling was alive with cobwebs, and the many paintings and photographs arranged on the walls looked comically crooked.

"Oh… *dear*," murmured Maude.

"Tell me what you really think," mumbled Elizabeth. "But honestly—I know exactly where everything is." They continued to stand before the anarchy. The pause went on uncomfortably, until Elizabeth declared, "Let's find that cezve, shall we?"

The kitchen was no less disastrous, except that Elizabeth only used a handful of dishes and rarely seemed to cook. The crockery was stashed away, along with most of the silverware, but what little Elizabeth had used was soaking in a murky sink. Elizabeth rinsed out a copper cup the shape of a decanter, then filled a kettle of water and lit the gas range. As she opened a tin and started to scoop finely ground coffee into the cezve, she said, "Let's call a spade a spade, shall we?"

"I—" Maude looked alarmed. "I don't really play cards."

Elizabeth leered at this, then dribbled steaming water over the coffee. "You were looking for me, weren't you? In the library?"

"I… yes."

"Then you know what I do?"

"Well, no, not really."

Elizabeth swirled the cezve, then balanced the handle over two copper cups the size of shot glasses.

"Then how come you were looking for me?"

"Well," said Maude sheepishly. "My friend… Helen… we work together…"

"Helen…" Elizabeth murmured to herself. "Helen… *Gaines?*"

"Yes, that's right!"

"Used to work in a wool factory, right?"

"Yes," Maude said. "But she was let go."

"Helen used to live down the street," said Elizabeth, handing the cup to Maude, who nodded her appreciation but looked too timid to sip. "She would sweep our porch and beat the rugs for extra money. Very spirited girl. Always spoke her mind. What's she up to now?"

"She... *we*..." Maude set the coffee cup down. "I'm sorry, Ms. Crowne, I'm discombobulated."

"*Gesundheit*," Elizabeth said. "That's a rather long word for a wool factory girl."

"Oh, I don't... I never worked in a factory. But I needed a job. I saw an ad in the paper. No experience necessary. Free room and board. The wage was fair enough, I thought. So that's where I met Helen."

Elizabeth sipped her coffee coolly. Then her expression changed—one second meditative, the next second alit. She slapped her coffee on the counter and folded her arms.

"I have half a mind," said Elizabeth slowly, "to say I bought a scarf because of you."

Maude looked away, seeming to shrink even farther from the scene. But Elizabeth persisted.

"That was *you*, wasn't it? I thought I recognized that face! There's nobody in the world that has an expression like yours."

"Ms. Crowne, I think this was a mist—"

"You're the *Reichers girl*, aren't you?"

Maude let out a long sigh, a mix of shame and forfeiture. That mousy exhalation was all the confirmation Elizabeth needed.

"My God, so *this* is where you are! I swear, for months I couldn't open a magazine without seeing your face. And the billboards! Everywhere! You must've been the most famous girl in Pittsburgh!" Elizabeth folded her arms and smiled ecstatically, studying her guest with fresh eyes. "Truth be told, I couldn't care less about department stores. All those phonies with their perfume bottles, saying *how lovely you look today*. Can't stand them, never could stand them. And I would never have stepped foot in a Reichers store. But then I saw that sign. Right on Fifth Avenue, in the middle of Uptown. I could've looked at that sign for hours. You looked..." Elizabeth permitted a rare blush. "Well, *you* actually did look lovely."

"Thank you," said Maude meekly.

"So what happened? Where'd you disappear to? I haven't seen your Reichers ads in ages!"

"Well..." Maude said. "I had some trouble."

"A man, I assume."

"Yes," said Maude pensively. "But not in... the usual way. You see, the man who hired me, his name is Lyndon Baker."

"Of course. The photographer."

"Yes! He... he found me at the railway station. When I first came here. I didn't know anyone. I had twenty-two dollars and a suitcase. I don't know what I expected. I was standing on the platform, and... and... all I wanted to do was turn around and take the sleeper back to Columbus."

"Columbus, eh?" Elizabeth sniffed. "Well, I won't begrudge you that."

"But then he saw me. Mr. Baker, I mean. He came over and said, 'You! You're exactly the girl I've been looking for!'"

"To photograph?"

"Yes."

"And..." Elizabeth grimaced. "*More* than photograph."

"Well, it didn't start that way," Maude confessed. "He treated me so well. So many clothes! I've been a seamstress my whole life, Ms. Crowne. I could make clothes out of... *anything*, really."

"You're a regular Rumpelstiltskin, eh?"

"I would have settled for that," said Maude distantly. "I pictured myself in a boutique. Making clothing for elegant ladies. I cherished that dream, Ms. Crowne, I really did."

"But he offered you something more," said Elizabeth. "He made you a star."

"Yes. I'm not vain, Ms. Crowne, I'm truly not! But when a man says you're beautiful, he dresses you in such wonderful clothes... and the parties, Ms. Crowne! I'm not the type for parties, not really. I'm a wallflower, believe it or not."

"Oh," said Elizabeth, "I believe it."

Maude hugged herself and caressed her forearms. "When men are toasting you, you feel so wonderful. Every night, I went to my apartment—the one he rented for me—and I would think to myself, 'What girl deserves such treatment? How could I possibly be so lucky?'"

"And then he made the ultimatum?" concluded Elizabeth.

"Well... not exactly. But it wasn't... *polite*, what he did. We were at a party, very late... he offered to take me home in his car. Then he walked me to my door. I'm terribly shy, Ms. Crowne. I never know what to do in those situations. And he was so tipsy, I thought he might fall over. But he tried to... well, I ran away. Just ran to the stairs, and into the street... and I haven't been back."

"You're missing a key detail," said Elizabeth.

"I... I am?"

"Yes. You see, I've met Mr. Baker. He's a very skilled photographer. But there's a reason he takes the pictures and doesn't pose for them."

Maude's head fell sideways as she pondered Elizabeth's meaning, and then it struck her all at once—and she laughed. An unpreventable guffaw. Then she giggled, girlishly, inciting Elizabeth to snicker as well, and soon they were laughing together, like old friends, at the expense of fat, balding, pockmarked Lyndon Baker, the homeliest photographer alive.

Elizabeth rounded her desk and plopped into a large, leather-backed chair. The chair swiveled slightly, and she steadied herself before opening a drawer and rooting inside it.

Maude was reluctant to sit across from Elizabeth—not for diffidence, but from curiosity. Elizabeth's office was a museum unto itself: A mounted boar's head extended from the old wallpaper, and a magnificent grandfather clock ticked in the corner. The walls were staggered with wooden masks and framed drawings, mounted antique maps and even a suit of armor, albeit missing one gauntlet. Maude leaned into a document hanging above a vase of hopelessly wilted tulips.

"That's my father's diploma," said Elizabeth from behind her mountain of papers.

"He's a... doctor?"

"Doctor of Philosophy," she said. "Upsettingly brilliant. He can lecture about anything. But he's useless in every other way. He hasn't got the common sense to boil and egg." Elizabeth stared long at the diploma, then drew a marijuana roach from her drawer. She pinched the roach between her teeth and spoke through the rolled paper: "I never finished mine."

"Oh, no?" said Maude, shifting focus back to Elizabeth.

Elizabeth struck a match and lit the roach, then exhaled a spiral of smoke.

"Medical school," said Elizabeth. "I should have finished, but I got... sidetracked."

"Ms. Crowne," said Maude. "I really hate to ask this, but could I come back another time?"

Elizabeth lurched forward in the chair, startled by the request. "Another time? Why?"

"Well, you see... I have a curfew of six o'clock."

"A what at *what?*" Elizabeth burst. "What kind of nonsense is that? Where do you work, on a submarine?"

Maude shifted her feet uncomfortably. "No. I work... at the Mt. Ruby Sanitarium."

Elizabeth gawped at her for a moment, then sank back into her chair. She took another long, slow drag, then let the smoke coil into the still air.

"Mt. Ruby," she said. "Where they treat the tuberculosis

patients?"

"Yes. And the criminally insane."

"Do they, now? I wasn't aware. But they're treated in separate wards, I presume."

"They should be," said Maude. "But they mix them all together. That's what's so strange, Ms. Crowne... it's the reason I'm here, you see."

"Mixed together? Disease and madness? Sounds like a recipe for mass extinction," said Elizabeth. "I can't imagine any patients get *better*."

"Well, what happened was," started Maude, "I answered an ad in the paper, like I said. I needed a place to stay, I needed money. I was so frightened. I thought I'd have to sleep in the street, like a tramp. But they hired me on the spot."

"Who hired you?"

"Dr. Lundqvist," whispered Maude, as if the man might hear her. "He owns the sanitarium."

"He *owns* it?"

"That's what the other girls told me. You see, it's like a fortress, the sanitarium. All the workers, we eat there, we sleep there. We almost never leave. We have to work six days a week, and half of a seventh day."

"Sounds typically barbaric," muttered Elizabeth.

"But Dr. Lundqvist... they say he *owns* it. The building. The land. Everything. They say he even renovated the building himself."

"Curiouser and curiouser," said Elizabeth. "So he renovated a sanitarium, he controls everyone inside it—and he doesn't care if the patients get better."

"Well, you see... I'm not an expert..." Maude abruptly moved to the second chair and sat down, looking more eager than ever. "But I don't think he *wants* them to get better."

"Go on."

"Well... I can't explain it. You see... he locks them in their cells. They're never allowed out, not even for a little sun. At first I thought it was because of cold weather... the tuberculosis... but he barely feeds them. They're locked away, like animals. And then..."

"Then what?"

Maude looked distant, as if lost in a memory. "At night, we can hear some of the workers. The men, I mean. There aren't many, and we rarely see them. We're kept separate, all the time. But we hear them... late at night, when we're supposed to be sleeping. I think they take the patients away... just before they... they..."

"Pass on?"

"Yes. I think they carry them in stretchers... put them on gurneys... and take them away."

"Why do you think that?"

"Because..." Maude took a breath. "Helen saw them. She sneaked out one night. She watched the men moving down the hall. She saw three patients. They were still breathing, but barely alive."

"Where did they go?"

Maude looked up, directly into Elizabeth's eyes. The innocence melted away, replaced by a cold and weary expression. Maude whispered, in a voice that might have been winter wind through the trees, "Ward Seven."

Elizabeth stubbed her roach into an ashtray and pressed her fingertips together. After a long pause, she said, "Well, you're not going back there, that's for certain."

"Oh, but Ms. Crowne—"

"No, Maude, your life is in danger, and I won't have you crawling back to a hive of iniquity. Whoever this Dr. Lundqvist is, he's up to no good, and you're best not to be mixed up in it."

"But—where will I go? It's the only work I've found!"

"Well, how about this," said Elizabeth. "You need a job, and I need an assistant."

Maude's jaw dropped, her mouth forming a small round "O", and her head drifted from side to side, incredulous.

"Oh, don't look so surprised," said Elizabeth. She gestured to the room and its piles of books and papers. "I think it's *obvious* I need an assistant. And if you're really desperate enough to sleep in a bunk surrounded by madmen choking on their own blood, I hope that working for me is a decent alternative." Elizabeth waited a moment, then added, "Please, say I'm better company than tuberculosis patients."

"Well, *yes!*" blurted Maude. "Of course! *Thank* you! But... where will I stay?"

"We have maid's quarters," said Elizabeth. Then she winced and shook her head. "What am I saying? We have an entire master bedroom, and three children's rooms, and they're all available. There's plenty of space. And if you get sick of it, save some dough and find your own digs. Either way, you can work with me as long as you can stomach it. And I guarantee I pay better than some old lunatic asylum."

"Ms. Crowne, you—"

"And knock it off with that *Ms. Crowne*. My name's Elizabeth, and I won't hear anything different."

"But..." Maude could barely breathe. "But why?"

"Well," said Elizabeth, standing and smoothing her skirt. "I'm not much of a homemaker. Oh, I like a man with broad shoulders, and I cook a decent coq au vin, but otherwise I'm as feminine as a border collie. I need someone decent and hardworking and gracious, and you frankly fit the bill. The last thing I need is some professional maid in here, polishing one candlestick before filching the silverware. I need someone..." Elizabeth broke off, then absentmindedly rubbed her palm with a thumb. She looked toward the window, beyond which the sun was turning red and violet. "The truth is, Maude, my parents separated not long ago. They just couldn't share a roof anymore. My siblings are off to seek their fortunes, and—the house just feels a little empty. So yes, I need an assistant. But I suppose I also just need someone around." She simpered inwardly. "And to top it all off, your billboard inspired me to buy a scarf, and I'll be damned if it isn't the best thing in my wardrobe."

Maude stood up slowly. She had rarely raised her voice in her life, but in that moment she could have shrieked with joy. But she didn't shriek. She said only, "Ms. Crowne— *Elizabeth*—I might be the happiest girl in the world right now."

"Understandable," said Elizabeth. "I haven't put you to work yet."

And they both laughed like people forever meant to meet.

As Maude chopped onions and tomatoes in the kitchen, Elizabeth lingered nearby, flipping through a dog-eared telephone directory.

"Ruby Hill, you say?"

"That's right," said Maude.

"Well, then, time to make a phone call."

Maude stopped cutting. The knife started to quaver in her hand. She was hungry, yes, but the mere mention of the sanitarium's name infused her with dread. She watched in silence as Elizabeth picked up the receiver, then said, "Yes, Central, I'd like Homewood-727."

They waited, until a deep voice crackled through: "Hello?"

"Hello," said Elizabeth. "I'm looking for Dr. Lundqvist."

The receiver was filled with nondescript noise, like a seashell. "Dr. Lundqvist is not available."

"Then tell him this," said Elizabeth. "I'm interested in buying his product. A *great deal* of his product. And I'll be stopping in at five o'clock tomorrow to discuss it."

Another long pause, amplified by the swirl of sound.

"Tomorrow at five o'clock," said the voice. "Dr. Lundqvist will meet with you then."

"Very good."

Elizabeth slammed down the receiver and nodded. "Nine parts confidence," she said, "one part luck."

"I..." Maude wrung her hands. "I don't understand."

"You will tomorrow," said Elizabeth. "But I have to know something — when you talked to Helen, when she advised you to come to me, what did she say?"

"Oh," said Maude. "Only... only that you could help."

"Not what I do?"

"Well... no."

Elizabeth bit her lip. "I specialize," she said, "in the uncanny."

"The un... un..."

"Uncanny. Strange events. Unlikely sightings. Stories that defy belief. There are occurrences in this world, Maude, that most people are unprepared to accept. Some of those occurrences are fairytales. Others — well, they're as real as you and me."

"What... what kinds of things?"

"I have a feeling," said Elizabeth, "you've already seen one — in Ward Seven."

Maude flinched, then bobbed her head in affirmation.

"Well, then, why don't you tell me exactly what happened."

Maude flung back her sheets and punched at the air. She sat up straight, gasping for breath in the dark room. But then she felt the soft mattress beneath her, the fresh-smelling blanket. The borrowed cloth nightgown felt warm and snug against her skin. She wiped hair from her face, and realized that it had been stuck there with cold sweat. Maude looked around at the unfamiliar room and at last remembered where she was.

"Helen," she mumbled to herself.

She had dreamt of Helen. The dream had been vague: Maude had only seen only her friend's face, the dimples and curled red hair, the light blue eyes. Around her, there had only been mist, no people or setting. But Maude had felt herself well up with fear, and then the face had vanished, and then —

Yet now she was here, in this comfortable room, and all was well. The windows were dressed in gauzy white curtains, and streetlight cast pleasing shapes across the smooth ceiling. Maude felt disoriented but protected, far from the windowless barracks of the sanitarium, where she had shivered herself to sleep in a tiny bunk.

But she was also alone. That had been the only comfort at Ruby Hill—the presence of Helen. They hadn't talked much. They weren't allowed to chat during work hours, and their suppers were spent in silence. It was only after curfew, during those minutes before the lights switched off, that they lay in their beds, only a few feet from each other, and spoke in hushed but honest tones.

Did you ever think of going back to Columbus? Helen had said.

Sometimes, Maude said. *But there's not much there for me, either. Anything's better than this sty.*

Ssh! They'll hear you!

Let 'em hear me. I got better treatment on the factory line. I'd still be there if they didn't find out my family was Mick.

Are you going to quit?

Quit? Helen sneered. *Escape, is more like it. This place gives me an ulcer. It isn't like any sanitarium I've ever heard of. I told you about the bodies, right?*

Please, don't.

Well, I think something crazy's going on, and I'm not sticking around to find out. But if things get any kookier, you should talk to this lady I know. Really swell dame. Elizabeth Crowne.

Elizabeth...?

Crowne. Must be the smartest woman in Pittsburgh. Has a lovely house in Oakland, like a mansion. Reads all the time. Practically lives at the library. But folks are always sayin' she'll lend a hand, 'specially if your circumstances are—a little strange. Helen sniffed and rubbed her nose. *But I'm gettin' out of here. I don't care where I go, long as I leave this dungeon behind.* She twisted her head toward Maude. *Wish you could tag along. You got a raw deal, like me. And you're a good egg, Maude. Don't let anybody tell you different.*

Maude opened her mouth, ready to speak. *Yes*, she wanted to say. *I'll go with you.* But then the ceiling lamps shut off, and the room was black, and the voices died with the light.

Nearly a week had passed since that conversation. Maude had felt some comfort in Helen's advice, and Maude missed her street smarts, her fortitude. She wondered where Helen had gone. But tonight, Maude could drift back to sleep with relative ease. For the first time since she could remember, Maude did not fear the coming of dawn.

The taxi bumbled its way along the chalky dirt road, and Elizabeth struggled to apply her makeup.

"Damned potholes," she cursed, pressing base into her cheeks.

"Let me help you," offered Maude, who gingerly took the compact and awkwardly applied it from the side.

"I suppose it's obvious how little I do this."

Maude evened out the base and then proceeded to the rouge. When she was satisfied, she closed the set and said, "All done." Then she glanced through the windshield, at the road that twisted up an increasingly familiar hill. Beneath an overcast sky, the grassy slopes looked dark and damp. Out here, the telephone poles leaned at oblique angles, and the few signs were pecked and worn by the elements. "Are you *sure* we have to do this?" Maude whispered. "Couldn't we just call the police?"

"If my theory holds," said Elizabeth, "the police won't do us any good."

"Then what can we do?"

Elizabeth pocketed her makeup set and drew her lambskin gloves over her hands. "There are three possibilities, in all interactions with the uncanny," she said professorially. "First, you alleviate pain. Say someone is sick or tormented, you may try to cure the thing that ails him. Second, you may resolve to do nothing. A seemingly nefarious thing may turn out to be benign. The third is the most unpleasant, and a last resort, to be sure."

"You mean —"

"Destroy it. I have no patience for malevolent forces. And unless I've missed my guess, Dr. Lundqvist is precisely that."

The walls of Ruby Hill had emerged on the horizon, great stretches of black stone topped with green-rusted copper roofs. An afternoon fog had swallowed the far corners, given a sense of infinite size. The structure was far bigger than Elizabeth had anticipated, and it was only when the car had stopped before its main gate that she could digest its volume.

"It doesn't exactly say, 'Tender love and care,' does it?" said Elizabeth as she exited the car and leaned against its roof, studying the bleak environs.

"The girls say it's a former prison," Maude noted, trying to hide the shake in her voice.

"Surprise, surprise." Elizabeth turned to Maude. "All right, let's get a look at you."

The taxi drove off, descending into the mist. The two women were alone in the gravel lot, enabling Elizabeth to assess Maude without distraction: The young woman had been restored to her former exquisiteness, exchanging the drab workwoman's garb for one of Elizabeth's own outfits — a flowing velvet dress that shimmered violet, even in the dimming light. Maude had wrapped around herself a black cloak, which accentuated the bourgeois guise, and her perfect hair was pressed beneath a pillbox hat, whose netted veil covered her long lashes.

"You clean up well," said Elizabeth.

"You don't think they'll recognize me?" Maude whispered, looking askance at the asylum's black gate.

"They employ twenty girls and a handful of men," said Elizabeth. "And you say you met Dr. Lundqvist only once."

"Yes, for my training," said Maude.

"Then I think we're golden."

When they reached the massive front door, Elizabeth knocked boldly. They waited a full minute before a tiny hatch slid open, and a pair of suspicious eyes peeked out.

"What is it?" said a gruff voice.

"We're here to see Dr. Lundqvist. I believe we spoke on the phone."

The eyes lowered slightly, indicating a nod of recognition. The hatch shut, followed by the sound of drawing bars, clicking locks. The eight-foot door opened with a deep groan, cracking only wide enough to admit the two women, who stepped into a dark atrium. Then the door clanked shut.

The man looming over them was surreally huge, and his blue uniform barely contained his dense musculature. He was unshaven, but the scruff along his puttied jaw had grown in uneven patches, suggesting that a full beard was a lofty goal.

"Your bag," he groaned.

"My what?"

"Your *bag*." He pointed a fat and callused finger at Elizabeth's purse, which was strung over her shoulder.

"What about it?"

He made a motion with his hands, as if stretching something open. Elizabeth scoffed at this, then sighed, irritated, and opened the purse wide, presenting its interior to the giant. The man leaned in and saw the jumble of feminine effects, including the makeup kit.

"What's this?" he demanded.

"This?"

Elizabeth snatched the object at the bottom of her purse and brought it roughly into the air. It was a wooden tube, about a foot long and an inch in diameter, its exterior carved with primitive figures. Maude hadn't noticed the tube, and it struck her as exotic and strange. A feather was tied to one end with a leather cord, and it flapped around in the wind.

"It's an Amazonian flute," said Elizabeth. "A gift for my nephew."

The man glared at it, confused, as if debating whether a musical instrument could be lethal.

"I'm just having it wrapped this evening," Elizabeth went on. "But don't ask me to play it. I play decent piano, but nothing from the woodwind section."

The giant fluttered his eyes, then turned sideways. His body was so large that this simple rotation seemed like the turning of a battleship.

"This way," he groaned.

The courtyard was large and open, surrounded on all sides by blackened walls, but it was clear that a once-busy recreational space had been abandoned for some time: Overgrown tufts of grass framed stagnant gray puddles, and an old pigskin had deflated and lost its stitching. Elizabeth stifled the urge to comment, but nevertheless she thought: *Funny that once being a penitentiary should constitute "the good old days."*

They climbed a wide stone staircase and proceeded through an iron gate, which the giant took care to lock behind them. Elizabeth silently cursed this action, for now they were trapped inside—except for the giant's key. Indeed, the man carried a hoop of keys on his belt, which jangled loudly in the corridor. When they reached a final door, the giant slammed his knuckles against it, knocking with the force of a gale.

"Enter," came a frail voice from within.

The office was large and designed like a castle's great hall. A massive stone hearth yawned from the opposite side of the room, where a well-built fire burned. The pelt of a polar bear had been spread across the floor, its limbs extended, its mouth fiercely opened. Behind the white fur stood a desk, where a small man wrote. He wore a dense turtleneck sweater, but his skinny neck and sunken cheeks betrayed a fragile figure. His knobby knuckles dragged his fountain pen across thick stationary, until he finally jabbed a period into the end of a sentence and tossed the writing implement away.

"Ladies," he hissed, then gestured to the two chairs in front of him. "If you please."

His accent was difficult to place, a base layer of Scandinavian tempered by years of American English. He removed his bifocals and rubbed the red ovals around his eyes. The desk lamp illuminated the many spots that blemished his vellum-like skin.

"Thank you for taking the time," Elizabeth said amiably, and she and Maude seated themselves. The giant moved silently, but Elizabeth could sense his presence directly behind them. She could practically feel the heat of his breath permeating through her scarf and into the back of her neck.

"My name is Theodora Quinley, of the Quinley family," said Elizabeth quickly, but then she raised an eyebrow. "You may have heard of us?"

"I'm afraid I have not," said Dr. Lundqvist slowly.

"Well, you will. You see, we've spent a great deal of time in California. We love it out there, of course. You can't beat a hacienda in Napa. But I don't think it's any secret that times are changing."

"Changing?" said Dr. Lundqvist.

"We've made do with our wine and oranges," said Elizabeth. "We've broken enough horses to start our own cavalry. It's a simple life, Dr. Lundqvist. But we're no naïfs. In this day and age, a family business has got to stay competitive."

"Yes," Dr. Lundqvist said, his cracked lips curling into a smile. "Now more than ever."

"I'm talking about industry, of course," Elizabeth went on. "Factories. Manufacturing. Which is to say, the Quinleys are preparing to come back East."

Dr. Lundqvist leaned forward and folded his hands on the desk. He searched for words, his mouth pantomiming speech, as if to rehearse his next thought.

"Then... how can *I* help you?"

Elizabeth fingered a knit on her scarf and pulled it away, examining it with abandon. "I have friends, Dr. Lundqvist," she said. "They pointed me in your direction."

"Did they?" said the doctor.

Maude tensed. She had willed herself to stay calm, for Elizabeth seemed so self-assured, but where was she going with this dialogue? The uncannologist had still revealed nothing of her plan, only that they should meet with Dr. Lundqvist and dress in the fashionable garments of heiresses.

"They knew to keep things private," said Elizabeth, now staring furtively into the old man's eyes. "They were light on details. But I'm keen on arithmetic, doctor, and I think I know what your business adds up to."

"My... *business?*"

"Consumption and lunacy," declared Elizabeth. "Two things no one likes to see. Sick men, mad men, both must be quarantined. So they come here, to Ruby Hill. But you only accept the lost ones. The ones without papers. The ones without families. The ones—*no one will miss.*"

Dr. Lundqvist's smile broadened as he glared back to her.

Then he shrugged his shoulders. "Any sanitarium is full of such people."

"But I think," continued Elizabeth, "that you keep them all together. All that sickness. All that dementia. You crowd it in one place, feed them only enough nourishment to live. And then, when they're on the cusp of dying—of natural causes, of course—you steal them away."

"And..." Lundqvist shook his head vaguely, rolling his fountain pen back and forth with a finger. "And what would be the point of all this? What value is there in a dead man?"

"But that's the trick," said Elizabeth. "They're not exactly dead. Nor are they alive. They're *undead*." Then she waved a hand, as if bored by the idea. "It's a common thing, more common than we'd like to accept. A contagion arrives in some place. Someone dies, carrying the infection—and then, to the chagrin of everyone around him, that man comes back to life. He crawls out of his grave, mindless and starving. He wanders around, in search of carrion to devour. And if he bites a living person, he spreads that contagion. Too soon, there's an outbreak, and all hell breaks loose. But what if—" Elizabeth could barely contain her excitement. "What if you didn't *stop* the outbreak, but *contained* it. What if you *harvested* these undead bodies and kept them in a secret place. What if you let the health of these sick patients decline, and then, at the final moments of their lives, exposed their bodies to the contagion, ensuring that they would *become* undead."

"Suppose you're right," said Dr. Lundqvist, in the voice of a skeptical academic. "And this contagion causes—let's call it what it is—*mass zombification*. Who would ever *want* such a thing?"

Elizabeth smiled knowingly. "Who would want a zombie? A creature that doesn't think or sleep? A creature that craves only human flesh, no matter how decomposed? It feels nothing, especially pain. Indeed, who would find a use for zombies?" Elizabeth paused, then threw up her hands. "Why, factory owners, of course."

Dr. Lundqvist bit into his blue cuticle, then grasped his bifocals.

"Factory owners."

"Exactly. You see, Dr. Lundqvist, I think you're selling *labor*. Chain a zombie to a treadmill, hang some flesh from a meat hook, and he'll walk forever. Like a mule following a carrot. Endless manpower, all day and all night. They don't drink, they don't fraternize, and they certainly can't strike. It's the perfect workforce, if automation is all you're after. And if I'm right, I want in."

Dr. Lundqvist exchanged a glance with the giant, which Elizabeth assumed the giant returned. Then he smiled in a grandfatherly way.

"And if I *could* provide such a workforce, how many specimens would you need?"

Maude's mind reeled. *Elizabeth was right!* She had figured out Dr. Lundqvist's scheme without ever meeting the man. Maude never imagined that such deduction was possible, much less deducing something so horrid and strange. The very idea that a human being could be both alive and dead sounded like fantasy, and yet here they were, discussing a transaction based on that very fact.

"I'll need two hundred to start," said Elizabeth. "If all goes well, we'll double it."

Lundqvist's eyes bulged with surprise. "Two *hundred?* We have never supplied more than twenty at a time!"

"Well, seems like we've both hit the jackpot," said Elizabeth. "I have faith in you, Dr. Lundqvist. I dare say that undead workers are the way of the future. Oh, I understand why you've been so quiet. Unions, newspapermen, Catholics — they'll never understand it. But the most efficient workforce is the one you don't have to pay, or house, or feed. You're the first to harness the human body for pure labor, and I think it's brilliant."

Lundqvist beamed. He looked vindicated, as if a thousand doubts had dissipated. He pressed his palms into the desk and pushed himself into a standing position, then extended a hand.

"In that case, Ms. Quinley, I should be very pleased to do business with you."

"Very good," said Elizabeth, but she didn't accept the handshake. Instead she gestured to Maude. "We do have one problem, though."

"A problem?"

"Well, I'm a trusting type. Most of us Quinleys are. But my sister here—she's a bit more skeptical. Georgina isn't as trusting as I am, which is why she makes such a good business partner. I would be happy to make a verbal agreement, sight-unseen. But Georgina—well, she has one condition."

"A condition? You mean a contract?"

"Oh, nothing like that. I think we can all agree, the less paperwork, the better. No, not a contract. But we *should* like to see this workforce firsthand."

"Ah!" Lundqvist tossed his head back, understanding, then snapped his fingers at the giant and said something quickly in a sharply consonantal language. He groped the brass handle of a cane and extricated himself from his chair. "But of course. Let us inspect them together."

Maude forced her feet forward, down the long corridor, as the voices reverberated in her ears. Now that Maude had escaped this place, her repulsion was doubled. She wanted to flee, to go anywhere but here.

She knew this place so well, after three months inside. She had walked this same unmopped floor a hundred times, past these same sealed metal doors. She knew which cells contained which voices—the maniacal laughter in 15, the uncontrolled weeping in 4, the gibbering in 12, the pleading in 2, the nonsensical prayers and monologues delivered in-between. She knew the patients who sang lullabies, the ones who spat profanities as she passed, the ones who crouched in the corners of their empty rooms like gargoyles, seeming not to breathe. Some hatches were always open, to admit air and to monitor the patients within. Others were sealed shut, and God only knew what transpired in those suffocating lockups. Violent patients were kept alone, docile ones in trios. The true lunatics might jump from cot to cot, ripping open pillows and hurling feathers into the air. But the tuberculosis patients were too weak to move. They stayed bedridden until—

Maude quashed the thought. She couldn't believe she had returned, and now she felt partly responsible for the suffering here. She had cooked their gruel, slid trays under their doors, and laundered their soiled blankets. She had helped Dr. Lundqvist—this calculating monster—neglect his patients to the point of death, then transform them into mindless slaves. In exchange for a meager wage and a place to rest her head, Maude had abetted the sale of living corpses.

"This is where we cultivate the patients," said Dr. Lundqvist in a singsong voice, stretching his arms wide, encompassing the whole corridor. "The old prison architecture is perfect for my purposes. And we have many empty wards to spare. As we grow, we may expand into the vacant space as well. There is room for five hundred patients, at least..."

Walking behind Dr. Lundqvist, it all felt so eerily natural. This could have been a visit to a hospital like any other. He was a businessman, using a resource to innovate the workplace. He hobbled forward, so elated by his lecture that his legs and cane failed to match each other's rhythm, and he stumbled more than once. The second time he nearly fell, caught at the last second by the giant's bulging arms.

"Thank you, Bjorn!" he chuckled. "I'm afraid you've made me giddy, Ms. Quinley. I have so little opportunity…" He coughed into his fist, struggling to catch his breath, then went quiet. "My workers, they know nothing. I keep them isolated. They think this is a common sanitarium. I don't care for questions. But you, Ms. Quinley—you have a rare intelligence. You can appreciate what I have done. All these useless bodies, sick and mad. No one wants them. Now, *they have purpose!*"

A moment later, they reached the door. The same heavy metal door that Maude had opened and closed so many times. The same hatch Dr. Lundqvist had forbidden her to look through. The same threshold between the standard revulsions of a modern sanitarium and the horrors of an inhuman trade.

"And that, I have forgotten to say," huffed Lundqvist, just before he coughed again. "The most ingenious part. The undead, they eat human flesh, yes? And this is abundant! Mortuaries! Graveyards! The many schools of medicine! What use is a cadaver? Now, we feed them to the workers. You see?"

Maude could feel her eyes rolling back in her head, the blood draining from her face. She wanted to obey gravity, to simply fall backward, slamming insentiently against the floor. But again she refused to faint. She suppressed the memory of those "slop buckets"—the basins full of dissected bodies, severed limbs, hands and heads and organs that had once belonged to living people. It was Maude herself who had dragged the basins into this room, pretending that the flimsy cloth that covered it was not saturated in blood and embalming fluid. But when she'd opened the hatch and looked inside, she could no longer stifle the truth: The undead were devouring the dead, feasting on human flesh every infernal day, in the cavernous bowels of Ward Seven. And it was Dr. Lundqvist, the smiling old man standing before them, who had resigned these poor souls to savage degradation.

Bjorn pulled open the door, and all four stepped inside. They crossed the vast expanse of concrete, and as they did so, a chorus of snarling voices erupted in the shadows. Lundqvist made his way to the cells, where the undead gathered behind their cages. There were dozens of them, silhouetted in the darkness, barely visible in the unlit chambers. Their arms stretched between the bars, mangled hands and broken fingers reaching for anything they could grasp.

"So you see, they require little," explained Lundqvist. "The holding pens have no need for light or beds. We waste nothing. The only reason even to feed them to is keep their bodies nourished. But the undead—by definition—cannot die. Only a head trauma, which destroys what remains of the brain, can terminate them." He smiled contentedly. "We have forty-three at this moment, but soon, Ms. Quinley, you will have a full supply. I will make your purchase a priority."

Maude could not tear her eyes away. She had refused to look at them before, those creatures in the darkness, but here they were—faces and bodies, soulless eyes that seemed to glow with carnivorous desire, unkempt hair and the sweat-soaked garments in which they had died. Maude surveyed those diverse visages, of old and young men, scattered women, even a sickly boy in his ragged suspenders. They were strangers, but they had once been alive, like anyone Maude might pass on the streets of Pittsburgh.

Then she saw it—a familiar face. Emaciated and colorless, clawing at the air like a starving animal. The face had completely transformed, but still Maude recognized its owner. She remembered how the face appeared before, healthy and sweet, a girl with Irish dimples and curly red hair, as alive as herself.

"Helen..." Maude said, her voice cracking.

"What was that?" Lundqvist said. The old man was still smiling, merely distracted by the errant name. But then he saw

Maude, and his mirth instantly faded. "What did you say?"

Maude stepped back, too consumed with horror to hide her emotions. She raised her hands to her cheeks, where tears were already streaming, and she felt her repulsion surge upward from her heart, into her throat, then explode from her lips as an ear-piercing scream. The scream filled the room, overpowering the undead hubbub, replacing all those primal groans with the voice of woe.

Then Maude knew that all was lost. She had blown their cover, and Lundqvist would now destroy them. Yet she couldn't stay silent. She stared at Helen, the friend she had once adored. She yearned to go back, to save Helen from this fate. She would trade her own life for Helen's, if fortune required the exchange—*But please*, Maude silently begged, *preserve Helen from this miserable end.*

Maude sensed Bjorn moving behind her, and she knew she could do nothing. She had always been powerless, and now she would die that way. She turned slowly around, ready to accept her doom. Maybe she would see Helen again, once the shock of death was over. Maybe this was all for the best.

Then, in the corner of her eye, she saw Elizabeth move. The uncannologist swung her purse forward, tore it open, and drew the wooden tube. It looked the same as before, small and ornately carved. But then Elizabeth raised it to her lips. She bit down on one end. She puffed out her cheeks.

A blowpipe, Maude thought.

Bjorn jolted. He looked down at his barrel chest, where a dart now protruded. He lifted a hand, as if to rip the projectile from his own skin, but his hand never reached it. Instead Bjorn teetered, looked blankly toward the ceiling, and slumped heavily to the floor.

"*Run!*" shouted Elizabeth.

Maude did—she ran, watching the open door ahead of her. Her body flailed as she went, a frenzied windmill of arms and legs. But she also felt a tinge of excitement, joy; she was running away now, away from the cells and undead and toilsome jobs, away from the men who had lorded over her existence, away from the stench of rigor mortis and the nauseating helplessness of life. Now she was running on her own two feet, and beyond that door, a great new future waited.

Maude looked back only once. She couldn't see Elizabeth, and she wanted to stop and turn around, to rescue her new mentor from this terrible place—but then she saw Elizabeth again, trailing just a few steps behind—and beyond her, Dr. Lundqvist, who stumbled over his cane and fell to his wobbling knees.

"*Stop! Damn you!*" Lundqvist called, but his voice was hoarse with age and exertion. What followed was a string of foreign expletives, as meaningless to Maude as they were ineffectual.

Elizabeth caught up to Maude, clapped her assistant on the back, and together they flew through the open doorway. They pivoted around and rammed their svelte bodies against the iron door, pushing with all their might, until it slammed into place. A profound boom reverberating through the lithic vacuum. The last sound was the click of the lock.

They leaned against the metal, panting. Maude felt blood rush to her head, but also relief, euphoria. She had lost her friend, and that loss would taint her days for years to come. But she was alive, and she would live for both of them, as fully as this bright new world would allow.

"Maude..." huffed Elizabeth.

"Yes...?" Maude huffed back.

"Would you... do the honors?"

Maude was only confused for a moment. Then she fervently shook her head. "Oh... no... I couldn't."

"Not that kind of girl?" said Elizabeth.

"I... no... not really..."

"That's all right. You've done enough unpleasant things

here. I think you deserve a substitute."

Elizabeth peeled herself off the door and strode over to the lever, the same lever Maude had forced herself to use so many times. Elizabeth clasped its handle with both hands, contorted her face, and pulled.

As before, Maude could hear the grinding of machinery, the slide of opening gates, the beastly excitement building as the undead sensed their freedom. She heard the shuffling of eighty-six feet across the bare floor. She heard the undead converging in the middle of the room, clustering together in a tight circle. She knew what would happen, thought she couldn't see it: She heard Lundqvist's voice—not words, but abstract groans of protest. The undead moans grew louder, rising into a crescendo of mindless gluttony, and it was only then that Lunqvist screamed—a breathy shriek of terror, followed by recurring wails of agony, protests of "No! *No!*" He vocalized his suffering for long minutes. The undead knew nothing of mercy, only hunger. From the savage sounds, Maude knew they were digging their teeth into his flesh, ripping him apart. Only when he had been quartered, skinned, and gutted would the doctor finally be allowed to die.

"Come on," Elizabeth said. "Let's leave them be."

"P-p-p-please…" Maude stuttered. "L-l-l-let's do!"

"And let's give the police a call," Elizabeth added. "They can handle unlocking the doors."

"But how do we get out?" Maude said, suddenly remembering.

Elizabeth smiled, wiping her brow. "With these, of course." And she lifted the ring of keys, which she had filched at the last moment from the fallen giant's belt.

Maude poured coffee into the cezve, then hurried to her crackling pan full of eggs. She slipped the eggs onto a plate and carried it to the breakfast nook, where Elizabeth was reading a newspaper.

"Will you look at this," said Elizabeth, smacking the edge of the paper. "'Police Raid Closed Penitentiary, Free Madmen.' Right here on the front page." She shook her head. "And nothing about Ward Seven."

"Nothing?"

"The undead fellows in the back? Not a word."

Maude set Elizabeth's coffee on the table, next to the untouched plate.

"Why wouldn't they... I mean..."

"It's *uncanny*," opined Elizabeth, folding the paper and tossing on the tablecloth. "Folks would never believe it. It's a double-edged sword. The things they don't believe could be their undoing. But it's that disbelief that keeps me in business."

Maude went back to the kitchen, slipped two more eggs onto a plate, then poured a second cup of coffee for herself. She moved past the newly wiped counters and appliances, across the freshly swept floors, toward the vestibule that Maude was now busy organizing. Light poured through the windows, and the floorboards seemed to glow.

Maude headed toward the front door. She wanted to sit on the porch swing and watch the traffic go by. To bask in the morning sun. It was the first warm spring day of 1921, and she wanted to relish every second of it. Just as she grasped the door's handle, she heard Elizabeth call from her nook.

"Stick with me, kid. We're going to have a lot of fun."

Maude pushed through the door, plate balanced in her hand. She was instantly immersed in solar warmth. Horses clacked past, drawing a carriage. Two young boys tossed baseballs in the street. Distantly, dogs barked, as if welcoming the day.

Maude smiled.

A lot of fun, indeed.

THE BOOTLEGGER'S MYSTERY

May, 1921

TRANSCRIPT

PATIENT: Thank you for meeting with me. I know it was short notice.

ANALYST: Of course. I had a cancellation, anyway. Would you like some tea? A glass of water?

PATIENT: I'm fine.

ANALYST: I was reviewing our notes before you arrived. I must say, I think we've made some progress.

PATIENT: Oh?

ANALYST: Don't you agree?

PATIENT: I don't know.

ANALYST: Well—when you first came to me, you struck me as *guarded*.

PATIENT: I suppose that's true.

ANALYST: You were schmoozing me.

PATIENT: Schmoozing?

ANALYST: You wanted me to like you. You wanted to seem charming. Successful. That's normal, of course. Everyone wants to look his best. But I feel that you've been opening up. About your family, for instance.

PATIENT: I don't… I don't like to talk about them.

ANALYST: I can tell. But you have. And that's important. What's more, you mentioned your—what was the word you used?—ah, yes, your *appetites*. Maybe we could talk about those appetites today?

PATIENT: What do you want to know?

ANALYST: Could you describe them? What does that mean, appetite?

PATIENT: Well… I have dreams. Vivid dreams.

ANALYST: What happens in these dreams?

PATIENT: I lose control of myself. I transform. It's like I'm no longer human. I become—an animal. I'm hungry. Ravenous. I'm filled with a kind of rage. But not a human rage. It isn't anger, exactly. It's a desire to destroy. To kill. I take pleasure in it.

ANALYST: In these dreams, do you ever take anyone's life?

PATIENT: Yes. But only recently. For years, I could control myself.

ANALYST: A lucid dream.

PATIENT: Come again?

ANALYST: That's the technical term—a lucid dream. We know we're dreaming, and we can take the reins, as it were.

PATIENT: But it's not like that anymore.

ANALYST: You have no control?

PATIENT: No. None at all. It's like my body isn't my body anymore. When I see with my eyes, it's as if I'm looking through a haze. My voice, my hands, even my skin—they act of their own accord. Have you ever been drunk, doctor?

ANALYST: I've been known to indulge, from time to time.

PATIENT: Have you ever been so drunk that you don't know what you're doing? You say things you don't mean? You lose track of your surroundings?

ANALYST: Not often, but I know the feeling.

PATIENT: It's like that, but a thousand time worse.

ANALYST: It's good of you to share this. But you should take heart—they're only dreams. They can't harm you. Dreams exist to help you understand

yourself. Your subconscious is trying to tell you
something. When you feel yourself transform into an
animal, it's a metaphor. Don't you see? You've denied
a desire. You've buried it. But that desire refuses
to go away. This is very common. You have no reason
to be ashamed. You have only to decode its meaning,
and those dreams will help you become a better man.
    PATIENT: What if…
    ANALYST: What was that?
    PATIENT: What if they're not dreams?

"There's a Mr. Lombardi here to see you," said Maude, poking her head from behind the door.

Elizabeth furrowed her brow. She decided that now was not the best time to blow some gage, so she slipped her roach into her desk drawer and folded her hands. Her chair squeaked as she leaned forward.

"No appointment?" asked Elizabeth.

"I… I don't think so," said Maude.

"Well, send him in."

A moment later the door opened. It swung outward slowly, pushed by a casual hand. A man stood in its opening, wearing black pinstripes and a gray fedora. His shirt was pressed white. His tie was a narrow line that bisected his slim torso, flanked by thick red suspenders. His jacket was folded like a newspaper over his forearm. He smiled, and his pencil mustache adjusted accordingly.

"Ms. Crowne," he said.

"That would be me."

At first glance, Elizabeth felt divided about this man. His fedora was too wide, his air too confident. She didn't like to judge, but with his cocky bearing and a name like Lombardi, she guessed the man plied an unpleasant trade. But she also noticed his slim physique, athletic shoulders, and the low growl of his voice. He didn't distort the diphthong of her name, as so many gangsters might. He looked distinguished in a way that few men had of late.

"Pleased to meet you," he said, removing his hat. "I like your office."

"I'm afraid it's not for sale," Elizabeth said.

The man chuckled deep inside his throat. His pronounced Adam's apple juddered, but otherwise he was statuesque. "They told me about that wit of yours."

"*They* give me too much credit, but I'd love to know who they are."

"Abner Cohen," said Lombardi. He drew a pocket watch from his shirt and flipped it open, then replaced it. "He spoke highly of you."

"Abner," murmured Elizabeth fondly. She permitted herself a sidelong smile. "Well, any friend of Abner's is someone worth meeting. Mr. Lombardi?"

"Please, call me Ennio." He stepped forward, guided by an extended hand. Elizabeth was comfortable in her high-backed chair, but she made the effort to rise and allowed Lombardi to kiss her knuckles, as tacky as she found the gesture. Then the visitor sank into a chair and crossed his legs in a gentlemanly way. Elizabeth noted his freshly polished wingtips.

"How can I help you?" Elizabeth said.

Lombardi looked away, toward the small window. The day was unseasonably warm, and Elizabeth had opened the window to admit fresh air and abundant sunlight. Now Lombardi looked pained, and crow's feet emerged at the tips of his eyes.

"I'm an attorney by profession," he began.

"A common affliction," Elizabeth said. Lombardi smiled at this, but Elizabeth still decided to soften the blow. "Having a profession, I mean."

"I'm second generation, and a Philadelphian," said Lombardi. "And I suppose you can guess what that means."

"Don't worry," said Elizabeth. "I have a weakness for

hooch."

"But please understand," said Lombardi, "it's a family obligation more than anything. I'm an advisor."

"A consigliere?"

He chuckled and brushed a hand across the rim of his shoe. "Nothing so grand. But there's always advice to dole out. My family—they think with their fists. They make a lot of mistakes. It doesn't matter how business is going. Good or bad, it's not long before I get a phone call and have to iron things out."

"And I presume you got a call recently?"

"I did." He cleared his throat. "My family has a regular route, between Philadelphia and Pittsburgh. We distill the product in basements, bottle it, and store it in trucks. Milk trucks, actually."

"Nice touch."

"They thought so. So they drive across the state, unload in the Strip District, and receive wholesale prices. It's a simple business. No dealing with speakeasies or gambling outfits—not directly, anyway. My family is bare-knuckled, but they don't break fingers."

"Well, that's a relief," said Elizabeth, flexing hers.

"We haven't had problems since the law changed," Lombardi went on. "We run a clean operation, all things considered. But a few months ago—we had an incident."

"G-men?"

"No," said Lombardi slowly. "I wish it was that simple. You see, there's a wooded stretch of road, just a few miles past Kinship. It's not far from Pittsburgh, only a few hours by car, but it feels like the wilderness. To make a long story short, Ms. Crowne, we lost two men out there."

"Attacked?"

"More than attacked." Lombardi took a long breath. "They were torn apart. Limb from limb. I'll spare you're the details, but the coroner confessed he'd never seen anything like it."

"You needn't spare details, Mr. Lombardi. I have a strong stomach."

"It's not that," he countered. "They were—they were cousins of mine. I don't like to think of them that way."

Elizabeth nodded. "Of course."

"My family grieved terribly. They know the risks of their business, but this was different."

"Different in what way?"

"Well," said Lombardi, his eyebrows rising. "For starters, nobody touched the bottles. Their wallets were still in their pockets. My one cousin, Tony, he had a gold cigarette case." Lombardi slipped a hand into his trousers and produced a shining metal box. "This one, in fact."

"No robbery," Elizabeth murmured. "And they were disemboweled, you say?"

"Yes. The car was full of blood. They found Tony's head…" He faltered, then looked back toward the sunlit window. "They found his head fifty yards away. It had been pulled out of his body. Took half his spine along with it." Lombardi shook his head. "I couldn't even look at the pictures. The coroner's report alone…"

"It's an awful thing," said Elizabeth lowly.

"My family couldn't lose any more of their own. So they decided to hire other men. Men outside the family. They had never done it before, but you can't buy back a loved one, so they spent the money. The trouble was, the next month, it happened again."

"Again?"

"Indeed. Then the month after that. Three attacks. Every time, the same place."

Elizabeth leaned back in her chair. She drew her finger across her lips.

"Well," she said. "If you're coming to me, I suppose you've

ruled out coyotes."

Lombardi grimaced. "The violence was animal," he said. "But a natural predator? Something that strong and vicious in Pennsylvania? It seems impossible."

"It does at that," said Elizabeth. "Even mountain lions aren't so aggressive. Well, then, what do you propose?"

Lombardi looked relieved by the question, and he gestured with his fedora. "With your permission, I'd like to take you out there."

"In a milk truck?"

He laughed fully at this. "In my car, actually. I drove here."

"From Philadelphia?"

"Yes, indeed."

"That's a long trip."

"Well, I trust Abner's opinion. If he says a woman is extraordinary, I'd drive to the moon to meet her."

"Hopefully it won't come to that."

"Frankly," said Lombardi, "given your area of expertise, I doubt anyone else could help me. What's happening out there—it's just not natural. And if it's paranormal, you're *the only one* I can turn to." He stared at her, insistent.

"And you want to visit the scene of the murders?"

"Exactly."

"We would be driving together?"

"That's the idea."

"I hope you don't take offense," said Elizabeth, "but given your line of work, I'd like to bring some company."

Lombardi smirked and said smoothly, "You don't trust a bootlegger's son?"

"I trust bootleggers fine," said Elizabeth. "It's lawyers that make me cagey."

And with that, they both beamed amiably, stood, and shook hands.

"Maude!" Elizabeth called from her bedroom closet. "Where did I put the damned silver bullets?"

Maude stuck her head into the room, but all she saw was a cascade of clothes gushing from the closet. "Have you tried the library?"

The clothes stopped tumbling, and Elizabeth emerged from the closet. With one hand she dusted off her skirt. In the other hand she held a violet glass sphere.

"The library," she huffed. "Of course." Then Elizabeth held the orb aloft. "On the bright side, I found my crystal ball."

"You... you can tell the future?" whispered Maude.

"Don't get excited," said Elizabeth, tossing the ball into the ruffled sheets of her unmade bed. "It's defective."

Elizabeth strode into the library and rolled the ladder along its runners until she reached the proper section. As she climbed to the highest rungs, Maude instinctively grasped the bottom to keep the ladder steady. Elizabeth scraped a finger along the spines until she found one volume, then removed it.

"*Varieties of Lycanthropy*," she said, blowing dust off the cover. "Dreadful book." She opened it, revealing the hollowed out pages within. A small wooden box was inserted snugly into the empty paper square. Elizabeth dug the box out, returned the book to its shelf, and descended to the worn carpet. "Makes for decent storage, though."

Elizabeth leaned over her cluttered desk and opened the box, where a handful of bullets glinted. They looked reflective and flawless, like freshly minted dollars.

"Oh, dear," said Maude sheepishly. "Do you really think you'll need them?"

"It stands to reason," said Elizabeth, plucking up a bullet and holding it to the light. "Lombardi said three attacks, once a month. Something big and clawed. And it always happens at night. My guess is a lycanthrope."

"But... it always happens in the same place?" asked Maude.

"That *is* odd, isn't it?" said Elizabeth. "Always the same stretch of road. The car is always there at the same time of the month, and always after dark."

"Why wouldn't they drive the day after?" said Maude. "Or the day before?"

Elizabeth shrugged. "A schedule is a schedule. Capitalism waits for no werewolf."

Maude shuddered. "I don't like the sound of this."

"I don't either, which is why Lombardi's handling the gun."

Elizabeth opened the desk's bottom drawer and dug through some papers until her fingers brushed the handle of a revolver. She drew it out, a compact six-shooter with the floral patterns of a bygone day engraved into its barrel.

"My grandfather's," said Elizabeth. "Just your typical Colt single action. Nothing special. But I love a good heirloom."

"I... I wish you weren't going alone," said Maude.

"I'm not."

"Oh, no?"

"Of course not. I don't know Lombardi well enough to trust him. And I'm not too keen on werewolves, either."

"So who's going with you?"

Elizabeth flipped out the cylinder and examined its empty cartridge holes. Then she flicked her wrist, and the cylinder locked back into place.

"Why," said Elizabeth, "you are, my dear."

TRANSCRIPT

PATIENT: What I'm about to tell you is my most closely guarded secret. You must swear to me you'll tell no one.

ANALYST: We've discussed this. I'm your analyst. Nothing you say will ever leave this room.

PATIENT: Eight years ago, I was walking alone at

night. I was still a student. I was studying for my examinations, and I wasn't feeling up to the task. I had to clear my head. It was winter, by the way. A few weeks after Christmas. I was walking in the park. It was snowing. I've always loved watching snow fall past the streetlamps. I find it so calming. There was no one there. The park was completely empty. Even the lowliest bums had found shelter.

ANALYST: It sounds very nice.

PATIENT: All of a sudden, I saw a dog. Or that's what I thought. It was big—bigger than any dog I'd seen in the city. I thought it might be a husky or an elkhound. It had no collar, no license. But it looked too healthy to be a stray. I love dogs, you understand. I hate to see them wandering alone. So I came closer, thinking I could help. I said soothing words. You know, "Here, boy. That's a good pup." Things like that. But he only growled at me. It was the most savage growl I'd ever heard. And his eyes— they burned in the night like embers. I'd never seen such a malicious dog in my life. It started moving toward me. I tried to run away, but it jumped in the air. It knocked me to the ground.

ANALYST: The dog?

PATIENT: But it wasn't a dog. I could see that now. It was a *wolf*. I tried to push it away, but the wolf bit into my arm. Its teeth were like razors. Here, I still have the scars. Look at this.

ANALYST: My God!

PATIENT: You see? I was lucky to get away with my life. I had to punch the creature in the head, and even then I had to use all my strength to get away. I nearly fainted on the way to the hospital, the pain was so terrible. I left a trail of blood in the snow.

ANALYST: Are you saying what I think you're saying?

PATIENT: Yes. I think it infected me. I think that thing was… the stuff of legend. But it's *real*, I tell you! Every month, every full moon, I transform.

ANALYST: Maybe you're just—

PATIENT: It started simply. I had nightmares. I *imagined* myself doing terrible things. But it got worse. Some mornings, I'd wake up to find my bedroom

destroyed. Two landlords evicted me. Then I tried
hotel rooms, where I used assumed names. Can you
imagine the horror? Waking up, exhausted, naked, and
you've wrecked an entire room? The furniture
overturned, shattered, gnawed-on? And you can barely
remember what happened. Like I said, my body wasn't
my own.

ANALYST: Listen to me. What have you been eating
lately? Have you ever experienced hallucinations?
Heard voices that we're there?

PATIENT: That's *not* what this is!

ANALYST: Do you have insomnia, maybe?

PATIENT: You want proof, doctor? Just look at
this! *Look at it!*

ANALYST: What is this? A newspaper?

PATIENT: Look at the headline.

ANALYST: "Third Bootlegger Attack in Three
Months."

PATIENT: You see? No *man* could do that. Not even
an animal. And do you know how I know? Because *I* did
it. (*Pause*). I killed those men. I tore them apart. I
can almost remember doing it. I can almost taste
their blood. I can almost feel the—the *euphoria*.

ANALYST: There must be some explanation...

PATIENT: Doctor, I *know* the explanation. *This* is
why I'm here. I need someone to understand. *I am a
werewolf.* And it's become so much worse than I ever
feared. You don't know what it's like, to wake up on
the road, naked and trembling, a headache so fierce
you'd think your skull was split. Then you look
around, and there are body parts everywhere. Men
shredded like pork. It's maddening, doctor, to know
that *you're* the one who's done this loathsome thing.
You are the animal.

ANALYST: But how is that possible? This took place
near Kinship. That must be a hundred miles away.

PATIENT: Believe me, I was there.

ANALYST: But what were you doing out there?

PATIENT: It doesn't matter. (*Pause*). No, it *does*
matter. I wanted to distance myself. I wanted to keep
my family safe. If I was found out in my own
neighborhood—anyway, it was too dangerous.

ANALYST: You swear this isn't a hoax?

PATIENT: I swear on my life. I swear on the honor of my late grandfather. This is the truth. This is what I've become. (*Pause*). I know you don't believe me. But please don't have me committed. An asylum won't do me any good. I just need someone to know.
ANALYST: To be honest…
PATIENT: Yes?
ANALYST: I may know someone who can help.

"I don't mind saying it," said Elizabeth. "You have a very nice car, Mr. Lombardi."

Lombardi's expression was proud, as it should be: His Moon 6-40 was a stunner, with its long body and spotless red exterior. Lombardi had clearly had the vehicle waxed, as its metal glinted sunlight like lake water.

"Had it shipped from St. Louis," Lombardi said. "I saw it in a catalogue and knew I had to have it," He tugged at the end of his mustache, then let his hand fall limp in his lap. "You'd be surprised how quickly a man adapts to luxury."

Elizabeth decided not to respond to this statement. She never cared for men who bragged about their social climb. Instead, Elizabeth reached a hand through the open window and adjusted the rearview mirror. She saw Maude, sitting in the backseat, looking ebullient. Her eyes were affixed to the passing horizon.

"You look like you've never seen trees before," Elizabeth exclaimed.

"Well…" said Maude, bobbing her head. "None like these!"

Maude had barely left the city, and the sight of forest-carpeted hills no doubt astonished her. Now and again the woods would separate like curtains, revealing little farmhouses and red barns, men in straw hats and overalls emerging from freshly tilled fields. Tractors nestled in meadows. Crows flapped away from midget corn stalks, startled by the passing motor.

"Pretty as a picture," declared Lombardi. "I'm a city man, of course, but nothing makes me happier than fresh air. Sometimes I'll pass through one of these valleys at daybreak. Not by coincidence, mind you, but because I time it out. Driving these long roads is all about timing. If you find the right valley at the right hour, you'll see the mist. It stretches over the land like silk. You'll never see anything more beautiful in your life."

"We have a fair share of mist in Pittsburgh," scoffed Elizabeth. "It just comes out of smokestacks."

"We should be coming up on Kinship in a few minutes," said Lombardi.

"Really?" said Elizabeth. "Seems a little soon."

"If there's anything this road needs, it's some decent signage," said Lombardi. "But trust me, it's just a pace up the road. And I'll be delighted to treat you ladies to some lunch."

True to his prediction, the town emerged a couple miles later, a quaint little crossroads of small shops and cottages. Outside the clapboard general store, some men sat in rocking chairs and smoked pipes. A young boy perched on a wooden barrel, fiddling with a yoyo. The largest building was the Grossman Hotel, its weathered façade ringed with verandahs. The dirt roads converged at an intersection of dried mud, the tire tracks and hoof marks fossilized in the summer sun.

On a patch of grass, smoke billowed from an old steel drum. Three brawny men stood around it as flames licked the air, and when a breeze pushed the smolder aside, Elizabeth could make out the samples of meat crackling atop an iron grill.

Lombardi ordered three fat sausages, which the men forked into pieces of bread. One of the men took out an old Coca-Cola bottle, half-filled with mustard, and rammed its back with a palm until yellow paste poured onto the glistening casings.

"I have a weakness for German food," said Lombardi. "Those fellows know their meats."

It took only two bites for Maude to drip grease onto her blouse. "Oh, bother," she murmured, smudging the dollop into the fabric with a finger.

Elizabeth chewed and gazed at the distant hills. "How often do you pass through?"

"Oh, just now and again," said Lombardi. "Business trips."

"So walk me through the scene," said Elizabeth.

"Well, the first time, we found the car…" Lombardi raised a hand, as if to correct himself. "I mean a local farmer found the car. An Amish fellow, riding his horse, they tell me. Anyway, he saw the car early in the morning. Got scared, rode to town and telephoned the police. Took almost the whole day to get a sheriff out there, then another day to fetch a decent coroner. We didn't get the call until two nights after."

"So the attacks happened at night?"

"That's what I understand."

"Your operation runs better than a Swiss watch."

"How do you mean?"

"I mean," said Elizabeth, examining the last bite of her sausage, "your men always passed this same road, the same time of the month, and always at night."

"We run a tight operation," said Lombardi, cooler than before.

"Sure. But a tight operation doesn't account for rough roads. It's three hundred miles between Philadelphia and Pittsburgh. Not one bridge out? Not a single bad rainstorm? In three months? Always exactly on schedule? I'm just impressed, is all."

Lombardi stiffened, his eyes narrowed. "Ms. Crowne, where I come from, a man is only as good as his word. I'm the first man in my family to ever see a written contract. If you say you'll do something, you'll do it, whether the bridge is out or not. And excuse the language, but nobody will hire a second-rate wop. Hardly anyone will hire a *first*-rate wop. I didn't earn a law degree by playing morra."

Elizabeth dropped her eyes. "Pardon me, Mr. Lombardi. I didn't mean to offend you."

He took a breath. "No," he said, looking away, then awkwardly stuffed a hand into his jacket pocket. "No, of course not. I hate to be so sensitive. I should know better."

"How about an act of good faith?" said Elizabeth.

"Go on."

Elizabeth swallowed the last of her lunch, and then she ushered Lombardi toward the car. They rounded the hood, away from pedestrians in the street, and Elizabeth leaned in.

"Look here," said Elizabeth. "I think I know what your attacker was."

"You do?" puffed Lombardi. "Already?"

"Yes. All evidence points to…" Elizabeth paused, then touched Lombardi's shoulder comfortingly. "You'll have to bear with me, Ennio. You'll find my theory hard to believe, but I'm confident I know what happened."

"I trust your judgment," said Lombardi. "Abner says you're the best, and I believe it."

"Well, then, I think your attacker was a lycanthrope. That is, a werewolf."

Lombardi stared at her stoically for a moment, and then, just when it seemed he had frozen completely, his head drifted into a nod.

"I'm glad I'm not alone," he said.

"You mean…?" Maude piped up. "You mean, you thought so, too?"

"I don't know much about the macabre," said Lombardi. "It all sounds like fairy tales to me. But it just makes sense. Three nights, all full moons. Once a month. And such monstrous violence." Lombardi gestured toward the hills. "And those woods—God knows what could be lurking out there. Beauty can hide the darkest things."

"Tonight is a full moon," said Elizabeth, "so we can probably expect the same thing to happen again."

Lombardi shook his head. "I'm sorry, Elizabeth. This was a fool's idea. Let me take you back."

"No. You conscripted me, and I want to test my theory."

"But it's dangerous—"

"I don't blush at danger," said Elizabeth. "I don't blush at much, actually. And we should deal with this. You can change your shipping schedule, but that *thing* could just as easily harm someone else." She leered. "It took your cousins' lives. If anyone should pull the trigger, it's you."

With that, Elizabeth dug into her pocket and drew the revolver. She held it oddly, her thumb through the trigger ring, so that the handle hung below her wrist. Lombardi furrowed his brow and grasped the pistol from Elizabeth's finger. He held it near his beltline in both hands, like a pocket watch.

"Now that *is* an act of good faith," said Lombardi. He looked circumspectly, then opened the revolver. He examined the six casings for a moment, then shook a bullet out. The silver capsule was surprisingly dull-looking, like new nickel.

"The silver could use some polish," he said.

"They'll do the trick," retorted Elizabeth. "They're designed to kill lycanthropes, not for fancy dinners."

"Of course. And thank you." Lombardi pocketed the weapon, deep inside his jacket. He glanced at the lengthening shadows on the road, just as the sun disappeared behind a cloud, dimming the scenery. "We'd best be going. If we're going to face this thing, we'll have to be ready."

TRANSCRIPT

PATIENT: Who?

ANALYST: I have a friend in Pittsburgh. A close friend. We've known each other for years.

PATIENT: What does he do?

ANALYST: *She*, actually. Elizabeth Crowne. We've known each other since medical school. She isn't your typical specialist. She investigates the… uh…

PATIENT: The paranormal?

ANALYST: You could call it that. I like to say she has a broad spectrum of belief.

PATIENT: Where is she?

ANALYST: Pittsburgh. I'll write down her address.

PATIENT: And what does she charge?

ANALYST: Charge? You know, I'm not sure. I don't think she charges anything.

PATIENT: You must be joking.

ANALYST: I've never heard her mention it. If I were you, I would conveniently forget to bring it up. In any case, she's…

PATIENT: What?

ANALYST: She's one of the finest people I've ever met. And if anyone can help you, she can.

PATIENT: Just one question.

ANALYST: Of course.

PATIENT: You believe me, don't you?

ANALYST: I think I do, actually. Hard as it is.

PATIENT: If I'm right, if this is actually happening to me, and she learns that I'm… I'm…

ANALYST: You have taken lives, you mean.

PATIENT: Yes. What would keep her from calling the police?

ANALYST: Well—I don't know.

PATIENT: Mightn't she turn me in?

ANALYST: I suppose she could.

PATIENT: She's not an analyst. She doesn't have the same code of ethics.

ANALYST: Well—

PATIENT: And if she considers me a threat, she could call the bureau. She could shut down our entire operation. She could ruin us, *all* of us—

ANALYST: Look here! Calm yourself. Elizabeth is a very decent woman. And she's likely the only person who can help you. I trust her implicitly, do you understand? There's no reason to panic. Just talk to her. I can give you her number.

PATIENT: No, no phones. You never know who might be listening. I'll see her myself.

ANALYST: Good. Remember, we all have the same mission. We want to see you get better.
PATIENT: Yes, of course. I'm sorry—my temper.
ANALYST: It's all right. You've come a long way.
PATIENT: Thank you, Dr. Cohen.
ANALYST: My pleasure, Mr. Lombardi.

The road worsened, the dirt pavement scarified with potholes and trenches. The thick veins of tree roots bulged beneath the soil. The trio clunked along, until Lombardi stopped the car completely. Late afternoon sun poured through the foliage, blinding them, but still Elizabeth could discern a fallen tree trunk.

"No driving over that," said Lombardi.

"Can we get around it?" asked Elizabeth.

"We can try. I doubt we'd be the first."

Indeed, someone had chopped up the tree with an axe, but only along one end. The job was sloppy, the slapdash work of someone eager to keep moving. The tree was old and dead, thick as a factory chimney, but it had fallen recently, probably in the past few days. As Lombardi maneuvered the car, he edged toward the whittled part of the tree. The bottom of the car made a grinding sound, and the vehicle rocked from side to side, but with a final thump the rear wheels released themselves, and Lombardi returned to the road.

"Best engineering there is," said Lombardi, patting the dashboard.

"I'll be sure to write the Moon people a letter," said Elizabeth.

"I know it looks like a show car, but it handles well. Care to take the wheel?" He grinned at her lightheartedly.

"You're doing just fine," said Elizabeth.

"You're sure?"

"Well, the truth is..." Elizabeth bit her lip, annoyed. "I can't drive."

"That's nothing to be ashamed of!" burst Lombardi. "Plenty of people don't know how to drive! Especially women."

"Well, plenty of women," scowled Elizabeth, "don't know how to steer a yacht or ride a horse, and I damned well know how to do those things."

"I've always wanted to ride a horse," murmured Lombardi. "To be free like that."

"Well, maybe I'll teach you."

There was a strange silence, and it unnerved Elizabeth. Lombardi stared down the road, which was quickly darkening, the last beams of light winking out behind the passing copses. When Lombardi pressed the brake, Elizabeth felt a chill. They rolled up the windows, but the scene felt stagnant, cold, and far from anything familiar. She still marveled, after so much time in distant lands, that places close to home could seem lonely and remote.

Lombardi opened his door and stepped into the velvety dusk. Elizabeth turned her head to the side and whispered over her shoulder, "Maude, *you* can still drive, can't you?"

Maude looked startled. "Well... yes. I mean... not well, but..."

"*Not well* will do in a pinch." Elizabeth removed a pair of lambskin gloves from her pocket and began to pull them tightly over her fingers. "Now listen, Maude. Whatever happens, I want you to stay calm. All right?"

"O... o... okay..."

Elizabeth spoke so softly she worried Maude might not hear her. "When I get out of the car, I want you to reach over and grab the keys from the starter. Can you do that?"

"I... I think so."

"Good. Ready?"

"Yes?"

Elizabeth opened the door. She looked away, as if now

disinterested in the car, and stepped heavily down the road. "This way?" she said.

"That way?" said Lombardi, whose frame was only a silhouette. "What do you mean?"

"Where the creature was?"

"*Near* here, yes." Lombardi sucked audibly through his teeth. "I don't know exactly. But I know the monster was here."

"I wouldn't call it that," said Elizabeth.

"A monster?"

"No. Predatory? Yes. Man-eating? Yes. But not a monster."

"What would *you* call it, then?" Lombardi spat.

A beam of light slashed through the dark. Lombardi's flashlight switched on so abruptly that Elizabeth swallowed a breath.

"For one night a month, it's an animal," she said. "And like any animal, it can't control itself. It has impulses. Needs. It's hungry. But that doesn't make it a monster, any more than a lion or a bear is a monster."

The flashlight's beam migrated across the woods, dully illuminating tree bark and branches. Elizabeth saw a firefly flicker briefly near her hand.

"And the rest of the time?" murmured Lombardi.

"An ordinary man," said Elizabeth. "Maybe a decent man, for all we know. He didn't decide to be what he is. Lycanthropy is a disease. It comes from a bite. It's transmitted, like any other virus."

"You mean..." Lombardi swallowed hard. "It's not—I don't know..."

"Magic?"

"Exactly."

"No," said Elizabeth. "Nobody knows the precise science, but it's an infection. Like leprosy, or elephantiasis. It changes our chemistry. But once infected, it's beyond human control.

You can't blame a man for getting bitten."

"Can it... can it be cured?"

She hesitated. "No. Not to my knowledge."

Elizabeth heard a metallic sound. The snap of breaking steel. Her spine tingled, because she anticipated the sound that would follow—the thump of something heavy in the woods, then a second thump. Something rustled in the underbrush.

"What was that?" she said, as credibly as she could.

"What was what?"

"That sound?"

"I don't know," said Lombardi. "Maybe a squirrel. The way they dart through the leaves..." He chuckled dryly. "For such little things, they sure make some noise."

"That's funny," said Elizabeth hoarsely. "It sounded like you threw the gun in the woods."

Everything stopped in that moment. Even the chorus of crickets seemed to fall silent. Elizabeth turned around slowly, but by the time she faced the blinding eye of the flashlight, it had switched off. They stood in complete darkness. Above, the sky was navy blue, its smooth surface pierced by only a handful of stars. But everything around Elizabeth was invisible.

"I know it was you," said Elizabeth. "*You* are the lycanthrope."

There was another deathly pause before Lombardi said, "How?" Then, in a leonine purr, he added, "How did you know?"

"You knew the road too well," said Elizabeth. "You knew the road, because you were there during the attacks. You rode with the bootleggers, in the same car. You kept them to a schedule, so they would always be here on the same day and the same time. That way, it would seem like the attacker lived here—in the woods—and not in Philadelphia."

Elizabeth could hear the heavy breathing, the throaty

ejaculations.

"You knew what would happen," she went on. "You lured them here, and then you transformed, just as you're transforming now—"

But a sound cut her off, like the bark of a ferocious dog. She heard the stretch of fabric as Lombardi doubled over. She heard the sound of palms hitting the dirt, his fingers dragging across the packed soil.

"And you lured *me* here," said Elizabeth, "because you knew about my expertise. I was *the only one* who could help you, you said. But you meant that I was the only one who might try to stop you. One day, I might read about the attacks in the newspaper. And maybe I'd call the police. I'd say, 'It's a werewolf. Buy yourselves some silver bullets.' You couldn't risk the meddling of an uncannologist. You wanted to bring me here—not to find the werewolf, but to kill me."

Lombardi snarled savagely, but it sounded sullen, remorseful. He panted miserably into the blackness, his sound becoming higher pitched, like a whining hound.

"I... I didn't want to do it..." he stammered.

"I don't blame you," Elizabeth said quietly. She stepped forward, as nimbly as she could. "You have to survive."

"I didn't know... what to do..." Lombardi seethed. "It starts... and I can't stop it... for years now..."

"I know," said Elizabeth, circling around Lombardi's sunken form. But as her eyes adjusted, she could see the black mass of his body enlarging. She heard the squeal of seams, then the pop of a button. The leather of his wingtip shoes wailed as the stitching unraveled, making way for burgeoning claws.

"It's like... a nightmare... I don't know what I'm doing... and then... I wake up... naked... sick..."

Lombardi shrieked—not a howl exactly, but a superhuman scream, ejected toward the sky. Elizabeth moved, using that shrill note to cover the sound of her footsteps. She bypassed Lombardi and began to back away. Now nothing stood between her and the car. But how far was it? Without the flashlight, she couldn't gauge its distance.

"Lombardi, listen to me," said Elizabeth. She could hear the quavering in her own voice. "I know you got rid of the gun. I know you broke it into two pieces and threw it in the woods. But listen—those bullets were fakes. They were Hollywood blanks, painted silver. The real gun is still in the car, and it has real silver bullets. Can you still understand me?"

Lombardi heaved into the ground. Elizabeth could now see well enough to match the sound of ripping with the tears in his suit; she could see the spiked hair blooming through the lacerated fabric. His back arched grotesquely, not merely lupine but enormous, and she dared not imagine what he would look like in a few short minutes.

"Do you understand me, Lombardi?"

His voice sounded like steam issuing from a large machine, barely discernible as language. But she clearly heard the word: "*Yeeeessss…*"

"We're going to drive away now," she said. "Try to fight it. To fight the impulse. And if you can—if you keep yourself from chasing us—we'll drive right back and pick you up in the morning. We'll have…" She felt panic creep into her voice. "We'll have a blanket, and coffee… we'll have a fresh set of clothes… all you have to do is…"

The dark shape reared upward, crouching on its hind legs, and stretched its arms. Claws rent the last of the clothing from its body. Its maw opened like a vise, and a long howl—a deafening, haunting howl—blasted into the night. Strings of saliva beaded from one row of teeth to another.

Elizabeth whirled around and ran. Her flats slapped the ground as she sprinted toward the car, skirt swishing along her legs. She could feel the vibration of enormous feet hitting the earth. Bile swelled in her throat as she imagined the claws slicing into her, cleaving her apart.

Just then, Elizabeth heard the sound of an engine. Two headlights flared ahead of her. Her heart leapt as she flung herself at the passenger-side door, ripped it open, and scrambled inside. One shoe fell from her foot as she slammed the door closed.

"DRIVE! DAMN IT, DRIVE!" Elizabeth shrieked.

Maude yanked the stick into place.

Both of them looked up at the same time, just as the gray leviathan bounded toward them, its muscles throbbing in the splash of headlights. Maude and Elizabeth screamed at the tops of their lungs, screamed so loud that Elizabeth's ears rang. And then, just as the creature leapt into the air, the car jolted backward.

For a full second Elizabeth felt hysterical relief—the car reversed so fast that both their heads fell forward, nearly smacking the dashboard. Elizabeth wanted to cackle with joy, knowing that they were moving away from danger, away from the howls and claws.

But then the wolf landed. Its hulking body crashed down on the hood. The creature was colossal, larger than the largest man, a pulsing carpet of fur. The hood crumpled beneath its weight. Elizabeth recoiled as its claws pierced metal, scissoring through the car's roof. The car still bounded backward, zigzagging along the road, but the metal groaned, the windshield cracked.

The wolf's head came down, smashing against the window. Glass shards rained over them. Hot breath whooshed across Elizabeth's face, and she could see the rows of razor teeth, the slimy pink ridges of gums, the boiling red eyes, the rugged nostrils that expanded and contracted with every pant.

Then they felt the impact.

A violent pain jolted Elizabeth's spine. Her head slammed

against the seat. Her brain jostled inside her head.

But somehow she summoned the presence of mind to realize what was happening: The rear bumper had collided with the fallen tree. It hit so hard that the wolf launched into the air, flying over the roof of the car, and crashed into the darkness behind them.

Everything was quiet.

Elizabeth winced, feeling woozy. Her body ached from the whiplash. Her breaths came fast and low, like when she'd smoked too much ganja. But she felt herself lift her hand. She flopped her arm between the two seats. As she swiveled her body, Elizabeth could see Maude, slumped forward, eyes tightly closed.

But she's breathing, Elizabeth assured herself. *She'll be all right.*

Her fingers touched the floor of the car, just behind the back seat. At last she felt the familiar texture of the revolver — the *real* revolver. Her grandfather's Colt. The heirloom she would never entrust to anyone. She hefted it into her lap, inhaled deeply, and opened the door.

Elizabeth could see gusts of breath evaporate in front of her face. The air was cold now, never mind the chill in her bones. She hobbled forward, around the car, limping on her bare foot. She lifted one leg over the fallen tree, then another. The headlights were aimed the other way and did little good behind the car. But Elizabeth could make out the heaving mass before her; the wolf, dazed and confused, rocking slowly, wheezing into the oblivion of night.

She lifted the gun with both hands. The muzzle trembled before her, and Elizabeth realized how shaken she really was. She doubted she could hold it steady, but she knew she had to. Just one shot to the head. One silver bullet. She could end the violence. She could put him out of his misery.

Elizabeth's thumb pulled back the hammer. But she only

stood there, unsettled. Couldn't she let him live? Couldn't she forgive his shrewd plan? If they could only survive until morning, maybe she could help him. Yes, he had plotted to kill her, but he had waited until the transformation. He had wanted to assuage his guilt; he'd wanted the wolf to tear her asunder, not the real Ennio, the charismatic lawyer with the beautiful suits and splendid car. Surely she could spare him?

The wolf rolled over. He moved so swiftly in the darkness that Elizabeth could barely discern what was happening. His red eyes flashed in the night, as soulless and devilish as a bobcat's. The mouth peeled open. The limbs adjusted, poised to leap.

Elizabeth closed her eyes. Her finger was so numb that she could not feel the trigger pull, but the *bang* sent shockwaves through her hands. She felt the gun reverberate in her forearms. Sparks exploded in the dark, followed by the whiff of burnt powder.

But then she heard a growl, louder than before. The scarlet eyes flared again, the mouth opened wider. The rolls of fur seemed to uncoil.

She had missed.

Elizabeth gulped down terror as she aimed again, truer this time. She saw the barrel form a straight line to the creature's head. The wolf's face was fiercer than ever. There was no trace of the man it had been. This face was not Lombardi's. It was pure hunger. It was the face of the wilderness, cold and remorseless, hungry for her death.

Elizabeth fired.

Everything fell silent.

The sun rose slowly, reddening the landscape, as the Moon 6-40 chugged down the road. The hood was lumpy, and air seeped freely through the empty window frame. Yet the car's engine worked as well as ever.

"Best engineering there is," said Elizabeth. She chuckled, but it was a sad chuckle.

Maude clutched the steering wheel so tightly that her fingers whitened. Her eyes looked pried open, as if determined never to sleep again. Elizabeth sighed as the road dipped downward, into a defile between two hills.

"Pull over," Elizabeth ordered.

"Here?"

"That's right."

The car stopped by the side of the road, and a stream of dust settled behind them as they stepped out. Newly tilled soil piled darkly in the morning sun, and sprouts of grass were dotted with dew. Birds chirped excitedly in distant trees. A rooster called from the roof of a leaning barn.

They stood side by side, gazing at the fields, until Elizabeth finally spoke.

"It's not pretty. What I do." She shook her head. "You don't have to see these things, you know. I just thought…" She shrugged. "I don't know what I thought. I just like you around."

Maude gazed at the landscape, then turned her head to Elizabeth. She pushed a curl away from her ear.

"I'm not… really of sound mind…" she said. "But… I think you're *tremendous*. And… after something like this… I mean, it was frightening… *very* frightening, but… I don't think I could ever go back. To… you know… normal things."

Elizabeth cracked a smile, then adjusted a pebble with her naked toe.

"You're a glutton for punishment," she said. "So you're probably in the right place. Homeward?"

Maude said, "Home! I mean, *ward*. Homeward. Yes."

A minute later they were bouncing down the road, back toward Pittsburgh.

THE MYSTERIOUS TONGUE OF DR. VERMILION

July, 1921

"MAY I JOIN YOU?" said a deep voice.

Elizabeth looked up from her book. She squinted at the man standing before her: He was densely built and dressed in a khaki jacket with many pockets. He bore the squarest jaw Elizabeth had ever seen, and his dark hair was cropped short. He held an attaché case in one hand, and carried his peaked cap under his elbow.

"Seeing as how I don't know who you are," said Elizabeth, "I'd rather you didn't."

"I think you should reconsider, *Ms. Crowne.*"

Elizabeth sighed, snapped her book shut, and slid it across the table. She removed her reading glasses as well, folding and placing them in her handbag, as the man seated himself across from her. He moved with the jerky formality of a born soldier.

For a moment, Elizabeth was self-conscious about the man's presence, and she glanced about the busy diner to see if anyone had noticed her conspicuous company. Then again, Uncle Joe's was a casual spot, and people kept to themselves.

Workers munched their lunches at the counter, murmuring conversation over the sound of scraping forks and sizzling pans. A radio played music in the corner, though she could barely make out the song over the lunchtime patter.

She lifted her coffee cup toward the man. "Well, how do you do, Mr…?"

"Commander Benjamin Watts," he declared.

"Pleased to meet you," said Elizabeth dryly, and she sipped.

"I'll make this brief," said Watts. "I represent the United States military, and I have been asked to consult you about one of our veterans. He has been experiencing some psychological problems."

"Well, I can recommend an excellent shrink."

"I've been instructed to consult you, and only you, Ms. Crowne."

"I think there's been a mistake," she said coolly.

"Frankly, Ms. Crowne, so do I."

Elizabeth raised an eyebrow. She placed her coffee cup on its saucer and leaned forward, her face a jumble of unwelcome emotions.

"Could you elaborate, Commander?"

"I'll provide more detailed information upon our next meeting," he said perfunctorily.

"But why should there be a meeting, if you think this is a mistake?" countered Elizabeth. "That sounds to me like a waste of time."

"Agreed," said Watts. His rigid lips suggested this had been a sore topic. "But I'm under orders, and I intend to see this meeting carried out."

"Fine," said Elizabeth. "But why me?"

"It would be unwise to discuss this…" He trailed off for only a moment. "We should discuss this in a different environment."

"Oh, because some millwright might overhear us?"

Elizabeth jeered. "Let's be honest, Commander—you're only talking to me because some bigwig told you to. But I'm no analyst, so what's the game? Everything about you irritates me, and I trust the feeling's mutual, so why don't we just agree to never see each other again?"

Watts seemed to consider this, although his stony expression had barely changed since his arrival. At last he twisted sideways, opened the flap of his attaché case, and drew a single green folder. The file wasn't thick, but a substantial bundle of papers was sandwiched within.

"That *can't* be mine," scoffed Elizabeth. But she could hear the anxiety in her own voice.

"The trouble with this file," said Watts frostily, "is that it contains more questions than answers. Can you guess what some of those questions might be?"

"Well, I doubt it's whether I'm a Taurus," grumbled Elizabeth. "Which I am, by the way, so you can cross that off your list."

"My first question," continued Watts, "is why Elizabeth Crowne discontinued her medical studies after three years. The timing seems strange, considering you left the same week that a distinguished professor died under—let's say *suspicious circumstances*."

Elizabeth leaned back against the cushioned booth. She swallowed dourly at the Commander's granite countenance.

"I would also be curious why Elizabeth Crowne decided to travel alone for several years—to nations unfriendly to her homeland—even during a time of war. Why, I wonder, did Elizabeth Crowne not help with the war effort, but instead spent time in Europe, Africa, and Asia? Why did she only return when the war was over? The timing is rather convenient, wouldn't you say?"

Elizabeth continued to say nothing, but her eyes grew fiercer with every sentence.

"But mostly," said the Commander, placing a callused hand on the file and tapping it with a finger, "I wonder how she earns her money. You see, most of these documents consist of numbers and dates. Dull reading. The common man would go cross-eyed. But if you know what you're looking at, it's quite the story. Because Elizabeth Crowne has no real profession. She has no husband, no inheritance, and no income. And yet she lives in a three-story house in Oakland. How does she afford this? She's wired money, through Western Union transfers. The same deposit, over and over. So where does the money come from?"

He paused. The silence that followed was like a battering ram. It wasn't until Watts plucked up the file and slid it back into his case that Elizabeth let herself exhale.

"You and I both know your money comes from Europe," Watts said slowly. "Central Europe, to be precise. Now, I'm not sure if you were near a newspaper in 1917, but you may have heard that our government passed a little law called the Espionage Act. And I can assure you, Ms. Crowne, that you do not want this law to pertain to you."

Elizabeth curled her fingers, took a clandestine breath, and lifted her coffee cup to her lips. She sipped the lukewarm sludge and said, "We don't know each other very well, Commander, so I'll forgive your offensive tone. But a word of advice—calling me a spy would be a very big mistake."

"Good thing I haven't," said Watts with mock friendliness. "I'm sure there's a reasonable explanation for all of this. My superiors just thought these facts should be brought to your attention. And I hope you'll bear that in mind when we meet tomorrow at noon."

"Tomorrow? Where?"

Watts stood up abruptly. His uniform remained rigidly starched, without so much as a crease or a fold.

"I have your address as 206 Cressida Street. I assume that's still current?"

Elizabeth's smile was as strained as it had ever been in her life. "Why yes," she said. "And why don't you bring your friend?"

Watts replaced his cap, then stood at attention. His blank face was illegible.

"Believe me, Ms. Crowne, this man is *not* my friend."

The day was overcast and breezy, and Elizabeth watched leaves and crumpled newspapers skitter down the sidewalk. She lay sideways in her porch swing, boots tucked under her, as she idly nursed a cup of black coffee. Trees rustled, occasional cars rolled past, and even the power lines swayed like tropical hammocks. It was as tranquil a morning as she had seen in a year, that perfect time in Pittsburgh, when the air and sky and general mood seem heaven sent.

Maude stepped onto the floorboards and gingerly shut the front door. She carried a steaming mug of tea in her hand, and she looked like she was about to speak, but the cheep of a songbird distracted her. She lowered her head, examining the nearby sapling for a view of the tiny creature.

"Just a chipping sparrow," said Elizabeth. "They're a dime a dozen around here."

"Oh!" said Maude. "Are you—are you sure?"

"You can tell from its high trill. Pretty little voice, I have to admit. Each has a spot of brown on the top of its heads. Looks like a brushstroke."

Maude's eyes widened as she contemplated this unexpected trivia. She took another step toward the tree, but she couldn't see the tiny bird beyond the veil of leaves. She straightened, bit the inside of her lip, and said, "So this man is from... the army?"

"Between you and me, I think he's Black Chamber."

"Black…?"

"Chamber. And don't worry if you've never heard of them. They put some effort into not being known."

"But… who are they?"

"The short story is, they're spies." Elizabeth slurped the last of her coffee, placed her mug on the floor, and sat up on the swing. "You may recall that we—that is, our country—came late to the war, a decision I wish we'd stuck to. By the time we got involved, we had to catch up with everybody else. The Germans had their codes, the Brits had their code-breakers, and we had—well, nothing, really. So the army threw together Black Chamber. A bunch of nebby eggheads, if you ask me."

"But…" Maude continued to gnaw at her lip. "Isn't the war over?"

"Bingo," said Elizabeth. "Now they're based in New York. Nowadays, with all these two-bit mobsters smuggling booze, they track transactions and look out for funny business. Which is why I think this Watts fellow is Black Chamber. They spend most of their time watching Western Union. You could say they have their finger on the pulse."

"But what about Western Union?"

Elizabeth cleared her throat and stood up. "My parents like to wire me money, now and again. To help with the upkeep around here. I suppose that caught their eye. Let's get ready for our guests, shall we?"

"Private Gunderson is running late," Watts announce stoically. "His train was delayed."

Commander Watts stood at attention in the middle of Elizabeth's office. While Maude had done her best to rearrange the clutter and wipe away the duvets of dust, the room remained untidy, and Watts' pristine presence looked hopelessly out of place.

"Well, I guess it's just you and me," muttered Elizabeth.

"Actually, Ms. Crowne, there's another man I'd like you to meet."

"Another? How many shell-shocked privates do you have? And feel free to interpret that question however you like."

"I—" Watts began, but then he hesitated. He ground his jaw, as if slowly absorbing Elizabeth's words and struggling to find a reply. "I..."

"Never mind," said Elizabeth, who compulsively began to reorder the papers on her desk. "Who's *this* one, then?"

"His name is Blinker, ma'am."

"Does he have a first name?"

"Eugene."

"Well, what's his story?"

"He was..."

As Watts struggled to find the right words, Elizabeth had a revelation about her new acquaintance: Watts did not like to leave sentences incomplete. Which was tragic, because the man wasn't naturally adept at public speaking. Despite the profundity of his voice, Watts was not a talker. Watts had required practice and training, surmised Elizabeth, to communicate as well as he did. But his own formality tripped him up.

"He was assigned an apartment in Milwaukee," Watts finally said. "He is sharing the tenement with Private Gunderson."

"They're roommates? But why? Are they friends?"

"I don't know, ma'am."

Elizabeth frowned, then stroked her chin with curled fingers. She leaned back in her chair and assessed the Commander. If it were even possible, the man seemed to stiffen. "How come you're so contrary about this, Watts? What's eating you?"

Again, the odd vacillation. This question was more personal, and she decided she liked prodding him.

"I don't believe in trauma, ma'am."

"You don't *believe* in it?"

"I think it's a lot of bunk."

"Do you? And why is that?"

Watts looked uncertain whether to proceed, but he couldn't seem to help himself. "When I was a boy, there was no such thing. All of sudden, these *civilian* doctors start talking their nonsense—about trauma and nerve damage and so on. Some European Jew writes a book about it and everybody goes weak at the knees. But I think it's just an excuse for feeble men."

"Well," said Elizabeth. "When I was a girl, there was no such thing as mustard gas. Do you believe in *that?*"

Their conversation was interrupted by a knock, and then the door opened slowly. A face popped inside, but Elizabeth was surprised by its latitude: Either the man was leaning low behind the door, or he was alarmingly short.

"Ms. Crowne?" he said. "Ms. Elizabeth Crowne?"

He shimmied inside, closing the door behind him. Eugene Blinker had a mousy face, including large, detached ears. He stood only about five feet tall, but his black three-piece suit had been flatteringly tailored. He carried a bowler hat in his hands, and as he marched excitedly across the room, Elizabeth noticed the prim leather spats that covered his spotless shoes. He extended a hand so fervently that he might have been directing traffic.

"*So* pleased to finally meet you, Ms. Crowne!" he exclaimed, leaning over the desk until Elizabeth finally shook the tips of his fingers. "I've heard such wonderful things about you!"

"You... have?" Elizabeth stared at him uncertainly.

"Just what they told me at the office," said Blinker. "I mean, about the paranormal stuff."

Watts cleared his throat dramatically. It sounded like two

distinct syllables, "Ah-*hem*," in the manner of a comics character.

"Oh, Commander, it's all right," exclaimed Blinker, collapsing into a chair and letting his upper limbs dangle over its armrests. "Ms. Crowne is here to help *us*, remember? No reason to keep her in the dark. And truth be told, Ms. Crowne, I really admire what you do."

"I'll leave you two alone," said Watts.

"Alone? Why?" asked Elizabeth. Then the uncannologist rolled her eyes. "Were you *ordered* to give us privacy?"

Watts shot daggers at Elizabeth. Now that he was about to leave, he no longer hid his antipathy. "I'll be downstairs," he said faintly, and closed the door behind him.

Elizabeth decided not to dwell on Watts, who was clearly just the messenger. She turned her attention to Blinker.

"I'm curious," said Elizabeth, "what is it you think I do?"

"Well," said Blinker, who could barely contain his enthusiasm. "They say you're an *uncannologist*. Which I assume is a made-up word. But the profession is really pretty old, wouldn't you say? With the ghost-hunters and exorcists and whatnot?"

"I suppose it is," admitted Elizabeth. "So tell me about yourself. What brings you all this way from Milwaukee?"

Blinker nodded emphatically, then touched his fingertips together. "It's about Pete, you see. Swell kid, I like him a lot. I'm really glad they arranged for us to live together. See, Pete and I did some intelligence work during the war. Not together. We didn't even know each other. But we have that in common. My work was easy, but I guess his didn't turn out so well. He's had some problems. Honestly, I think he lost some marbles. I don't judge. I think he's just a sensitive type, and he bit off more than he could chew. Anyhow, I don't have much family, and once I was discharged, I didn't have anything to do. So someone upstairs must've thought, 'That Peter Gunderson could use a friend.' Or a *cohabitant*, anyway. Someone to watch after him. Someone to help him out. So they asked me, and I said yes. Always love to help a fellow out. And I get free room and board—what's not to like?"

The monologue came so fast, so fully formed, that Elizabeth struggled to keep up. Now Blinker paused. His face was so boyish and strange. His skin was slightly pimpled, and his nose looked like a drop of tapioca that had run down his face. His head was shaped like a football, wide and compressed. He wasn't attractive, but his buoyant demeanor was charming.

"I'm not going too fast, am I? It's one of my bad habits. Comes from growing up in a crowd."

"Lots of siblings?"

"No siblings, actually. I grew up in the circus."

Elizabeth nearly sputtered at this reply. "The... circus?"

"That's right. The ringmaster found my cradle in front of the big top one morning. There wasn't an orphanage nearby, so they took me in. Raised me like one of their own."

"You—*must* be joking."

"Something you should know about me, Ms. Crowne," said Blinker. "I don't joke much. I'm much too genuine. People call me 'forthright,' and I think that's just the word for me. And as surely as the sky is blue, I was raised in the Xander & Xerxes Traveling Circus."

"But—by whom?"

"By everyone! You see, the owners were a pair of Greek fellows. As circuses go, I guess you could say it was a little low-rent. A Bengal tiger, but no lions. Strongmen, but no trapeze. They cut a lot of corners. Still, it was a marvelous life, Ms. Crowne! I lived on the road, free as could be. And I did everything—I swept the floors, fed the animals, sold tickets, whatever they needed. At night, I'd read in my bed. I'm self-taught, in almost every way. You have to be, when you live that life. But I'll tell you what I never lacked: a family. That's what I had in spades."

"Well," said Elizabeth dryly. "You make a good case for it. If I come back as an orphan, I hope it's a circus that takes me in. Seems like quite the transformation, though. Not a lot of carnies end up doing intelligence work."

"Oh, it didn't start that way. See, Xander & Xerxes went out of business. It was a sad day, let me tell you. I was sixteen, and I remember it like yesterday. Everybody hugged and said their goodbyes, and then I was alone. Just me and a bindle, by the side of the road. I'd saved up $113, which was all I had to my name. I thought, what should I do? Where should I go? I'd taught myself to read. I was pretty well studied, if I say so myself. But I hadn't had a day of real schooling. So I thought — I'll join the merchant marines."

"Prudent choice," said Elizabeth.

"You can say that again! I sailed all over the world, Ms. Crowne. But it was Asia that struck my fancy. What a continent! So much history. Such exotic races. We sailed everywhere, from Pondicherry to Hong Kong. It was hard work, but I liked it. Everyone thought I didn't have the body for it — I'm not exactly tall, of course — but sure as shooting, I kept up with some of the biggest mates on the ship."

"But how did you end up in the army?" asked Elizabeth impatiently.

"Well, by the time we reached Japan, I'd made a good amount of money. So I said *sayonara* to the skipper, he wished me well, and I stayed on in Tokyo. Amazing city! I fell in love right away. I traveled all over the country. I spent *three years* there, Ms. Crowne. I even learned the language pretty well. I had an apartment in Tokyo and everything. And it was about then that I ran into some..." He stopped, then chuckled inwardly. Finally he shrugged, as if none of his admissions really mattered anyway. "I met some fellows in a sake bar. I thought they were just prowling for geisha girls, but then they started chatting me up. Turns out they'd been watching me for a while. They saw I was good with languages, I'd met a lot of people..."

"So they asked you to spy?"

"Well, not *spy*, exactly. See, the Japanese are a proud people. You can tell that the second you arrive. They're humble, polite, they love to bow to each other and show respect—but they're a tough bunch. So once the war started, everybody wondered what Japan was going to do. Would they join the fight? Who would they side with? That kind of thing. So I kept an eye on things. I sent reports. They paid me a pretty penny. In the end, Japan didn't do a thing. No harm, no foul. And that was it."

"So you weren't really *in* the army?" Elizabeth concluded.

Blinker smiled peculiarly. He reached into his jacket pocket and drew a loaded pipe and a matchbook. He lit the match, which sent an eerie glow across his puerile cheeks, and he said, "Ms. Crowne, in the intelligence business, no one is really doing anything."

Elizabeth prickled. As Blinker puffed his pipe, and the smoke cloaked his face, Elizabeth felt compelled to do something with herself. She searched her desk until she found a small, flat stone with a smooth imprint. It was her Mesopotamian worry rock, a gift from a long-ago friend. She took it in her grasp and began to rub her thumb into its center. Slowly, her anxiety dissipated, and she felt she could speak once more.

"So they gave you this apartment?"

"That's right," said Blinker with a flash of pride. "And I think it's the best thing for both of us. I wasn't any use in Japan, and Pete... well, he's seen better days. This way we each get some company."

"That's charitable of you," said Elizabeth. "What's he like, anyway?"

"Pete? Oh, he's as gentle as a lamb. Nicest guy you'll ever meet. A little nervous, maybe. He had it pretty rough. But I'd trust him with my life. You can tell those Gundersons are good stock."

"Do you..." Elizabeth sighed. "Do you know why they're sending him to me? I mean, I don't feel equipped for this."

"I think you'll understand when you hear his story. He didn't have a typical experience, if you catch my meaning."

"I don't catch your meaning at all, actually. What are you saying?"

"You'll have to hear it from him," said Blinker with cordial finality. "But brace yourself. It ain't pretty."

"Just one last question, Blinker," said Elizabeth. "Why are *you* here? That must be quite the trip from Milwaukee."

"Ah," said Blinker through a nimbus of sweet-smelling smoke. "I understand, you're confused. I mean, I barely know the guy, really. What's the angle?" He looked away, dreamily. "Ms. Crowne, the army has given me a place to live. Three meals a day. A monthly stipend. All I have to do is help a guy out. Now I didn't *have* to come all this way, but I felt I ought to. I'm a transient fellow. In my life, people come and go, carrying the same burdens every day. But I'm a can-do type. And if I can stand by Pete, give him the pat on the back he needs, that's what I'm gonna do." He cradled his pipe for a moment, then snickered self-consciously. "I don't know if that makes any sense."

"It does, actually," said Elizabeth. She set down the worry rock. "You're a good man, Blinker. I think you're doing a selfless thing. You're quite the interesting fellow."

"I take pride in it," said Blinker. And he winked.

This final gesture took Elizabeth by surprise. She was about to stand up, but the wink held her fast. What did *that* mean? That quickly closed eye could suggest so many things, but none of them made sense to her. Was there another joke she hadn't understood? Was there a subtext she should have detected, a hidden meaning that only the two of them shared? Or was this his vaudevillian personality, his flamboyant style, his showman's friendliness?

Again, there was a knock. The door cracked open just wide enough for Watts' face to peer through.

"Private Gunderson's train just arrived," croaked Watts' bass voice. "If it's all the same to you, he'll get some rest and come tomorrow morning."

"Good, we were just finishing up," said Elizabeth. "Pleased to meet you, Mr. Blinker."

Blinker stood up and shook her hand. And then, as if to confirm all her uneasy feelings, Blinker winked again. Then he turned around and quickly left the room.

"Maude!"

Maude was chopping cucumber in the kitchen when she heard Elizabeth's call. She hurriedly wiped the knife with a rag and set it on the chopping block, then dashed up the staircase to the bathroom, where she heard the sound of water spraying in the shower.

"Is everything all right?"

"Thank God you're here," Elizabeth muttered. "Could you find me a towel? I plum forgot to get one."

"Oh! Yes! Be right back!"

Maude flew back down the stairs, then opened the cellar door. The old staircase creaked with each rapid step. The cellar was spacious, mostly packed with wood crates and moldering trunks. A wash basin stood on a bench in the corner, surrounded by puddles of water on the concrete floor. The ceiling was festooned with drying lines, and every kind of dress, blouse, and undergarment dangled in the musty air. Maude scanned the line until she found a towel that looked dry enough, grabbed it away, and stomped back up the stairs.

She arrived at the bathroom again, huffing. "Got it!" she called through the cracked door.

"You're a godsend! Just leave it on the sink, if you would."

Maude nudged the door farther open. By happenstance, she had never set foot in the second floor bathroom, which was evident from the black grime that had infected its seams and tiles, and she promised herself to scrub it down soon. Thick steam filled the air, obscuring the shower curtain beyond. Maude didn't realize how far the sink would stand from the door, and when she placed the towel on its porcelain edge, she saw a silvery string fall to the floor, followed by a tiny clink of metal.

The towel securely positioned, Maude instinctively crouched low to pick up whatever had fallen. She seized a small necklace and placed it atop the bundled towel. But before she could quit the room, something caught her eye: The necklace itself was unremarkable, only a strand of ball chain, but it was strung through a ring.

How old was the ring? Maude pondered this as she turned it around in her fingers, its rugged metal the color of pewter. The ring was topped with a disc, which showed an emblem: It looked like a star, with seven branches radiating outward. The figure rested on a vertical line, and a crescent arced above.

Maude had never seen such a pictogram before, and she marveled at the insignia's simple power. She might have stayed there indefinitely, hypnotized by this strange new jewelry, were it not for the turning of the faucet.

The water stopped spraying, and Maude snapped out of her trance. Just then Elizabeth pulled the shower curtain back. She didn't make a sound, but she did cock an eyebrow. The half-drawn curtain draped over her slick body like a toga.

"Making sure I dry off?" asked Elizabeth.

"Oh... I was just..." Maude had no idea what to say next.

Just *what*, exactly?

Elizabeth then made an odd expression—distant and pensive, as if a strange epiphany had entered her head, and she was now lost in reverie. After a few silent seconds, Maude realized Elizabeth was looking at the necklace, which was still coiled in her palm. But Elizabeth could have been thinking anything in that moment, for her flattened eyebrows and lips betrayed no particular emotion. Rivulets of water continued to slide down her face and shoulder, and it was only now that Maude realized how peculiar this was—for Elizabeth to stand stock-still in the middle of a shower and not reach for the towel that Maude had rushed to retrieve.

At last her lips split and she said, "May I?"

Maude was relieved to hand the necklace over, but once she'd dumped the ring and chain into Elizabeth's palm, the uncannologist only held them, gazing at their dull metal with wistful eyes. At last she curled her fingers over the bundle, batted her lashes—as if waking from a daze—and said, "What's for lunch, anyhow?"

"Cucumber sandwiches!" exclaimed Maude, grateful that this surreal exchange had drawn to a close. She then grabbed the towel from the sink and passed it to Elizabeth, who began to pat herself down. She raised the necklace so fluently over her head that Maude barely noticed the motion. But as the chain settled into a V over Elizabeth's pastel neckline, Maude had an unavoidable notion—that the necklace was always there, dangling over her heart, hidden beneath her garments.

"Cucumber sandwiches," echoed Elizabeth. "Looking forward to it. All this intrigue is giving me an appetite."

Elizabeth was writing a note when she heard the knock at the door. But it wasn't a knock so much as a flutter of knuckles against wood. Soft and quick, like a child nervous to disturb his parents.

"Come in," called Elizabeth, setting aside the paper and pen and folding her hands over the desk.

Gunderson entered the room slightly hunched, his wrists bundled over his chest, like an old woman. He was tall, but he was also a beanpole, which accentuated his height. He looked both ways, as if scoping traffic, then shuffled quickly toward the chair, his baggy slacks billowing as he went. He sat quickly, then fell into himself, his fingertips tapping his knee, jouncing feverishly.

"I would offer you some coffee," said Elizabeth. "But you seem well caffeinated."

"*What?*" he chirruped.

"Nothing." Elizabeth leaned back in her chair, groping the Mesopotamian worry rock in her fingers. "How can I help you, Mr. Gunderson?"

"You can call me Peter," he said, but the invitation sounded forced, as if he'd been instructed to be informal in her presence.

"Well, then, Peter. What brings you here? Aside from a federal order?"

"To be honest," he stuttered, "I don't know that you can help me at all, Ms. Crowne."

"Neither do I, but we can give it a whirl, can't we?"

He tried to smile at this, but his lips did not obey.

"Listen, Peter, I don't know you from Adam, but I'm here to listen. And even if I'm useless to you, I'm not going to judge or spread gossip around town. Whatever you say is between us. So…" Elizabeth set down the stone and opened her drawer, drawing a bottle of bourbon. "Maybe we could start at the beginning."

"I don't really drink, Ms. Crowne."

"It's not for you," she said, producing two tumblers but pouring into only one. "If you're this nervous to talk, I should take any precaution."

This time he did crack a slight smile, and Elizabeth took an inward breath of relief. She sipped, smacked her lips loudly, and said, "No breakfast is complete without a good nip. That's my rule. So? Shall we begin?"

Peter's knee halted, as if by sheer will, and he smoothed the fabric of his trousers with his long, long fingers. Peter was youthful, no older than twenty-five, but his pale pallor betrayed an aged soul.

"I grew up in Wisconsin," he said. "A small wheat farm, not near any place you'd know. I grew up in overalls, and so did my father. We are a proud family, you see."

"My mother is the same way," said Elizabeth. "I know the type."

"Then you know we love our land," he said, straightening. "We love our country. We are humble, or we try to be humble, but if you take that one thing away, we are nothing without it. My grandmother, she made me a quilt of the American flag. Sewed every star and stripe. And I'll be damned if I didn't sleep under it till the day I left home." His head dropped. "Sorry. My language."

"I've made Pullman porters blush," said Elizabeth. "Say what you like."

"Well, I have a certain gift," Peter said. "If you can call it that. You see, I have a strong memory."

"Do you?" Elizabeth smirked. "How strong?"

"How strong?" Peter looked around, then drew back in his chair, hands on knees. "Well, I guess I could demonstrate."

"Try this." Elizabeth grabbed a book from her desk and threw it toward him, the pages flapping freely in the air. Peter recoiled at the sudden movement but managed to catch the book in his lap. "Look at the first page," instructed Elizabeth.

Peter opened the book gingerly. His eyes darted swiftly for only a few seconds, and then he closed the cover.

"Well, you can take your time—"

"A quail takes wing above a glassy pond," said Peter in a slow, deliberate voice. "As jays trade harmonies in avian song. The quail floats above its reflected twin, 'til both birds meet at the water's skin. Sun and moon share a velvet sky, though roving sheets of fog are nigh. My boat's misplaced on this reedy shore, and I regret the ripples of my offending oar. A mallard floats in sleepy peace, 'til man, clumsy man, makes liquid crease, and my small prow stirs bird to flight. Its frantic wings are lost to night."

Peter closed his eyes and kept them closed. When his lids at last peeled open, they revealed bloodshot whites and swollen pupils.

"Who wrote it?" he asked.

"A friend," said Elizabeth quickly. "So it seems your memory is impeccable."

"I'm not artful," said Peter. "I'm really very stupid, in most ways. But I remember everything. Words, numbers. I never forget a face."

"I should be so lucky," grumbled Elizabeth.

"But it's a curse, too! You think it's such a fantastical thing, like a magic trick. And I did. I showed off, especially to—you know. The girls I met. They could say anything, just a bunch of letters, or even just nonsense words, and I could say every syllable back, even an hour later, or the next day."

Peter was excited now, his eyes bolted open and gazing askew, as if remembering the exploits of a mystical stranger.

"How did you join the Army?"

Peter deflated again, seeming like a shamed child.

"I wanted to fight," he said. "I was eager to fight. The day I enlisted, my father was so proud. I had never *seen* him so proud. We went to the enlistment office together and—he'd never so much as sniffled, Ms. Crowne, but he *bawled*, he was so happy. He bought me my first whiskey…" He paused and wrung his hands, as if pantomiming cross-stitch. "Which is to say, I fibbed to you before. I'm really pretty fond of the drink, Ms. Crowne."

"It's an open bar, Peter."

He sighed deeply and reached for the bottle, then poured whiskey into the tumbler. His fingers shook so much that the glass clinked alarmingly against the bottle's mouth, but he didn't spill a drop. He swallowed hard, his throat throbbing, but he stopped himself from draining the glass in a single swig, as he clearly yearned to do. Then he studied the remaining liquid, lopsided in the angled tumbler.

"I started training," he went on. "And I was strong, I knew. I baled hay my whole life. And I wanted to fight. I did. But…" He sucked down the last of his bourbon and wiped his lips with a fist, then kept his hand pressed against his chin, lost in thought. "I could tell I wasn't as tough as the other doughboys. They could throw fists, but I—I always hesitated. They were like dogs, just always ready to pounce. But I'm polite, Ms. Crowne. I say please and thank you. They made fun of me. I needed to show them I was good at something."

"So you showed off your memory."

He nodded, ever so slightly.

"In the barracks, they would take out an entire deck of cards and spread them out on a bunk. They'd turn the cards over, and I could name all fifty-two. They would move them around, but I could still do it. They'd laugh and pat me on the back. They even gave me a name." He sniffed—a stifled laugh. "They called me Houdini, Jr. But then it was just Huey. And, to be truthful, Ms. Crowne, I loved it. It didn't matter that I couldn't hit a damned scarecrow with a bayonet, or I couldn't shoot a target at ten yards. Guys thought I was the bee's knees, showing off my memory like I did."

"A brain like yours," said Elizabeth, "somebody's bound to notice."

"Well, we had some smart fellas. Jimmy Pataki? He could draw anything. That guy was a genuine artist." Peter fell silent, then covered his face in his fingers. "He died at the front. Mustard gas."

"But they noticed *you*," Elizabeth reiterated.

"One day," Peter said grimly, "they ordered me to report to this office, on the other side of the camp. I didn't even know it was there. This special room. Just a desk. I honestly thought I was in trouble. I don't have but a few years of school, Ms. Crowne, but I felt like the schoolmaster was about to scold me. That's exactly what it felt like."

"Was it Commander Watts?"

"Yes," Peter whispered. "The way he talks, it's like a voice on the radio. He just makes you freeze up and listen. He said, 'We need you for a special mission.'"

He faltered, then reached for the bottle. Elizabeth watched him pour, his hands shaking with guilt and trepidation. It pained her to watch him, so she said, "You can top me off, too."

He obliged, then cradled his drink protectively.

"Ms. Crowne, I'm a sucker for duty. And when Commander Watts said I could help my country, I jumped at the chance. You can understand that, can't you? I just wanted to help win the war, in any way I could. Doesn't that seem right? If I could help lick the Krauts, if I could —"

"Everybody likes to feel valued, Peter," said Elizabeth hurriedly. "But I'll reserve judgment until I have all the facts. So then what happened?"

"I said yes," Peter said. "And then — that very night — they woke me up. In the barracks. They put a blindfold over my eyes. I got in a car, or maybe a truck. And then they drove for a long time. Then they brought me into a room, and they took the blindfold off. And then I saw—it was a classroom."

"A classroom?"

"Just one desk, like you'd see in a schoolhouse. One notebook, one pencil. And there was a big blackboard."

"That was all?"

"Yes. For a while, I was just alone. Maybe two hours, sitting there. I had no idea what to do, so I just stayed put. And then…"

When Peter trailed off, Elizabeth leaned forward. "And then?"

"*He* came in."

Peter bent forward and his cheeks blew out, and for a moment Elizabeth thought he might be sick. He lingered there for a long time, until his head swung upward, his face whiter than ever.

"When he came in, it's like he took up the whole room. He was big—*enormous*. He wore all black, and he had a black cape. Well, black on the outside, but inside it was all shiny, the color of… of…" He coughed, then shook his head, his mouth stretched widely. "The color of blood."

"What did his face look like? Can you describe it?"

"It was… it was a mask."

"You mean *like* a mask?"

"No, it was a *real* mask. Smooth and white, but painted to look—almost like a demon. The cape had a hood, and it covered up his head, so the mask had a shadow over it. And it had… a mustache."

"A mustache?"

"But more like whiskers. They pointed straight out."

"Straight out? Are you sure?"

"I'll never forget it," Peter murmured. "And that's my curse, Ms. Crowne. I *can* never forget it. It's like he's right here now, watching over me."

"What did he say?"

"He said, '*My name is Dr. Vermilion.*'"

A shiver rocked Peter's body, and he drank so sloppily that bourbon spattered on the floor.

"Dr. Vermilion?"

"Yes. But his voice... it was like nothing I'd ever heard before. So deep, like a bullfrog's croak. I swear to God, it was unholy, Ms. Crowne. Like something out of Hell itself."

"What else did he say?"

"He said, 'Your mission is to learn a language. A special language, created only for you.' And then—he started to write on the chalkboard. English words, then other words."

"What kinds of words?"

"Well, just one example—'boat' was *tushenaga*. And 'sight' was *bofasendi*. They were just nonsense words. But we spent hours, writing and memorizing. Thousands of words."

"It was a real language?"

"Well, yes. Not just a code, but an entire language, with its own rules. *Complicated* rules. So, you see, if I wanted to say, 'I'm going to the bank,' it would be, *Chi salvash ko besheni twa.* But if I said, 'I went to the bank yesterday,' it would be, *Twaji chimesh salwashwei kaptek beshilo-wash-wei.* The rules were hard to follow. But I understood them. It felt good, in a way, because I had to put effort into it. It was actual work, memorizing all those words, more than I'd ever had to work at it before. There were all these special exceptions."

"How long were you there?"

"I don't know. I had a private room, in the back, where I slept and ate. The only person I saw was... Dr. Vermilion. But I slept twenty-eight times. So, I guess it was about a month. But there were no windows. They never let me outside. I only saw those two rooms. And they were so dark, Ms. Crowne. I thought I'd go blind."

"But you learned the language?"

"By the end, that's all we talked. I mean *spoke*. Just the secret language. Nothing else."

"Then what happened?"

"It was the strangest moment of my life. One day, the door to my room was open. I went into the classroom, and the door was open there, too. I went down a hallway, and—I saw the sun. It was so bright. I took me a long time to see anything straight. But then I saw the whole building. It was just a building in the middle of a big field. A cornfield, as far as the eye could see. It was so bright. And then I saw a car coming up. It came down the dirt road and stopped in front of me. A man came out. Commander Watts. He walked up to me and saluted. Can you imagine? An officer saluting *me?* And all he said was, 'You're a lucky man, private. You're about to go to Switzerland.'"

"Switzerland?"

"Ms. Crowne, I had never so much as left Wisconsin! And suddenly I was taking a train to Baltimore, and then I was on a steamship to Europe! It was beyond anything I'd ever dreamed of. Ten days on a boat, then London, then another boat to Italy, then a train to Geneva. I don't know how to describe it. I couldn't believe the things I saw. I'd never even seen a decent hill before, and now I was seeing mountains. It was like walking into a moving picture show, Ms. Crowne. And all I had was an address, for an apartment. And a key. The second I put that key in the door, I couldn't believe it opened. And it was a *big* apartment. Lots of furniture, so old and—*beautiful*. I touched the..." He raised a finger in the air, as if touching a plush surface.

"The upholstery?"

"Yes! It had these shapes and patterns. I could've sat in those chairs all day, I really could. There was even a balcony. I'd stand out there, smoke a cigarette, and look at the Alps."

He paused, and kept pausing. The silence was so long that Elizabeth found herself distracted by particles of dust caught in the light.

"Peter?"

He curled his back, like a cat, and arranged himself awkwardly in the chair.

"I thought I was in heaven. When I got that first envelope, I actually shouted, I was so excited. I opened it, and there was a telegram — *written in the secret language*. And do you know, I felt something I had never felt before. I could read this language, and it was *just mine*. Nobody else could understand it. Not a soul in the world. It was like someone had handed me a power that... that..." He wobbled his head, then gave up and drank.

"What was the message?"

"It said to go to a church," said Peter. "Go to a specific church, then to go inside a specific confessional. I should sit down and say, 'Father, the sins of the flock do not compare with the sins of the single sheep.'"

"In English?"

"Yes."

"Do you know what it meant?"

Peter suddenly smiled. He looked self-effacingly amused.

"I have no idea." He chuckled humorlessly. "But the message told me that the priest, or whoever it was, would say, 'Bless you, magnificent child.' Also in English. And then I should leave. And I did exactly as I was told! I sat down, said what I was to say, and — I couldn't believe when I heard him answer exactly that. 'Bless you, magnificent child.' I had never been inside a Catholic church in my life. I grew up Calvinist, truth be told. But at that moment, I thought I'd heard the Word of God."

"How many messages did you deliver?"

"Seven. One per week. Always written on an envelope. Always the same church."

"Was there a pattern?"

"None that I could tell. I can tell them to you, but they would only make as much sense as the first."

"What did you do in the meantime?"

"I kept to myself. I felt like a spy, because I suppose that's what I was. I walked around. They gave me money, slid under the door, so I bought a Kodak. I took some pictures and had them sent away to be developed. I gave my father's farm as a return address." He sighed. "The prints never arrived, I found out."

"Then what happened?"

"Well, in a word, I was found out."

Peter paused to pour another glass of whiskey. He had hit his stride now, and the shaking had died out. He looked neither wary nor confident, only resigned to the tidal pull of his own narrative.

"I guess that's the way to put it," Peter continued. "Some men came to the apartment, in the middle of the day. They grabbed me, and..." He inhaled deeply. "They hit me. A lot. It hurt." He hugged himself. "It hurt so much."

"They took you away?"

"After they worked me over, they injected me. With a needle, I mean. I felt it go in. There's a lot I don't remember." He sniffed. "I'm not used to not remembering things. Then I woke up in a room. It was..." He swallowed hard. "I was strapped to a chair. Big leather bonds. It reminded me of that picture show. The one about the monster that comes to life?"

"*Frankenstein.*"

"That's the one! I tried to watch it, back in Wisconsin. We had a Nickelodeon. I wanted to see that movie, but when it got to that point—with the monster strapped to the bed, in that castle, with the lightning—I ran out. Scared the wits out of me. But it wasn't the monster that scared me. It was the idea of being trapped. Strapped down. And there I was, exactly like

Frankenstein's monster. There was even a strop over my head."

Peter breathed hard and fast. The glass dropped from his hand. Bourbon bled into the Persian rug, but he seemed not to notice.

"Peter, do you need a mom—"

"I was there for five days," Peter droned. "There was a window. A big one, with iron bars. I watched the sun move across it. I could smell fresh air. It looked so close. But I couldn't get out. And then, on the second day—" His lip curled, threatening a breakdown. "The door opened, and it was *him*."

"Him?"

"Dr. Vermilion."

Elizabeth nearly jumped out of her chair. "*Dr. Vermilion?*"

"He was there. With two others. Two men in white aprons. Dressed like doctors, with masks over their faces."

"What did he say?"

"He held up a sheet of paper. He said, 'Tell them what this means.' It was written in the language, *our* language. I was frantic, *frantic*, Ms. Crowne. I couldn't understand what was happening. 'You must now betray your country. You are the key that will destroy the world. You are the Shiva of the modern age. Speak, and unleash Pandora's suffering.' That's exactly what he said, word for word."

"Peter," said Elizabeth, "if he was wearing a mask, can you be sure it was him?"

"Yes."

"How?"

"The way he walked."

"How do you mean?"

"He took these long steps." Peter abruptly rose from the chair and threw out his leg, then slammed his foot down. He repeated the movement with the second leg, making a slow circle about the room. "Like a stork. It was the strangest walk I'd ever seen. It was the only thing about him that didn't frighten me—at first, anyway. I knew, or at least I thought I knew, if I had to, I could outrun him. He walked around like a man with a broke hip." He smacked his temple hard. "I mean a *broken* hip."

"Let me ponder that," said Elizabeth. "Then what happened?"

"Ms. Crowne, I'd rather not say."

"Peter, I understand your discomfort—"

"No, *you don't!*" Peter exploded. "No one *can* understand! *The things they did!*"

Elizabeth stopped. She arrested her every muscle. She knew better than to poke a man in agony. It was vital to stay still, to speak delicately.

"This may be the most important thing," said Elizabeth. "If we wish to decipher what happened, and *why*, we must know their methods. And understand, Peter, that I have no more desire to hear these particulars than you have to recount them. But without your testimony, the rest is incomplete. Do you understand?"

Tears issued down his cheeks, and Peter's face crumpled. He wagged his head, but finally he nodded in anguished compliance.

"They used *sound*," he gargled.

"Sound?"

"They left the room, and then the air was filled with sound. Sound like the world has never heard. A shrieking, howling noise, as if every animal was shrieking at once, and at a pitch that could... it could break your spirit, Ms. Crowne. I really thought my ears would burst."

"How long?"

"An hour? Maybe two?"

"An *hour?*" Elizabeth asked, incredulous.

Peter's lip quivered as he punched away his tears.

"*An hour*, you say? *Yes!* You don't know what kind of sound this was. It was *torture*, I tell you! Even the open window was no relief. That window *mocked* me! I screamed, I could feel my throat burn, for all the screaming. But I couldn't hear my own voice! An hour? Yes, an hour! It was all I could take! Could *anyone* endure more?"

His body was like a gnarled tree, curling into itself, fully and completely wrecked by the memory.

"An hour, then," said Elizabeth. "And what would I know? I've never known torture."

"Yes, what *would* you know?" Peter spat. He looked askew, toward the window. "What would anyone know? Five days in a room in some strange country, never knowing if you'll see your home again. I'd sooner have — I'd sooner have taken a hundred bullets from some Kraut Gatling gun than..."

"But why did they stop? Why end the torture, if you didn't break?"

Peter shivered. He looked queasy.

Then, suddenly, he lifted his chair from the floor and hurled it at the wall. The wood exploded into a rain of legs and backing, landing on the floor in a crippled pile. Elizabeth recoiled with surprise.

"Because I *did* break!" Peter screamed. "Don't you see? I gave in! I gave up everything! For three days, they brought me messages, and I translated every word! Every syllable! I told them all the secrets — the church, the priest, all the messages I had sent! I gave everything up! Just the threat of the noise, and I buckled. I'm a spineless traitor! *I betrayed everyone!*"

He doubled over, shrieking and weeping with unprecedented loathing. He crawled across the floor, in no particular direction, sobbing so forcefully that spittle flew from his pried-open mouth.

"I'm a *disgrace!*" he wailed. "I deserve to die! Kill me! Kill me! *Kill me!*"

Elizabeth opened a window and finally lit a long-anticipated joint, then tossed her match into the street below. Cars moved effervescently down the dark pavement, framed by gridded wreaths of light, each lamp haloed in the gathering fog. The evening chill seeped into her house robe, but Elizabeth was too preoccupied to notice.

She weighed Peter's sordid tale in her mind. She considered the double appearance of Dr. Vermilion, his debut as American agent and encore as German mastermind.

But a queerer fact loomed large: Peter had been rescued. After five days, a platoon of U.S. soldiers barged through the door and ripped Peter from his cell. Once he was safe, they secreted him to Paris. And what had awaited him? A hero's welcome. He was treated in a hospital for minor wounds, then was given a private hotel on the Champs Élysées. During debriefings, he confessed to betraying his country; the shame had torn him apart. The thought of lying to his superiors had overwhelmed him. And yet the Army had granted him an honorable discharge and a hefty bonus. Generals decorated him in private ceremonies. A special long-distance call had been scheduled with the President, who showered him with praise.

It doesn't make sense, Elizabeth thought, rubbing her temples.

Peter had shared state secrets. The torture didn't matter. He should have been tried and convicted. He should have been led before a firing squad. So why had the Army spared Peter? Why the special treatment? Surely not out of the kindness of their hearts. What game were they playing?

Elizabeth exhaled into the night, felt the buzz of ganja overtake her mind, and then a thought surfaced, so pure and true that she spoke it aloud.

"They wanted him to fail," she said. And slowly, as she stared into the mist, everything started to fall into place.

The next day, Elizabeth closed the same window.

It was nearly noon, yet the sky had turned gray and threatening. Storm clouds and coal smoke pooled in the atmosphere, swirling above the rooftops and choking out the sunlight. Raindrops slashed the glass, and the darkening landscape of slate roofs compelled Elizabeth to draw the curtains completely. She returned to her desk, but she lingered at its corner, absently jabbing a finger into the polished wood. The air felt heavy and stifling inside the room. She was cornered now, and there was only one escape.

She heard a firm knock at the door.

"It's open, Watts!" beckoned Elizabeth.

The commander entered the room with angular steps, as if his legs were reluctant to bend. He then pivoted forty-five degrees and stood rigidly as Eugene Blinker followed. Blinker had forfeited his dark three-piece suit for a plaid jacket and matching slacks. The outfit had the tacky pattern of a pitchman, yet the style was so handsomely cut that Blinker looked strangely dashing. He had a bounce to his step; he appeared even jauntier than before. Blinker placed himself in one of the chairs and sat up straight. With his erect spine and hands on kneecaps, Blinker looked like an eager schoolboy.

"Care for a seat, Commander?" asked Elizabeth.

"I would prefer to stand," he asserted.

"Of course you would." Elizabeth dropped into her chair and examined the room. "Let's get down to business, shall we? Commander, explain something to me—why is it you're here?"

Watts didn't move, except for a flinch of one cheek. "As I explained before, I was asked to introduce you to Private Gunderson in order to assess his psychol—"

"Yes, yes, of course," said Elizabeth, waving off the rest of his speech. "But what do you expect to gain from this meeting? Surely not a better state of mind. Military intelligence may be a contradiction, but even Black Chamber is smart enough to find a decent shrink."

Watts' eyes narrowed. "I'm only following orders, Ms. Crowne."

"Yes, but *whose* orders? That's what I'd like to know. And of course you won't tell me, because you don't really know. Some pencil-pusher told you, because some bigwig told him, and for all we know it was Harding himself who came up with this cockamamie idea."

"Ms. Crowne, I would advise you not to disrespect the president—"

"Stuff it, Watts," Elizabeth shot back. "*You* tracked *me* down. *You* stalked *me* to my favorite diner. *You* insulted me, and then *you* accused me of anti-American activities. Disrespect? I think *you're* the expert here."

Watts only blinked. He looked too stunned to move any other muscle.

"Back at the diner," Elizabeth resumed, "during our charming introduction, you said, 'This man is not my friend.' What did you mean by that?"

Watts ran his tongue over his teeth as he debated how to respond. "I don't think my personal feelings are relevant to this investigation."

"No? You don't, perhaps, consider Gunderson a *traitor?* You don't feel he gave up secret messages to save his own skin? You don't think him a coward? A yellowbelly? A stupid farm boy pretending to defend his country, when all he did was take a free trip to Switzerland and get himself arrested?"

"Ms. Crowne, Private Gunderson served his country—"

"Don't you wonder," Elizabeth interrupted, "why some hayseed from Wisconsin received a medal of valor, and all you got was a chance to be his babysitter?"

Elizabeth had never noticed the thickness of Watts' neck until this moment, when he swallowed hard, and his Adam's apple bobbed powerfully.

Watts said, "My role in this matter is not—"

"I think you *despise* him," proclaimed Elizabeth. "Because he's *not* a spy. He's not clever, he's not brave, and he squealed the first chance he got. If it were you…" Elizabeth stood up and leaned over the desk, propping herself against her outstretched arms. "But it *wasn't* you, was it? They didn't pick you. You had to stay back and guard the home front, like any good housewife—"

"THAT'S ENOUGH!" screamed Watts. He lunged forward and slammed his fist into the desk. He towered over Elizabeth. But the uncannologist didn't budge. Their faces hovered so close that their breaths mingled between them. Their eyes locked, like rival bulldogs in an alley. Only then did it sink in that Watts' stentorian voice had cracked. He had broken. He had shown his hand. His face was suddenly awash in red.

"I've never struck a woman," he growled. "Never in my life. But…"

"But *what?*" sneered Elizabeth. "Do you want to hit me, Watts? Is that what you want? Because I *dare you*. Imagine the headlines tomorrow—*spy beats civilian woman to save face*. What would your higher-ups think of *that*, Watts?"

Watts broke their gaze by whirling around. He stomped past the chairs and planted himself in the middle of the room, facing away. Then he punched his fist into his palm, once, then twice. The smacking sound was luridly violent.

"Keep it up, Watts," Elizabeth said, easing back into her

chair. "It'll make you feel better."

Elizabeth smiled victoriously. She took the Mesopotamian worry rock from her desk and clutched it in her hand like a baseball. Then she looked over at Blinker, and her smile leveled out. She looked contemplative as she studied the small man before her.

He was giggling. It was a silent giggle, yet it pulsated through his body. He doubled over with hysterics, until he was obliged to cover his face with his hands. More than ever, Blinker looked like a fun-loving child, silly and carefree.

"It's funny, isn't it?" said Elizabeth quietly.

"Oh, Ms. Crowne, you're a *crackup!*" Blinker cackled, no longer concealing his amusement. "You should have been a comedienne, I swear!"

Elizabeth waited a moment, then opened her desk drawer. "You know, Blinker," said Elizabeth, "I didn't tell you—when we met the other day—but I'm actually very fond of the circus."

With this comment, Blinker calmed himself, his laughter diminishing into scattered titters. "It's a wonderful place, isn't it?"

"*I* thought so. My parents took me, when I was young. My brother and sister, too. It was one of the few things we all did together. We saw—which one again?—ah, yes, the Ringling Brothers."

"Oh, that's a good one!" affirmed Blinker, nodding. "One of the best!"

"But I'll tell you my favorite part," Elizabeth persisted. "It wasn't the clowns or the animals that we loved. And it wasn't the musicians or the human cannonball or any of that. It was the acrobats."

"Really? How come?" Blinker leaned forward, placing his jaw in his hands, like a child waiting for a story to begin.

"I'm no expert," said Elizabeth. "But if I recall, every

routine has three distinct stages. In the first, the acrobat does something simple. It's not so simple that *I* could do it, but it's simple enough for anyone to watch and understand. For example, maybe he places a wine glass on his nose."

"Ah, I know that one!" said Blinker. "A classic balancing act! Our man was named Shane the Human Chandelier."

"Let's use that as an example, then," said Elizabeth, privately annoyed by his interjection. "In the second stage, the acrobat raises the stakes. He places more glasses on top of the wine glass, or even plates, ceramic bowls. The pile grows higher and higher. With each new object, our trepidation grows. Out in the audience, we can hardly believe his talent. We think back to that first wine glass, resting on his nose, and it seems so simple, now. That trifling little trick, which no normal person could ever learn, is something the acrobat could do in his sleep. The second stage builds suspense. With each passing moment, we respect him more."

"So what's the third stage?" said Blinker, starry-eyed.

"The third is the climax," answered Elizabeth. She reached into the drawer and drew out a curved object. Bright colors were splayed across its convex side, but Elizabeth held it close, toward herself, and examined it ponderously. "There's always a final trick, a feat that seems impossible. In this case, the acrobat already has a pile of fragile flatware balanced on his nose. And you're right, it looks like a chandelier, teetering back and forth, as if it could crash to the floor at any moment. So then, just as we're biting our fingernails, an assistant joins him onstage — pushing a unicycle."

"Ooh, I love it!" cried Blinker, shaking his fists with delight.

"And this is important," said Elizabeth darkly, "because we now realize just how skilled the acrobat is. The first wine glass was nothing. The chandelier? Difficult, but something he does every day. Yet when he mounts that unicycle, and he pedals across the stage carrying thirty pieces of glass on his narrow septum, we realize this man is something *special*. He has a skill that none of us will ever possess. He can concentrate with the rarest intensity. We are nothing compared to him. All of us, out in the audience, must suddenly accept ourselves as mere mortals."

The room went silent. Watts still faced away, his arm folded. Blinker sat in his chair, mesmerized by Elizabeth's speech. The room was as still as a vacant library.

Finally Elizabeth said, "How much did Private Gunderson tell you about Dr. Vermilion?"

Blinker curled his lip and shrugged. "He told me a little. I think it's kind of a lousy memory for him."

"Believe me, it is," said Elizabeth. "But you know the gist, yes?"

"I think so."

"Dr. Vermilion," mused Elizabeth, "is like that acrobat. The first stage is simple. He invents his own language. A brilliant idea, in a time of war. You can crack a code, but you can't crack a language. Better still, you can't learn a language that no one speaks. So there it is—the mysterious tongue of Dr. Vermilion. He teaches the language to *only one man*. This way, he can transmit messages from Washington to Europe any way he likes. Anyone who intercepts a message will find only gibberish. It's a perfect system—except for one problem." Elizabeth raised her voice: "Maybe Commander Watts knows what that problem is?"

Watts lurched with surprise. He had clearly not expected to hear his name. He angled his head sideways, but his body refused to turn around. He said nothing.

"What the Commander smartly pointed out," Elizabeth continued, "is that Peter Gunderson is a *terrible* spy. He's anxious. He's shy. Worst of all, he's a chicken. Not that *I* would fare well under torture, but *real* spies are trained to endure anything. They bury their secrets so deeply within themselves that nothing, not even excruciating pain, can unearth them. A real spy assumes a role. He is the consummate actor. He tells lies every minute, to everyone he meets. But Gunderson? He couldn't lie to an orangutan. Some people are born spies. Others have to settle for being decent men, and Gunderson is one of them.

"Which begs the question—why would anyone conscript such a sap? Surely, in an army of nearly five million men, Black Chamber could have found someone braver than Peter Gunderson. Sure, he has a photographic memory, but lots of men do. Gunderson hadn't left his hometown. What business did he have sending secret messages in Europe?"

She looked up to see Watts, who had angled his body toward Elizabeth, as if to hear better. She knew his interest was piqued. It was time.

"Now we begin the second stage," said Elizabeth. "They picked Peter Gunderson *because* he was weak. The messages he sent were all decoys. They didn't mean anything. They benefitted no one. But as long as Gunderson *thought* he was transmitting top-secret information, he would do anything he could to keep them safe. Because, despite everything, Gunderson is a devoted patriot.

"Which is why the enemy captured him—because he was *supposed* to be captured. I'd believe it was Black Chamber itself that tipped the enemy off. They probably sent his address and a convenient time to abduct him. The Germans showed up, captured him, and took him to a secret hideaway. Which is where Peter again met Dr. Vermilion."

"So this is the third stage?" exclaimed Blinker, who was now frantic with excitement. "This is the climax?"

"No," said Elizabeth coolly. "But it would appear that way. Because Dr. Vermilion *seemed* to be playing both sides. He worked for the Americans, but he *also* worked for the Germans. Was he a double agent? Yes—in a way. He pretended to betray the Americans, to confuse Gunderson. He tortured Gunderson, who spilled the beans—exactly as he was supposed to. Because the messages Dr. Vermilion ordered him to translate *were all fake*."

Watts whirled around. "What do you mean?"

"I mean, Dr. Vermilion created phony messages, and then he tortured Gunderson until he translated them. The Germans thought they'd broken Gunderson. They thought they had gained something, but instead the messages sent them on a wild goose chase—appropriate for the inventors of the goose step."

"How do you know the messages were false?" demanded Watts.

"I don't," avowed Elizabeth. "But why else would Gunderson receive a hero's welcome? Probably because Washington arranged the whole charade—with a little help from their friend, Dr. Vermilion. Black Chamber probably knew where he was imprisoned the whole time, and it was Dr. Vermilion who arranged his so-called rescue. The entire thing was choreographed, from beginning to end. But it was choreographed by the men at the top of the ladder. People like us, Watts, wouldn't know anything about it."

"Incredible!" said Blinker breathlessly. "So there it is, the third stage!"

"Again, no," said Elizabeth. "Although Dr. Vermilion would like us to think so. Because it leaves a final question—who *is* Dr. Vermilion? A clandestine creature, to be sure. He conceals his face with a mask. He appears only in secret rooms. He would seem impossible to identify, which is exactly what he wants." Elizabeth paused. "Or *is it*?"

She looked from Watts to Blinker, then back again.

"Well?" Watts blustered. "What do you think?"

"I think Dr. Vermilion is a free agent," said Elizabeth. "I think he worked with Black Chamber, but just once."

"Why?" asked Watts. "If he helped us win the war?"

"He didn't care about the war," said Elizabeth. "That's my guess. It's convenient that the allies won. Always nice to side with the winning team. But that wasn't important. Above all, he wanted one thing — *to test his sound weapon.*"

"His *what?*"

"Remember, Watts, that Gunderson was tortured *with sound.* I think Dr. Vermilion was testing a new technology, a machine that uses sound to destroy the human mind. He used the ruse as an excuse to try out his new invention — to see how far he could ruin an able-bodied man without killing him."

"My God," said Watts, flushing. "Gunderson was his lab rat."

"And maybe not the only one," Elizabeth said. "But the experiment was inconclusive. It's one thing to break a man, but what about after he's broken? You have to keep watching him, studying him, collecting data, like a good scientist. But how could Dr. Vermilion get close enough to such a wounded soul? How could he earn that poor young man's trust?" Elizabeth turned her eyes to Blinker. "I never asked you, what do you know about Noh?"

Blinker frowned. "You mean, the opposite of yes?"

"I mean Noh theater. You spent three years in Japan. You must have heard of it."

"I guess so," said Blinker indifferently.

"How about kabuki?"

"Now that I *have* heard of." He smiled in his cheerful way. "Good stuff, kabuki. I caught a couple of productions over there. Not everyone's cup of tea, but I enjoyed it."

"You see, Blinker," said Elizabeth slowly, "I've been to Japan myself. And I've also seen kabuki. I've even seen samurai armor, and I've taken in some Noh. And all of these Japanese traditions have something in common."

"Do tell," said Blinker, batting his eyelashes.

"They all wear masks."

Elizabeth turned the object around in her hands, and a fearsome face emerged. The surface was painted in fiery scarlet, the eyes were maniacally large, and the mouth was stoic and oblong. Beneath the monstrous nose sprouted a pair of straight, wiry whiskers.

"The mask!" exclaimed Watts.

"No," Elizabeth clarified. "*A* mask. Common in Japan, but almost unknown in America, let alone rural Wisconsin. Which is why, Blinker, *this* is the third stage. This mask is the real magic trick, the one that makes all the others seem elementary. But you know that. You've known the whole time. Because *you* are Dr. Vermilion."

Elizabeth had tried to anticipate his reaction. She had rehearsed her speech a hundred times since the previous night, and she felt herself trembling with rapture. But she'd had no idea what Blinker would do. She imagined him shouting his protests, storming from the room, hiding behind Watts, leaping through the window, or even breaking into tears. Perhaps he would try to laugh it off, call her foolish and paranoid, or swear to sue her for defamation. But none of these predictions matched what actually happened.

Blinker smiled, raised his hands, and clapped. The clap was slow and taunting, and it drained Elizabeth of her excitement. His smile swelled. He no longer looked sprightly or adolescent; now he seemed arrogant, superior, a demigod disguised as a dwarf. The clap continued at the same chilling tempo for longer than Elizabeth cared to reckon. When she could no longer endure his amused expression, Elizabeth looked up to see Watts, who looked calcified with shock.

At last Blinker let his arms flop into his lap. "Well done, Ms. Crowne. Well done."

"So you won't deny it?" quavered Elizabeth.

Blinker pursed his lips. Even his pout filled Elizabeth with fear. "But aren't I a little bit—*small?*"

"Stilts," murmured Elizabeth. "You stood on stilts, inside the costume. That's why you walked in such a strange way. *Like a stork*, Gunderson said."

Blinker dropped his chin only an inch, but it was a nod that confirmed everything. His eyes blazed.

"But if I were Dr. Vermilion," fumed Blinker, "why come here? Why risk exposing myself? I could have stayed in Milwaukee and no one would be the wiser."

"Because..." said Elizabeth, but she wavered.

"*Why*, Ms. Crowne?" demanded Blinker, his voice rising. "Say it! I know you know. But I want to hear the words."

"Because... you're testing me."

"BRAVO!" cried Blinker, who now leapt to his feet. "*Bravissimo*, Ms. Crowne. And now, I'm happy to say, *you've passed*."

"But passed what?" stammered Elizabeth. "For what purpose?"

She could barely finish the sentence, for now Blinker glowered at her with demonic eyes, a lusty sneer spread across his face. His hand snuck into his jacket pocket, the movement so smooth that Elizabeth couldn't think to protest. His hands remained there, groping something behind the layer of tweed.

"The game has begun, Ms. Crowne," he seethed. "Know thine enemy—that's the common wisdom, isn't it? Well, we've come to know each other, now. And someday soon, we'll meet again. Sooner than we think, perhaps."

"But why me?" Elizabeth said softly.

"Because you are an *uncannologist*," Blinker said triumphantly. "And *I* am the uncanny. You are the instrument of my destruction, and I am yours. There are no rules. The game board is as vast as the world. And the gauntlet, Ms. Crowne, is now thrown."

As he spoke, Elizabeth noticed Watts hovering in the

background. The commander moved slowly, reaching down to the leather holster attached to his belt. The flap silently snapped open, and Watts groped the curved handle of his M1917 revolver.

"If I didn't know you were mad," Elizabeth said breathlessly, "I'd try to reason with you."

"That's the trouble with you," Blinker snarled. "Your favorite act is the acrobat. The acrobat is nothing. His life is only somersaults and high wires. But the magician—*he's* the one who steals the show."

Watts drew the pistol and aimed it at the back of Blinker's head. "*Blinker!*" he called out.

But in the same moment Blinker drew his hand from his breast pocket and flung an object at the ground. A burst of light flared upward, and tendrils of colored smoke exploded from the floor. Only a second passed before the room was filled with pink and violet fog, which billowed everywhere, blinding Elizabeth. Her eyes stung, her throat burned. She gagged on the powdery texture of the air. She whipped her arms through invisible space until her hand brushed against a bookshelf, and then she felt her way along the wall, guiding herself toward the exit.

When she found it, the door was already ajar. Elizabeth continued to cough as she stumbled into the corridor and descended the steps. She grabbed her throat and gasped for breath. It was only when she reached the landing that she saw Watts, doubled over, hacking into the carpet. Her watery eyes could barely make out the scene, but she saw the front door open as well, admitting glum daylight into the vestibule. Watts looked up, his eyes a sickly red. He shook his head, and Elizabeth knew that Blinker—Dr. Vermilion—had escaped into the drizzling afternoon.

"How did you figure it out?" asked Watts, as he shoveled another forkful of scrambled eggs into his mouth. He looked exactly as before, the same impeccable uniform, but his eyes were puffy and maroon.

"I have a friend in the circus," said Elizabeth, sipping her coffee. "He's worked for the Hagenbeck-Wallace Circus for years. He knows all the lore, and carneys all seem to know each other. So after I talked with Blinker, I sent my friend a telegram. I asked about the Xander & Xerxes Circus. The story sounded fishy to me, and I wanted to make sure Blinker was telling the truth."

"So he lied about it?"

"No," said Elizabeth. "I think that part was true. The abandonment. The adoption. I'm sure he was actually raised on the road. But I doubt it was one big, happy family."

"Why not?" asked Watts, dabbing his mouth with a napkin.

"Because Blinker said the circus went belly-up. *It was a sad day*, he said. Everyone hugged and said goodbye. But it didn't go belly-up. The circus was doing quite well—until one night, when someone soaked the bleachers with kerosene."

"You mean..." Watts set down his fork, appalled. "You mean he set the big top on fire?"

"The whole place burned down," Elizabeth said morosely. "No one knows how many died, and how many more were burned so badly they wished they had died. The circus had shown up in some one-horse town in Mexico. It never made much ink. But it certainly put Xander & Xerxes out of business."

They were quiet for a while, eating their breakfast in silence. It was late morning, and the weather was gray and muggy. Uncle Joe's Diner was nearly vacant, except for a couple of old men in stools poring over their newspapers. Elizabeth allowed the streetcar to rumble brashly by, its bell clanging into the distance, before attempting to speak again.

141

"One thing concerns me," said Elizabeth. "If Black Chamber gave you orders to meet with me, and it was Dr. Vermilion who arranged the meeting..."

"Then someone at Black Chamber is working for Dr. Vermilion," concluded Watts. "And no doubt he's *been* working with Dr. Vermilion for some time."

"You don't know who it could be?"

"I don't." Watts sniffed. "I've been a damned fool. I trusted the chain of command. Even during the war, I thought, 'If the agency picked Gunderson, it must be for a good reason.' I had no idea."

"Why did they keep you stateside?" asked Elizabeth. "You could have gone to Europe. You're tough. You're loyal. You would've made a terrific spy."

Watts looked through the window. A bicyclist pedaled past, followed by a woman walking her dog.

"I have asthma," he said. "Not severe, but bad enough to..." He closed his swollen eyes. "They made a patsy out of me."

"It's all right," said Elizabeth. "You were just doing your job."

She touched a thumb against her blouse, and there she felt the hard circle of her ring. She pressed it against her solar plexus, felt its shape beneath the fabric of her clothes, and was comforted. Unmasking Dr. Vermilion had at least given the two of them a common enemy. Watts might not trust her, but he hadn't learned anything about her past. She had diverted his suspicions. For now, they could sit civilly together in her favorite diner, openly debriefing about the previous day. She removed her finger from that hidden ornament and took up her coffee.

"Just one request," said Elizabeth.

"Go on."

"You may not believe in shellshock. But torture is torture, and I think Gunderson could use a professional. I have a friend in New York. He's an analyst, and he's good. I would even pay the fees — "

"Just write down his name," Watts said. "I'll make the arrangements myself."

The bell above the front door tinkled, and a lanky young man appeared. He wore a simple gray uniform and carried a leather messenger bag. His brimmed cap was too large for his head and flopped sideways over his curly chestnut hair. He scanned the room until his eyes fell upon Elizabeth, and then he grinned toothily.

"Ms. Crowne?" he said, approaching their booth. "I've got a special delivery."

For a split-second, Elizabeth imagined the worst of this gangly youth, and when he reached into his bag, she could almost see the outline of a knife or handgun. She pictured herself screaming, Watts tackling the boy and scrambling for the weapon. She imagined a grenade skittering across the floor, then blowing them all to smithereens.

But it was a manila envelope that emerged, as harmless as any other, and he placed it on the table, saluted with two fingers, and said, "Have a swell day!"

Elizabeth and Watts both stared at the envelope, which was besmirched with ink stains and bent from its journey through the postal maze. At last Elizabeth took the envelope and tore it open. Again, she feared a burst of toxic powder, a ticking bomb, a venomous snake — but instead she felt a bundle of curved and rigid paper. She pulled it out at once, and its glossy surface glinted with light.

They were photographs. Several dozen, at least. The first showed a high cliff covered in pine trees. The next showed a lake, its placid surface broken by a single sailboat. Each landscape was slightly off-kilter, out of focus, as if taken by an amateur. She saw stately buildings and cobbled roads, street signs with elegant script. It wasn't until she saw the portrait of a man that her mouth fell open. She grabbed her throat. "Oh, God!" she gasped.

"What is it?" Watts said, leaning forward.

Then he saw it, too: The man was young and happy-looking. He wore a trench coat and leaned against a stone balustrade. He was alone, but he smiled broadly.

"Private Gunderson," said Watts.

"Peter," said Elizabeth. "These were the pictures. The ones he took on his Kodak. The ones that never..."

Elizabeth stood up in her booth. She felt her heart flutter with panic. She looked through the wide window, into the sheets of falling rain. But there was no one there. The street was empty.

THE CASE OF THE APOCALYPTIC ARIA

July, 1921

"**W**AKE UP, MAUDE!"

Maude's eyes fluttered open, and she rose from her mattress. She squinted in the dark compartment, trying to remember where she was, and then she looked through the window to see a concrete platform.

"Where... where are we?" she murmured woozily.

"We're here!" exclaimed Elizabeth.

Maude dropped her legs along the side of her bunk and let them dangle, then looked down to see Elizabeth struggling with her trunk. Elizabeth dragged the unwieldy luggage to the door, looked up and scowled.

"Are you coming or what?"

"Oh... yes!"

Maude suddenly swelled with excitement as she leapt to the floor and slipped on her boots. As she fastened the laces, the last remnants of her dreams melted away and she remembered what awaited her: *New York City.*

When she looked up, a long-limbed youth in a double-breasted suit emerged at the sliding door and leaned into the sleeper compartment.

"Help you with that, ma'am?"

Maude had little experience with porters, and it felt strange watching a pimply adolescent pick up her suitcase, doff his round cap, and barrel down the corridor. But Maude was relieved to watch him pick up Elizabeth's trunk as well, then hobble toward the exit with the double load.

When she'd caught up with Elizabeth, the uncannologist smirked at Maude and said, "They don't call it first class for nothing."

Maude could barely contain her astonishment: The two women stepped out of the train and headed down the busy causeway, the outside air dense with humidity. They passed through a tall doorway, and Maude beheld a voluminous hall—larger than any room she'd ever seen, with a curved ceiling and squared pillars of granite that receded into the distance. The stone floors clattered with the endless march of feet, hundreds of heels and dress shoes advancing in all directions at once, just as the mass of jackets and capes and shawls and fedoras throbbed like a single organism. Letters on the overhanging train schedule shuffled downward, a waterfall of destinations, times, and platform numbers. All around Maude hummed the din of voices, a thousand conversations echoing discordantly against the imperious walls, as strange and wondrous as the sound of her own breaths.

Maude had barely grasped the train station's size before the porter led them to the revolving doors. He struggled to fit the bags between the glass-and-copper frames, but somehow he managed to shimmy both himself and the luggage through the rotating panels. The door first whisked Elizabeth outside, followed by Maude. She emerged on the sidewalk, took one long look at her surroundings, and gasped, "My... *word*."

The wide avenue was flat and straight, enclosed between

two infinite walls of buildings. Traffic was a tangled web of cars and trucks, bicycles and carriages, and the pedestrians walked so hurriedly that Maude saw them only as blurs. The broad sidewalk was a galaxy of dark spots, and Maude could feel the spritz of rain on her hands and cheek. The sky was a perfect sheet of pewter gray, and the buildings were so tall that their upper echelons were lost in the gathering clouds.

But before she could swallow a full breath, she heard the porter call, "Here you go, miss!" Maude felt the boy's hand on her back, guiding her toward an open taxi. As she slipped awkwardly inside, the driver's cigar erupted all around her.

"Where ya headed, lady?" he said, belching smoke through his blackened teeth.

"The Clutterbuck Hotel," ordered Elizabeth, who promptly tumbled into the seat beside Maude. She tossed a coin out the window, which landed in the porter's gloved hands.

"A half-dollar!" he exclaimed. "Gee, thanks, lady!"

Elizabeth waved dismissively as the car jerked into motion, and the train station disappeared behind them.

"You got a garden or something?" said the cabbie as he scratched his scruffy neck.

"Not nearly," said Elizabeth. "Why do you ask?"

The cabbie leered. "'Cause you gotta have some serious cabbage if you're stayin' at the Clutterbuck."

Elizabeth couldn't help but smile at this. "Just good friends," she said.

"Well," said the cabbie, "if you ever got friends to spare, you send 'em my way."

"I'll do that," said Elizabeth. Then she leaned toward Maude and murmured, "I love New York."

Elizabeth tapped the reception desk with the tips of her fingers. When she realized she was doing so, she stuffed her hands into her jacket pockets. The clerk in front of her was tall and bulky and wore a graying mustache, and he listened intently to his telephone receiver.

"Yes," he said in a breathy voice. "I assure you, sir, our kitchen is one of the finest in New York. The Michelin Guide has recommended us no fewer than... no, sir, our chef has not yet arrived, but I can take down your number and have him ring you as soon as possible..."

At last he signed off and placed the receiver delicately on its hook.

"My apologies, ma'am," the concierge said. "Welcome to the Clutterbuck Hotel. Do you have a reservation?"

"Elizabeth Crowne," she said.

The concierge suddenly lit up and pressed a hand to his chest. He bowed slightly and said, "Ah, yes, Ms. Crowne, we've been expecting you."

"Have you, now?" Elizabeth raised an eyebrow. "If I didn't know better, I'd say you've confused me for a Rockefeller."

He smiled strangely—Elizabeth couldn't tell if he was amused or put off.

"It's an honor for the Clutterbuck to have made this reservation," he said slowly.

"That's flattering," Elizabeth said. "But I suppose I don't see why. I can't imagine I've become famous all of a sudden."

"Ah," said the concierge, who now seemed to understand. "You're quite right. I don't have any idea who *you* are. It's not the reservation itself. It's who *made* the reservation."

"I see," said Elizabeth. "And who might that be?"

"I'm—" The concierge gritted his teeth, discomfited. "I've been asked not to say. But I'm sure you'll find out sooner or later. It must be a surprise."

"Very good." Elizabeth sighed. "Might I know *your* name, then?"

"John Santorini," he said.

"Greek?" said Elizabeth.

"Mutt," he replied. "May I take your bags?"

The elevator chimed, and John Santorini pulled the luggage cart through the separating doors. Elizabeth and Maude wordlessly followed Santorini down the seventh floor hallway, whose walls were decked with watercolor paintings of fruit bowls. The curved ceiling and thick red carpets muffled all sound, making the passage nearly silent. When they arrived at room 727, Santorini drew a key from his pocket and pushed it into the lock.

But then he stopped, bit his upper lip, and turned to Elizabeth.

"Do you *really* not know who made the reservation?"

Elizabeth hid her surprise. She took a step closer. "Should I?"

"I don't know," said Santorini. "I don't know you from Adam. But I'm a little surprised, is all."

Santorini no longer sounded like a prim concierge. He had transformed into a befuddled, middle-aged man. He was convincing behind a desk, but it was clear that Santorini was clumsier and more endearing in real life.

"Maybe you could give me a hint," Elizabeth whispered.

"I wish that I could," Santorini whispered back. "But their instructions were specific."

"*Their* instructions?"

Santorini closed his eyes. He pinched his nose melodramatically. "Ms. Crowne, please don't put me in this position."

"I won't, Mr. Santorini," said Elizabeth. "But you must tell me—were there any *other* instructions?"

"Well, yes, actually."

Santorini turned the key and nudged the door open. He

cocked his head, ushering them to follow. The room revealed itself, and even Elizabeth was dumbstruck: The décor was designed in the Empire style, antique chairs with gold-tinted frames and royal blue upholstery. The dense drapes bundled around enormous windows, and although the rain now poured outside, daylight flooded the ornate Oriental carpets. Fleurs-de-lis were spread across the wallpaper in diamond patterns, and the room was vast enough to contain both a baby grand piano and pair of sofas.

"This is our French room. Over there," Santorini said, pointing to the far side, "is one boudoir. Over here is the second. You have your choice of two separate washrooms, and robes have been provided. The dining room is open from 6 p.m. onward, and room service has been comped." He spoke rapidly now, for his monologue was well rehearsed. Santorini approached a bucket of ice, from which the neck of a champagne bottle protruded. "And we have provided a bottle of Perrier Jouët, at the request of your..." He fumbled for the right word. "Your *benefactors*."

"This will certainly do," said Elizabeth. "But I assume that opening a bottle of bubbly was not your only instruction."

Santorini looked to the floor. He rifled inside his jacket, drawing a single lavender envelope.

Maude gasped. "It's the same..."

Elizabeth shot her a look and Maude stopped herself.

Santorini held the envelope out, and Elizabeth snatched it from his grasp. She dug her finger into the seam and tore savagely at the paper.

"We have a letter opener..." Santorini offered halfheartedly, but a second later Elizabeth had already slashed the envelope apart, and she unfolded a thick piece of paper.

Elizabeth scanned the letter, nodded once, then folded it slowly.

"Anything else?"

"No," said Santorini. "Just that."

"Then maybe you can do something for me," said Elizabeth. "I'd like to send a telegram to this address." She drew a shred of paper from her own pocket and handed it to Santorini. "How's your memory?"

"Worse every year," grumbled Santorini, rolling his eyes upward. "But decent enough."

"Good. I don't want this written anywhere but on the telegram. All it has to say is, 'Clutterbuck bar, quarter after six.'"

Santorini sniffed. "Not exactly code, is it?"

"It doesn't have to be," said Elizabeth. "Because if anybody else shows up, anyone unsavory, I'll know who let the cat out of the bag."

Elizabeth glared at Santorini meaningfully, until he finally straightened his jacket, linked his hands behind his back, and said, "I'm just a maître d', Ms. Crowne."

"We'll see about that," said Elizabeth. "I'm of the opinion that no one in this world is *just* anything."

"Will you be all right?" said Maude, her voice warbling.

"I'll be fine," said Elizabeth. "All this cloak and dagger business doesn't make a lick of sense. I think someone's just having fun with us. And for what it's worth, I don't think Santorini knows a thing. He's a teddy bear, as far as I can tell. But you can never be too careful."

"Just..." Maude faltered. She nervously squeezed the skin of her neck. "Call up, if anything happens?"

"You can bet on it," said Elizabeth. "Just be dressed and ready when I get back."

Elizabeth quit the room and headed toward the elevator. She had changed into a black dress, its fabric outlined in glass beads. She had never worn it before, nor the pillbox cap with its single red plume.

In mid-step, Elizabeth noticed how hastily she was charging down the hall, and she retarded her pace. "Slow down, Liz," she murmured to herself. Elizabeth felt her clogs press firmly into the carpet, and with each step, her stomach tightened. She concentrated on her breaths and swallowed hard. When she finally reached the elevator, she hesitated before pressing the button. She watched her painted fingernail quiver. A metallic taste welled in her mouth.

The door opened.

"Which floor, ma'am?" cheeped the elevator operator, a lanky boy with a lopsided cap.

"Lobby, please."

Before she knew it, the door had split open again, and the lobby emerged. She felt woozy. The room seemed larger than before, warped and malformed, and the polished floor rocked like the deck of a ship. She strode toward the restaurant's brass doors, passing sofas, travelers, and puffs of cigarette smoke. She held her chin high, but the pose felt unnatural, and she couldn't sustain it past the row of telephones. When she finally arrived at the restaurant doors, she realized she'd been holding her breath.

The doors opened, and a squat man appeared, wearing a tight-fitting jacket with lapels.

"Madame," he said.

"Just heading to the bar," stuttered Elizabeth. "For a drink," she added uselessly.

"But of course." The man kowtowed and gestured toward the interior. Elizabeth looked beyond the diminutive host and spotted the bar—a crescent of varnished wood lined with backed stools. Every metal surface looked as pure as liquid mercury.

Elizabeth leaned against the bar and absently pressed two fingers against her carotid artery. When the tall barman appeared, he was still wiping a wine glass with his towel.

"What can I fix you, ma'am?" he said.

"A Sidecar," she said.

"I think you mean a *lemonade*," the barman replied.

Elizabeth furrowed her brow, until she saw the barman wink.

"Ah… yes… of course. A lemonade."

Then she heard a voice behind her. "Two, please."

Elizabeth froze. Her spine sagged. For a moment, she couldn't turn around. She could sense the presence behind her. The fear she had felt now fermented into exhilaration. The moment had arrived, and she could no longer deny its gravity. Suddenly Elizabeth remembered who she was, where she was, and how far she had come. She straightened. The anxiety evaporated, replaced by a feeling of kinetic joy.

Elizabeth swiveled, leaning an elbow against the bar, and threw her head sideways, her hair fanning like a quickly drawn curtain.

"Hello, Sándor," she said.

She could barely force herself to perceive him, and when her eyes finally absorbed his image, she suppressed a warm shudder. Sándor was average height, but his slender frame was as elegant and agile as a wild cat's. His lower garments betrayed his Magyar origins — high black boots and slightly billowed breeches; a thick belt with a weathered gray buckle rounded his torso. But he also wore a simple jacket and dress shirt; a burgundy necktie bisected the outfit. His arms were akimbo, as if readied to dance. And then there was his face — a perfect oval of swarthy flesh, supple and firm in all the right places. As always, his mustache was waxed but not garish. His black hair was dashingly slicked.

If Elizabeth were just meeting him now, none of these features would occur to her. She would not notice his powerful handsomeness and exotic traces — the many rings that

ornamented his left hand, the lacquered cane he leaned against.
The only thing she would have seen, the only thing so many
strangers saw, was the patch that covered his right eye. That
single triangle of black leather, lashed efficiently around his
skull, drew all attention. Elizabeth wanted to wince, not
because of its peculiar imperfection, but because she
remembered the hazel eye that the patch now replaced. It had
been a world unto itself, the color and texture of a blood moon,
a vibrant circle in which she had many times lost herself.

Sándor lifted a hand into the air, fingers splayed, as if to
say, *Voilà!* His smile was resplendent. His single eye squinted
vivaciously. Elizabeth wondered for a moment whether she
might simply collapse.

"Elizabeth," he said. His voice crackled like a campfire. He
extended his hands and stepped forward, as if to embrace her,
but instead they touched each other's faces and kissed cheeks.
She felt the faintest hint of stubble against her skin; she
smelled the Egyptian musk he always wore.

"Sándor," she said again, then shook her head. "How far
you've fallen — meeting me in a hotel bar in New York City."

"Is that where we are?" said Sándor in his charcoal
baritone. "I had forgotten. All I see is you."

"You and your tawdry compliments," said Elizabeth.

"Your cocktails, madam," said the bartender, sliding two
glasses across the bar atop cloth napkins.

Elizabeth plucked one up, and Sándor followed suit. They
held them aloft for a moment. Elizabeth's mouth was slightly
open, as if preparing to speak. Then she said, "The hell with it.
Cheers."

They clinked glasses, but only Elizabeth sipped. Sándor
watched her, a cool smile crossing his lips.

"Let me try a toast," he said.

"Don't bother. Nothing would do. Especially not in your
second language."

"My fifth language, actually."

"That might impress other girls, but I've got a few languages myself."

Sándor shrugged his well-constructed shoulders and curled his lip. "Then I'll just say this—it has been much too long."

A thousand retorts entered Elizabeth's mind. A torrent of sarcasm poured through her, as it always did. But those phrases sounded so cheap, so meaningless. No quip seemed right in Sándor's presence. His genuineness disarmed her, blunting her wit. Elizabeth had always been a cut-up, no matter how grave the company. But Sándor was different.

"It *has* been too long," Elizabeth confessed. "And—I'm sorry."

Sándor dipped his head. "That is good to hear," he said. "And it needs only be said once."

He clinked his cocktail against hers, and they both drank, eyes locked beyond the rims of their glasses.

The waiter couldn't help but steal a glance as he poured water into their goblets, the ice cubes loudly tinkling against crystal. Elizabeth noticed the waiter's curious expression, which amused her. How odd they must look, a dolled-up biddy from Pittsburgh and a half-gentlemen, half-pirate with an ornamental cane, sipping glasses of contraband liquor at a corner table in a nearly empty restaurant.

"He's my chauffeur," said Elizabeth to the waiter. "He looked thirsty."

Sándor threw his head back and laughed heartily.

"It would help if I knew how to drive," he rejoined.

"Nobody's perfect."

The waiter grimaced curtly and shuffled toward the kitchen.

"Poor dear," said Elizabeth. "We've confused the stuffing out of him. Five more minutes of eavesdropping and he won't know right from left."

"You have that effect on people, I think," said Sándor, as he drew a nickel-plated case from his breast pocket and tapped a cigarette against its cover. "I myself am muddling present and past. It's as if two moments are occurring simultaneously. Care for one?"

"There's only one smoke I indulge, and now is hardly the time for it."

"Ah, yes, the green devil. I never asked you: How come you prefer this—what do you call it? —*cannabis sativa?*" His match flared, illuminating his face as smoke burst from his lips.

"Why, indeed." Elizabeth sipped her drink, then pressed it thoughtfully against her cheek. "When I was young, my mother taught me to swim."

"Not your father?"

"Dear Lord, no. He has hardly the coordination to cut a steak. But my mother—she took me to a farm one summer, and we would jump in the pond. It wasn't a pleasant pond, mind you. Lily pads everywhere. A thin veil of green scum. Dragonflies darting, mosquitoes everywhere. It was a murky pool, unfit to look at, much less swim in. It was one of those country ponds, where they dig a hole and fill it with water, in case of a barn fire. Handy, but hideous."

"Why did she take you there?"

"She's a tough bird, my mother," said Elizabeth wistfully. "She grew up on the prairie, back before all the fences and telephone poles. Her first word was Remington. Or so she likes to say."

"So you learned to swim in this... *pond.*"

"That's right." Elizabeth set the tumbler down and gazed distantly. "The days were hot and sticky. I spent entire afternoons sweating and slapping at horseflies. Even then, I always waited to jump in the water. But late in the day, when I couldn't bear the heat anymore, I went to the water's edge and dived right in. Quick as could be. The water was cold at first. Made me shiver all over. But then I was submerged. I loved feeling so weightless, my eyes squeezed tight. Couldn't see or feel a thing, just the water. Every sound was muted. Your mind works so differently, down there. You can really *think* underwater. Take away all the distractions, even gravity, and your brain takes the spotlight." She sniffed and traced the rim of the glass with her fingers. "And *that*, my dear Sándor, is why I fancy my cannabis sativa. It's like I'm taking that pond wherever I go."

Sándor nodded. At first he looked satisfied to contemplate these words. But there was something more to his expression.

"Why do you never respond to my letters?" he said.

Elizabeth sighed briskly. "I don't know, Sándor. You give a girl writer's block." She took a cleansing breath, then leaned forward and said slowly: "I have to ask you something."

"Anything, Elizabeth."

"Did you send me a letter written in cut newspaper?"

"Newspaper?"

"As in, the letters were clipped from a newspaper and arranged on a piece of stationery. Like a ransom note. You know, how gangsters are always trying to hide their penmanship?"

Sándor dragged on the cigarette, stupefied by the question, and then waved the smoke away. "I did not."

"Damn," murmured Elizabeth. "Well, there goes my theory."

"Perhaps you should tell me what is happening."

Elizabeth nodded reluctantly. "Yes, I will. After all, I might need your help."

"Is it something — dangerous?"

"That's the thing, I haven't a clue. It might all be a big joke, although I can't say I find it very funny."

"Let us start at the beginning."

"Right." Elizabeth beckoned the waiter with her empty glass, which was instantly carried away. When the waiter had disappeared fully into the kitchen, Elizabeth dug through her handbag. "A couple of weeks ago, I received a letter in the mails. It certainly stood out—a lavender envelope. The paper was bond, the kind you'd use for a wedding invitation. But the message was cryptic."

The envelope emerged from Elizabeth's purse, and Sándor opened it thoughtfully. He saw the collage of snipped-out letters.

Dear Ms. Crowne,

Enclosed you will find two trains tickets to New York, for yourself and another. A reservation has been made at the Clutterbuck Hotel. You will receive a second message upon arrival.

"That was all?" puffed Sándor.

"Well, there *were* tickets, just like it said. First class sleepers. And the reservation was genuine. The Clutterbuck staff is treating me like Cleopatra. Whoever this is, he wants me to travel in style." She shot Sándor a look of rueful disappointment. "Which is why I thought it might be you."

Sándor looked disarmed, and he took a moment to collect himself. At last he said, "Did you receive the second message?"

"The moment we arrived," said Elizabeth. She pinched the

second envelope between index and middle fingers, then held it aloft. "See what you make of it."

Sándor read.

Ms. Crowne,

go to the Clementine

Theatre at 9 p.m. Ask about

the private function. You are

on the guest list, plus one.

"This is all very mysterious," murmured Sándor.

"And pointlessly so," said Elizabeth. "Whoever it is, I wish he'd spill the beans. I feel like someone's toying with me, and I don't like it."

"The Clementine Theatre," said Sándor. "That is not a place for plebeians."

"Oh? I've never heard of it."

"Just so. The Clementine is small, but very elegant. It is famous for its operas."

"Operas?"

"Chamber operas, yes. It is very exclusive. They have no publicity or box office. The people who come, they are dignitaries, millionaires, politicians. Not just anyone may attend a production at the Clementine. It is by invitation only."

"Well, aren't I a lucky girl."

"Whoever this is," said Sándor, glancing about the room. "He is very powerful. He has connections. You must be careful. And if you like..." He looked away bashfully. "I will help you, if I can."

"I'd like that very much, actually."

As Elizabeth said these words, she was startled by her tone. Its meaning was deeper than even she expected. But it was also undeniable—she needed Sándor, not just to assist her, but to be close. So many years had passed, yet his presence felt familiar, *necessary*. She swallowed hard and tried to bury the sensation.

"But you can't come with me," said Elizabeth. "Not tonight."

"Elizabeth," said Sándor urgently, "you cannot go alone."

She cracked a smile. "Oh, I've got a date. And she's far cuter than you are."

Elizabeth knocked on the door to room 727, feeling both tired and harried. The day's travels and transitions had worn her down, and a part of her yearned for a five-star bubble bath. But when the door opened, all her misgivings evaporated.

Maude stood in the doorway, completely transformed. Her narrow body was draped in a dress of silver lamé, whose fine fibers twinkled in the lamplight. Several necklaces hung between her shoulders in concentric ovals, and each strand was studded with seashells. In place of a hat, a narrow band rounded her head, and a small bouquet of violets blossomed on one side. Makeup had smoothed her already magnificent skin; she looked like a statue carved from varnished pine.

"Oh... Maude..." said Elizabeth, though she was incapable of finishing the sentence.

"Do I look all right?" said Maude faint-heartedly.

"You look..." The more Elizabeth perceived Maude, the less she knew what to say. At least she blurted, "You look *resplendent*, Maude."

"Oh," said Maude, smoothing her skirt. "Is that a good thing?"

"Maude, you're a *vision*. Where did you find that thing?"

"This?" Maude looked timorously to the floor. "I found some cloth in the Strip District. I was running errands, but I loved it so much, I just knew I had to buy some."

"You *made* it?"

"Well... yes?" Maude spoke as if she wasn't sure herself. "I used your mother's sewing machine. The one in the attic, I mean. It was dusty, but it works just fine. I hope you don't mind."

"I don't mind at all," said Elizabeth reverently. "As long as you make me one, too."

"Oh, of course!"

Suddenly Elizabeth remembered that she was not alone. Disconcerted by the delay in introductions, she jutted a thumb toward Sándor and murmured, "This is my friend Sándor."

"It is an *honor* to meet you," ejected Sándor, who strode forward, grasped Maude's wrist, and kissed it with excessive flourish. Elizabeth balked at the exaggerated gesture.

"Pleased to meet you, Mr. Sander," said Maude. "How... how do you know Elizabeth?"

"Well," he said, wielding his debonair smile. "That story requires some time to tell. Perhaps when you return from the theater."

"I think I'd like that..."

But the final words trailed off. Maude studied the fingers that still squeezed her hand. Each digit wore a different ring, most of them studded with colorful stones. But one ring was different — it bore an insignia, a seven-pointed star resting on a vertical line, a crescent arcing above. Maude was transfixed; her head wafted from side to side.

"Mr. Sander," she said. "Your ring..."

Elizabeth launched forward and grabbed Maude by her free hand, then guided her away from Sándor, into the corridor.

"Well, we really must be going," said Elizabeth. "Already running late, and if there's anything New York abhors, it's dawdlers. We'll see you in the morning, Sándor?"

"Yes," affirmed Sándor quietly, waving to the women as they sauntered down the hall, toward the waiting elevator.

"Just keep your wits about you," said Elizabeth as she rifled through her purse. "I can't imagine we'll get ambushed in a place like the Clementine, but this whole thing seems fishy, and I can't say I like it." Elizabeth snapped her handbag shut. "Mind if I borrow your lipstick?"

Maude said nothing as she opened her own bag and instantly drew the small copper capsule from its depths. She looked absently out the window of the taxi, watching colossal buildings flash past. The rain-washed asphalt reflected their impossibly vertical outlines, their lit windows, the warm glow of the streetlamps, and the rippled shapes of pedestrians queued along the sidewalk.

"You're a quiet girl, Maude," said Elizabeth, puckering her lips and applying the pink stick. "But I'd say this is a different kind of quiet. What's eating you?"

"Oh, nothing," said Maude self-consciously. But then she bit the side of her lip, glanced nervously at Elizabeth, and said, "I didn't mean to… to…"

"Didn't mean to what?"

Maude closed her eyes and belted, "I didn't mean to notice the ring. It just surprised me, is all."

Elizabeth silently capped the lipstick and grasped it in her hands. They let a wordless minute pass. The taxi turned off Amsterdam Avenue and veered onto a side street.

"I used to think I had a lot of friends," said Elizabeth. "And it's almost true. I know a lot of folks. They're scattered from here to Timbuktu. Everywhere I go, there's someone I can ring up. When I get into a scrape, I can always call in a favor. All these ten-odd years, gallivanting the globe, I've taken pride in that. All these people, this network of names and faces, showing up when I need them. People like…" She munched her cuticle, then examined it. "Well, there's no one like Sándor. He's a special case. But it's always the same routine. They pop up somewhere—say a hotel bar—and they help me out. But soon they're gone again. I dust my hands and say, *Job well done.* I never minded. I never stopped to think about it. Until I met you."

Maude looked sideways, eyebrows raised.

"What I mean is," said Elizabeth, holding the lipstick in the air, "you've taught me what a real friend is. I know it hasn't been much time. Just a few months. But it's embarrassing to recall what life was like before you."

Maude's cheeks reddened beneath her foundation. Her lips moved, as if they might spring words at any moment.

"Which is to say," continued Elizabeth, interrupting Maude's pantomimed speech, "that I *want* to tell you what that ring is about. I know you're wondering. The thing is, it's a secret. And I promised to keep that secret till the day I die. But you've made me reconsider. I think of all those so-called friends, and they don't hold a candle to you. I could lie to all their faces and say that ring means nothing. It's just a novelty, or a joke, or Sándor found it in a box of Cracker Jacks. But I don't want to lie to *you*, Maude. Keeping a secret from you is like trying not to blink."

Maude took the lipstick and placed it gently in her bag. "Thank you," she said. "You don't have to tell me. I don't want you to break your promise."

"Well," said Elizabeth. "Let me see what Sándor thinks." Then she leaned forward and tapped the driver's shoulder. "Straight ahead, my good man! If I'm not mistaken, that's just the marquee we're looking for."

One after another, limousines rolled in front of the theater, and valets in maroon jackets hustled toward the doors, opening them with servile aplomb. Men stepped out, capping themselves with top hats before leading opulently dressed women from their vehicles. The theater bore a neoclassical façade of inlaid pillars and stone walls. Its architecture was concise; the Clementine wasn't nearly so haughty as the great opera houses of Europe, but its stately columns commanded respect all the same.

Instead of a "marquee," a stone engraving was carved over the entrance: AURES DOMINI VERI MUSICAM QUAM CANIS NON POTEST AUDIUNT.

"What does it say?" inquired Maude, as they stepped from the cab and observed the scene from across a broad avenue.

"It's Latin," said Elizabeth. "It says, 'The ears of a true master hear music that the dog cannot.'"

"What does *that* mean?"

"It means they think very highly of themselves," grumbled Elizabeth. "And I think they're calling the rest of us bitches."

When they arrived at the entrance, they found a large man standing in the doorway. His girth was so great that he strained the buttons of his frock coat, and he wore a monocle and captainly side-whiskers. He nodded to everyone that passed, warmly murmuring their names: "Welcome, Senator Gary. Welcome, Lady Quarter…" But when he spotted Elizabeth and Maude, his mirth faded.

"Invitation only," he huffed.

"I'm on the list," said Elizabeth. "That is, *we're* on the list."

"Her, I'd almost believe," said the monocled man, pointing a white glove at Maude.

"Believe whatever you want," said Elizabeth. "But my name is Elizabeth Crowne, and I'll bet you a million dollars I'm on the list."

"What if you lose?" sniffed the man.

Elizabeth smirked. "I'm sure someone around here can spot me."

The man drew little amusement from this, and he turned slowly around, lumbering into the theater. Elizabeth and Maude stood on the sidewalk as the lavishly dressed guests flowed past them.

"Times like this, I wish I'd brought my flask," said Elizabeth.

Maude couldn't think of anything to say. She had never seen Elizabeth look so uncomfortable. The woman who had always seemed so confident, so chameleon-like, now stiffened her lips with tension. She groped the cord of her handbag so fervently that Maude worried she might snap it.

Then the man appeared again. His expression was the strangest Maude had ever seen—submissive and humiliated, a confusing mix of emotions that seemed to affect different parts of his face. It was only now that Maude spotted the thick veins that bulged beneath his comb-over.

"Ms. Crowne," he said in a deadpan. "Welcome to the Clementine Theatre."

"It's too late to feel welcome," snapped Elizabeth. "But do be a dear and go suck an egg."

She pushed past the man, making sure to bump his shoulder as she went. She moved quickly, and Maude scrambled to catch up.

"Goddamned parasites," Elizabeth seethed as she stormed through the lobby.

"Elizabeth, wait!" Maude called, following the uncannologist up the marble staircase that led to the mezzanine. Maude was anxious, but she also managed to take in her surroundings: A spongy red carpet covered the floor, then continued up the rounded steps. The space was deceptively ample, and Maude paused in mid-climb to gaze upward. The ceiling was layered in frescoes—but there were none of the usual cherubs and saints, no famous gentlemen or scenes of industry. Instead, there was a portrait of a man, dressed in robes and blackly bearded. In one hand, he held a scepter topped with a bull's head; in the other, an orb that glowed with stars, as if he balanced the universe in his palm. The man stood firmly atop a cliff, his sandals balanced on its edge. A profound mountain range and lush valley spread out before him; the peaks and forests were washed over with clouds. The sun gushed light over the landscape, and its amorphous shape was painted so brightly that Maude felt the urge to cover her eyes. The fresco was fearsome and proud, and not even the grand chandelier, with its thousands of glittering prisms, could outshine that formidable figure.

Maude was so dumbstruck that she didn't notice Elizabeth standing beside her.

"Zarathustra," said Elizabeth.

"Zara-*who?*"

"The ancient Persian mystic. I gather someone around here is a Strauss fan." Elizabeth touched Maude's shoulder. "Forgive my hysterics. Nothing pushes my buttons like an uppity simp. Let's see where everyone's headed, shall we?"

Scores of people flooded the atrium, sipping champagne and conversing in tight circles. Yet the place was not stifling. Elizabeth remembered the few operas she had attended, the deluges of men in bowties and women in boas, the throngs crammed so tightly at intermission that she ached for fresh air. Here there was breathing room; the elite clusters were spread out across the floors. It was only when they reached the entrance to the ballroom that the crowd became congested.

The ballroom was a garish chamber of portraits and mirrors. Nameless bourgeoisie posed in canvas after canvas, and guests had the chance to see themselves reflected in between. What Elizabeth had not anticipated were the tables, each dressed in tablecloth and attended by a separate waiter, who stood at stiff attention, like a yeoman warder. Plates and silverware were perfectly arranged, and centerpieces of bright flowers burst from copper vases embossed with Chinese dragons.

"Ma'am," announced a dapper adolescent in a tuxedo vest and sleeve garters. "May I escort you to your table?"

"You certainly may," said Elizabeth. "Otherwise, I might never find it."

The waiter laughed, in a way that seemed disingenuously accommodating. He led them to a table and pulled one of its chairs away. Elizabeth lowered herself, allowing the young man to seat her. Maude followed suit, looking more sheepish than ever.

Across their table sat two women, both young and finely gowned. For a moment, Elizabeth felt some wicked relief: Yes, the women had donned the latest fashions. One even wore a necklace of robust pearls. But no makeup could disguise their plainness. Their faces were equine and homely, neither ugly nor pleasing. One had straight blond hair and an unbecoming beauty mark on her cheek. The second girl was taller and thicker, but she radiated energy. Her hair fell in thick red curls, and her fleshy cheeks blossomed with color. The blonde might be boring, but the redhead was something to behold.

"Well, hello there," said the redhead. "You're a new one, aren't you?"

Her voice was loud and accented, like a mobster's moll. Despite herself, Elizabeth liked this introduction. Yes, they were besieged by stuff shirts, but at least this specimen could talk like a human being.

"Just arrived," said Elizabeth. "Fresh off the train."

"The train! How adventurous of you," said the redhead. "I'm Tabatha, and this is Ruby. We're with the McDonnoughs." A proud smile solidified across her face.

"Ah, the McDonnoughs," said Elizabeth, feigning

recognition. "You're sisters, then?"

"Cousins!" tweeted the blonde. "But we're just like sisters. Grew up together. Went to the same finishing school. We almost have the same birthday."

"Just a week apart," confirmed Tabatha. "But to tell the truth, we've *really* bonded over music."

"Music?"

"Why, yes! It's why we're here! But who's surprised? You must be here for the same reason."

"Well, yes, of course," said Elizabeth. "To see—well, the one everyone's been talking about."

"Can you believe it?" squealed Tabatha. "Herr Schteyrn is actually *here!* In the flesh!"

Elizabeth froze. She knew that name. But why? What had made the name Schteyrn so famous? And why should a pair of dopey society girls feel so gaga about him? They were *nouveaux riches*, the daughters of self-made tycoons, and couldn't be older than twenty. Elizabeth knew their type: They were being bred for marriage; they were coddled daily with fat allowances and fine clothes. For them, balancing a book on their head passed for education. What attracted such blithe succubi to a random German surname?

Then she remembered—*Alexander Schteyrn*. And with this full name came a deluge of recollections: He was a composer from Austria. He had produced several symphonies, which the European press had lauded as masterpieces. But wasn't there something odd about him? Something eccentric? The details escaped her.

A spoon clanged against a wine glass, and the din of conversation quieted. The portly man who stood in the center of the ballroom was brown-haired with hints of gray. His big mustache drooped down the sides of his small mouth. He had removed his top hat and pressed it to his heart.

"Ladies and gentlemen," he said in a gravelly English

accent. "Welcome, as ever, to the Clementine Theatre. It is an honor to host you tonight."

Elizabeth leaned toward the two girls. "And who might he be?"

"Who might *he* be?" Tabatha whispered, aghast. "Don't you know Alistair Bromley? The famous producer? He owns this place!"

"Ah," Elizabeth said, then muttered into Maude's ear, "I didn't know producers could get famous."

"When we opened our humble venue, some years afore," continued Bromley, "it was my dream—and the dream of my late wife—to produce only the finest and most original works. But it was not the art alone that we strove to cultivate. It was also our esteemed audience. We are discriminating in our tastes, and have always been. Our choice of company is no less selective than our choice of wine or china. It is you, dear friends, who make this theater possible. And Gracie..." Bromley looked up toward the ceiling now, as if speaking directly to the heavens. "My darling Gracie, wherever you are, take comfort, my sweet. We have gathered the city's finest people in a single room. We are statesmen, businessmen, forerunners in all fields. If New York is the Empire State, then we, surely, are its emperors."

He lifted his flute of champagne, and a hundred other glasses rose in unison. Clinking was heard all around. Laughter and kind sentiments bubbled through the room.

"To wit," said Mr. Bromley. "I should like to introduce our latest collaborator. He has come all the way from Vienna to join us tonight. Tomorrow evening, for the first time, Herr Schteyrn shall share with us his new opera. It is a premiere unlike any other. Herr Schteyrn's reputation precedes him, of course. He is among the most respected musical talents in Europe. Yet it is his privacy that makes him so unique..."

Ah, yes, though Elizabeth. *That was his quirk. Intense privacy. A recluse, in fact, forever toiling in secret.*

"… and now, on this rarest of occasions, Herr Schteyrn has come to join his public. A man who has never been photographed, who has declined all interviews, shall at last reveal himself. I am ecstatic to present the honorable Alexander Schteyrn!"

At first Elizabeth scanned the room for movement, but she couldn't tell one face from another. A tidal wave of applause followed, until a single man emerged from the clapping masses. He was tall, skinny, but shockingly handsome — a mane of gray hair poured around his pleasant, smiling face. He approached Mr. Bromley and gave him a vigorous handshake. Bromley backed away, withdrawing into the crowd. The applause persisted until Schteyrn, beaming graciously, raised his hands and signaled for silence. The crowd continued to clap, so Schteyrn drew his fingers horizontally through the air, in the manner of a conductor. Many recognized the gesture and chuckled.

"Ladies and gentlemen," said Schteyrn in a sandy voice. "I thank you. You are, as you say in English, too kind. And I have many thanks to express tonight. But first, I wish to tell you a story."

The room was deathly silent. All eyes trained on Schteyrn, the hermit-genius who seemed so strangely comfortable among these strangers. He was perhaps fifty years old, and so charming, the way he shifted his weight from one knee to another, gesticulating with his right hand as he pocketed the left.

"Years ago, I traveled to India. I was a young man, full of spirit. It is there that I learned of Kalki, the Hindu avatar. One day, it is said, Kalki shall arrive on earth riding a white horse. He shall carry a sword, which is covered in fire. And he shall destroy the world." Schteyrn scanned the room intensely, until faces in the audience turned away. "It is Kalki's right and his duty, as a god, to erase the errors of our age. He must sweep clean the rubbish. He must help rebuild this world from nothing."

Then he smiled innocently and shrugged his shoulders. "But I am not concerned, for I am not a Hindu."

After a brief pause, the audience erupted into laughter. Some stood and clapped, which caused a wave of ovation across the room.

"Yet we need no gods," Schteyrn said, louder than before. "It was but two years ago that our countries were drowning in war. My continent lies in ruins. My nation, my dear Austrian Empire, has been destroyed. So many are dead, and for nothing. It seemed, for four long years, that the end of the world was upon us." Then he smiled slyly. "And yet, *here we are.* Survivors of the apocalypse. We did not perish in the trenches. We did not drown in sinking ships. We live, each and every day, because the war did not destroy us. And from its ashes, we build a new life. And though I am not a Hindu, I believe in this cycle. Our era shall end, and another shall blossom. Kalki threatens our existence, but he has not won yet."

Again, claps and cheers of, "Hear, hear!"

"It is to honor this cycle that I have composed my opera. *Kalki, Der Gott der Vernichtung* is my ode to mortality. For without the threat of mortality, we cannot love our present moment. In order to appreciate existence, we must face annihilation."

Someone called from the audience, "Will you be conducting, Herr Schteyrn?"

"Ach, no, I cannot," said Schteyrn forlornly. "For reasons that are private. But be assured, my friends, that I shall be nearby. In my special box. You will not see me, but I am with you." He waved the thought away. "And anyway, I am a clumsy and ordinary man. To meet me is not to know me. But to hear to my music — that is to know my soul."

"Are the rumors true?" someone else called, more authoritatively than the first.

"The rumors?" Schteyrn called into the fray. "You must be more specific."

Over the chuckles, the same voice called: "Is it true you've cast Margaret Matzenauer for the lead role?"

"Oh, *this* rumor." Schteyrn leered. "No, it is not true. Frau Matzenauer has other engagements. But I would not ask her anyhow. She is an angel, to be sure. But not the ideal singer for this part."

"Then who?"

"Who's going to star?"

"Tell us!"

The crowd shouted with excitement, voices calling over voices, until it reached a crescendo that Schteyrn seemed to appreciate. At last he raised both hands.

"My friends, you have asked a wonderful question," he said. "Because I have for you a wonderful answer. May I present the star of my new opera—the woman who shall give a voice to the avatar Kalki—Frau Constance Violeta!"

All at once, the audience rose from their chairs, and the crowd parted down the middle, making way for the surprising new visitor. Elizabeth watched as Violeta appeared: She was a sturdy woman with a pinkish pallor and a round chin. Her curly blonde hair was piled high in the way of ancient Greece, and she strode slowly, hands splayed in both directions, like a follies girl. She moved with forced elegance, and her lowered lids revealed layers of blue eye shadow. Violeta showed little emotion; she looked introverted, bored. It was the face of a true diva, who is so enamored of herself that her surroundings seem irrelevant.

Elizabeth whispered to Maude, "This all feels very scripted, wouldn't you say?"

Maude replied, "Even *I* thought so, too."

Just then Elizabeth noticed the McDonnough girls across the table, and their reaction gave her pause. Instead of manic excitement, the color had drained from their faces. Tabatha covered her mouth with her hands; her eyes glazed with impending tears. This was not the enthusiasm of a fan. Something was terribly wrong.

"Are you all right, dear?" asked Elizabeth.

"I... I just can't believe it," said Tabatha under her breath.

"Can't believe what?"

"She just... how could she be singing? Why would she agree to it? It's just too awful!"

"What's too awful? What are you talking about?"

Tabatha shifted her eyes to Elizabeth, now overwhelmed with disbelief. "Don't you know? About the scandal?"

"What happened? What did she do?"

"Nothing! That's the trouble. *She's* innocent. They all say she's a delightful woman. But her baby daughter..."

"What about her?"

Tears rolled down Tabatha's face, and she sniffed into her bundled fingers. *"Her baby was kidnapped!"*

Elizabeth was eager to leave. She sucked down her soup and gobbled only half the rump steak before excusing herself. She had seen more than enough for one day, and now her head was swimming.

When she returned from the lavatory, Elizabeth stood in the corner, fingering the reefer in her purse. She was desperate to make a break for it.

But Elizabeth waited. She watched as a team of ushers wheeled a baby grand piano into the ballroom, inciting cheers from the dining crowd. Alistair Bromley escorted Herr Schteyrn through the throngs and pointed to the piano. Herr Schteyrn grimaced humbly and sat down at the bench. He stretched his fingers, then tested the keys with a few errant chords. Voices in the audience quieted expectantly. At last he began to play.

Elizabeth had dabbled in piano—just a few selections from a dusty old songbook. She knew only enough to appreciate Schteyrn's mastery: His fingers danced across the keys with the airy ease of a ballerina. His body swiveled forward and back, then to each side, as if the sound itself dictated his posture. With every jerk of his head, his long hair shifted madly.

Elizabeth shifted her attention on Violeta, who sat nearby. Her hands were folded in her lap like a matron. She wore a simple purplish gown, and her gait was stiff and formal. Violeta said nothing to anyone. A floral scarf was wrapped tightly around her plump neck.

"Are we ready?" asked Maude as she appeared from the ladies'.

"I've never been more ready," said Elizabeth. "Let's blow this joint."

Then, just as she was about to head off, Violeta turned her head. The singer gazed directly at Elizabeth. Their eyes met, and Elizabeth felt her heart skip.

There was no mistaking those eyes' intent: Violeta was looking *directly at her*, a stare that cut through the hubbub, past faces and candles and half-eaten entrées. Elizabeth felt a shiver, for the eyes followed her all the way to the exit.

The air was humid and cool as they climbed into the taxi and sped toward the hotel. Elizabeth considered that final look. Did Violeta know who she was? Or had she confused Elizabeth with someone else? She hoped, in the wake of that vile kidnapping, Violeta had not lost her mind. Surely a mother in such nightmarish circumstances sees a potential kidnapper in the face of every stranger. But why Elizabeth?

"May I ask?" said Maude.

"Ask me anything."

"Any idea who could have sent the letter?"

Elizabeth sighed. "It's been a long day, and a social one. Lots of new faces. But I'll be damned if I know who it was—or *why*, for that matter. If someone wanted me to have more culture in my life, they could have taken me to the Pittsburgh Symphony. No reason to come all the way out here."

"Poor Constance Violeta," murmured Maude.

"Am I the only person in the world who doesn't follow opera?" Elizabeth exclaimed. "Are *you* an expert, too?"

"Oh, not an expert!" Maude said. "It's just—it was such a terrible thing. It was in all the gossip magazines. Her husband died in the war, you see, so she's been raising their daughter alone. She was already well known. Everybody liked her. But when Mr. Violeta was killed, she became quite famous. The wife of a hero, and so on."

"Everybody likes a survivor story," mumbled Elizabeth. "Even the Hindus. So what happened with the baby?"

"Well," said Maude. "She comes from France, of course. She has a chateau there, somewhere in the countryside. Anyhow, one night someone snuck through an open window, and—well, they took the child. All the police found was an empty crib."

"How horrid," said Elizabeth. "How long ago was it?"

"Six months."

The taxi drew to a halt in front of the Clementine, and Elizabeth and Maude strolled to the front door. The lobby was quiet, except for a pair of men nursing snifters of brandy on the sofas. Just as the two women reached the elevators, Elizabeth caught movement in the corner of her eye: Santorini was waddling toward them, his finger raised.

"Just a moment, Ms. Crowne," he said, out of breath. "I'd

like to go with you, if that's all right."

"Go with us? What for?"

"Some guests were complaining on the seventh floor," he said. "They say there's a gas leak."

"A gas leak?" Elizabeth was incredulous.

"I know, it sounds absurd, but could I just check your room to make sure? It would give me peace of mind, you understand."

All at once Elizabeth wished she'd packed her revolver. She hadn't wanted to carry around a pistol like a madwoman, especially in the close quarters of Manhattan, but the lack of clues was starting to agitate her. Santorini still looked blameless enough, but this request struck her as suspicious.

"Well, let's go, then," Elizabeth said.

If anything went wrong, she decided, she could always pull a fire alarm.

Silently the elevator rose through the floors, until the doors opened and the garish corridor appeared. The trio moved down the hall, but Elizabeth slowed her pace, so that Santorini could walk ahead. When he reached their room, Santorini inserted the key and turned the handle. Elizabeth watched from a few feet away, gauging whether Santorini looked anxious or strange.

But then she saw something—straight ahead, through the open door, a man sat in an easy chair.

Elizabeth wanted to yelp, to run, to knock Santorini to the ground. But none of these maneuvers transpired. Because the man looked familiar. Elizabeth stepped forward, through the open door. She noted his simple gray suit, his crossed legs, his carefully trimmed mustache. His eyebrows raised slightly with recognition, and he stubbed his cigarette into an ashtray.

"Elizabeth," he said. "Come in. And close the door."

Elizabeth could barely speak, but somehow the words tumbled out. "Royce? Is that you?"

Royce stood up and adjusted his collar. He offered a somber smile before stepping forward and saying, "It's nice to see you, Liz."

"But what are you doing here?"

"Well," said Royce, "I wanted to explain why I sent you that letter." He snapped his fingers abruptly and pointed. "Santorini, watch the door. I don't want any peeping toms."

"You got it, Dr. Abbott," said Santorini, and he slipped into the corridor.

"Lay it on me, Royce," said Elizabeth huskily. "What in blazes in going on?"

Royce, Maude, and Elizabeth faced each other in separate chairs. Maude and Elizabeth had poured the champagne and were now sipping it liberally from glasses. Introductions had been made, but Elizabeth was bewildered. Royce looked completely different than he had in Cuba—he was fitter, sharper, and mustached. It was as if she were meeting a stranger who had climbed into her old classmate's skin.

"Forgive the secrecy," said Royce, lighting another cigarette and tossing away the match with élan. "But once you hear the story, I think you'll understand."

"So this isn't a practical joke?" asked Elizabeth.

"I'm afraid not," said Royce. "I wish that it were. But from what I gather, the situation is quite grave, and I've taken every precaution to keep people safe."

"But safe from what?"

"That's the trouble," confessed Royce through gritted teeth. "I don't know."

"Then what happened? Start at the beginning."

"Well, as you know, I came back to New York in January. I've done well. Cleaned up. Quit the drink. My practice is better than ever. The hospital is earning a good name, too.

We've drawn a better class of patients, you see.

"So one day, a woman came in," he continued. "She wasn't sick. She wasn't pregnant. But she couldn't tell me her problem."

"Why not? Was she ashamed?"

"No, quite the opposite. *She couldn't speak.* She was completely mute. But then she took off her scarf—it was still early spring, at the time—and I saw one of the most terrible scars I've ever laid eyes on. It ran the entire course of her larynx, from jaw to clavicle. It was a vertical line, but crudely drawn. At first I thought it was an accident, but it took only a moment to tell it was a deliberate incision. Someone had neglected its care, and now it was terribly infected. I used some hydrogen peroxide and replaced the stitches. The surgery had been recent, but they'd done a savage job. It was the shoddiest work I'd seen since medical school."

"Could she communicate?" asked Elizabeth.

"At first we used a kind of sign language," said Royce. "It felt like charades. It actually picked up her spirits a little. After a while I took out a notebook and asked her to write me. I wanted to know what happened. She hesitated, and then she started to cry. My heart broke, watching her. A lesser doctor might have left her alone. But I persisted. I had to know who had done this to her. At last she took the pen and wrote a simple message: *'Je ne peux pas vous dire.'*"

"Come again?" said Elizabeth.

"I can't tell you," said Maude.

"You know more than I did," said Royce.

Maude retreated into her shoulders. "My mother is French."

"Well," said Royce, "it never occurred to me that she came from another country. She had no paperwork, no identification. From the way she dressed, I assumed she was a well-heeled woman trying to prevent rumormongering. Which

I could understand—in this town, the wrong scandal can ruin lives faster than the Spanish flu."

"So what did you do?" Elizabeth asked.

"I knew she was in trouble, but writing would do no good. I didn't know anyone fluent in French. I only knew a few phrases, hardly enough to learn her story. But then I had an idea. Whatever had happened, it sounded very strange. The surgery was crude, but it was successful. This was the work of someone diabolical, someone who cared nothing about human suffering. This, I realized, was something *uncanny*."

Royce blew a long stream of smoke and doused his cigarette. Then he looked at Elizabeth with profound emotion.

"I told her, *I know someone who can help. I have a friend in Pittsburgh, and she can come straight away.* It took some time to explain, but eventually she understood. She squeezed my arm. She wept with joy. And then she wrote the letter. I had to translate it, and I had to make it look like a ransom note, to ensure no one could trace it back to us. If her life was truly in danger, I knew that mine could be as well. I bought the train tickets and made arrangements with the hotel. She put you on the list at the Clementine soiree tonight. It's all been very clean and quiet. With any luck, no one is the wiser."

Then Royce stood up. He brushed ashes off his trousers and buttoned his jacket.

"And now I'll take my leave."

"Take your leave?" Elizabeth said, startled. "But where are you going?"

"I'm going home," said Royce. Then he paused, aware of his curt transition. "Liz, you saved my life. I'll never forget that. More importantly, you reminded me how much I cherish living. Because of you, I not only survived that airship—I've become the man I always wanted to be. But I'm not like you. I'm still afraid of death. I'm a good physician, a *very* good physician. But a detective? An adventurer? That's where *you* excel. That's why I brought you here, to help this woman."

"But don't you want to know who she is?" Elizabeth coaxed.

"No, I don't. Liz, I've just asked a girl to marry me. A nurse in the hospital. She's beautiful. Fun. She's a modern girl who's not afraid to smile. She's everything Prudy wasn't. Anyway, she said yes. I can't throw that away. Life is really starting for me. I can't get mixed up in—something dreadful." He took a fedora from the nightstand and held it gingerly in his hands. "Please don't think me a coward."

Elizabeth smirked at this, shook her head once, and rose to her feet.

"You've never been a coward, Royce," she said. "You're a very decent man, who's done a decent thing. And if I want you to stay…" She shrugged. "It's because I can tell you're now the man you've always wanted to be. So chock it up to me being selfish."

Royce blushed, then turned to Maude. "After all these years, Liz Crowne finally asks me on a date. And what do I do? I must be the thickest man in Manhattan."

Royce offered his arm to Elizabeth, and they linked elbows, walking each other to the hotel room door. Royce put on his hat, took a final look at Elizabeth, and said, "You'll need this, too."

He handed her a small slip of paper, which Elizabeth folded into her hand.

Then Royce turned on his heel and walked slowly toward the elevator. Elizabeth watched him disappear behind its sliding doors.

Santorini was still standing in the corridor. Once he'd watched the scene unfold, he shook his head and said, "There goes one of the good ones."

Elizabeth spoke over her shoulder. "He's getting married, you know."

Santorini scoffed. "A guy can dream, can't he?" Then he ambled toward the elevator. "I'll ring up if I see anything strange."

"Thank you, Santorini."

When Elizabeth returned to the room, she groped her chin in thought. But then she yawned loudly, stretched her arms, and adjusted the curtains to make sure they were shut tight.

"What do we do now?" asked Maude.

"I'm going to get some shuteye," said Elizabeth, unfolding Royce's note. "And then tomorrow, we'll go to this address."

"Where did it come from?" asked Maude.

"I'd bet my life it came from the woman in Royce's hospital," said Elizabeth.

"But who is she?"

"But haven't you guessed?" said Elizabeth. "The woman in the hospital was none other than Constance Violeta."

Elizabeth held her teaspoon like a shovel and tapped its head repeatedly against the tablecloth. Sun poured over their breakfast table in the Clutterbuck's restaurant, and the potted orchid standing between Elizabeth and Maude looked vibrant enough to sing. Silverware tinkled all around them as guests conversed in their carefree way, sipping coffee and nibbling at scones.

"Where is he?" Elizabeth snarled.

"Well…" said Maude. "You *did* just call him."

Elizabeth threw a hand in the air and set her spoon down. "Being patient makes me so impatient."

Suddenly Sándor appeared at the restaurant entrance. He looked exactly as before, except for the sweat that dotted his forehead. He scanned the room with the intensity of someone self-consciously late. His eyes fell on Elizabeth, and his head snapped with recognition. He led with upturned palms, his visage pained and pleading.

"I do apologize," he said, leaning into Elizabeth and kissing her on the cheek. "These streetcars are worse every day."

Elizabeth was suddenly bemused. "You're the only Hungarian count I know who takes a trolley to an appointment."

Maude's jaw dropped, and then her head jerked from one face to the other, as if waiting for further explanation. "Mr. Sander, you're... a Hungarian count?"

"The word is actually *ispán*," he said, grinning affably as he adjusted in his chair and clasped his hands in front of his face. "But you could call this a count."

"You're in the presence of Magyar nobility," said Elizabeth. "And after all this time, he still can't keep an appointment."

"Each day I spend in New York City, I yearn to ride a horse," said Sándor wistfully. "Have you ever ridden a horse, Maude?"

"I... no, I can't say I have."

"You have never lived, if you have not felt such power between your legs."

"All right, now," interrupted Elizabeth. "That's enough of *that*."

They ordered, making chitchat before pumpernickel toast and eggs benedict were laid before them. Elizabeth had slept terribly, rolling over and over until the bed sheets were twisted hopelessly around her body. She had eaten so little at the banquet that her appetite was now ravenous, and she ate so sloppily that dollops of egg ran down her chin.

"Permit me," said Sándor sweetly as he raised a napkin to Elizabeth's face.

She batted the napkin away and used her own. "Sándor, you're an absolute cad this morning."

Sándor leaned mischievously toward Maude and said, "She was always like this. A secret romantic. Like a songbird in a cage."

"How long have you known each other?" asked Maude.

They spoke at once:

"Too long," said Elizabeth.

"Not long enough," said Sándor.

Then they looked at each other, allowed a moment to pass, and burst into laughter. Their laughter was bright and cheery, the kind shared between old friends who know each other better than anyone. As the merriment fizzled, everyone noticed that Elizabeth was now touching Sándor's elbow. She retracted her hand with conspicuous discretion.

"Were you…" Maude wavered.

"Were we…?" Sándor finished her thought: "Were we lovers? Yes."

"*No*," corrected Elizabeth. "We were *not* lovers."

"Were we not?" Sándor searched her face.

"No," said Elizabeth, looking exasperated. "Because *we weren't in love.*"

Silence fell over the table. Maude was so stricken by the power of this statement that she dared not move a muscle. Elizabeth herself looked away, toward the window. And Sándor did the most conspicuous thing of all: He raised two fingers to his eye patch and caressed its outline. He did this for only a second before grasping the coffee cup, raising it to his forced smile, and saying, "How was the theater?"

"We've learned some things," said Elizabeth carefully. "It seems that Constance Violeta was the one who sent us the note."

"Constance Violeta? The opera singer?"

"You, too!" exclaimed Elizabeth. "Is there no one in the western world as clueless about opera as I am?"

"I only know her from the headlines," admitted Sándor. "Her baby daughter, stolen from her room. A dreadful thing. But why should she write you? Could it be—she wants you to find her child?"

"I think something queerer is afoot," pondered Elizabeth. "See if you follow: A woman has an operation. A grotesque incision is made down the length of her neck. That's not for throat cancer, and it's a wretched excuse for a tracheotomy. I may not have finished medical school, but I know that much. Then what? What's the purpose of such a surgery?"

"And this is confirmed?" asked Sándor.

"My friend at the hospital, he's a physician. He helped Violeta contact me. But she can't speak, that's the thing."

"A mute opera singer?" Sándor chuckled humorlessly. "It is nonsensical."

"Precisely. If she can't speak, why would they hire her to sing the lead? Surely they must know."

"But..." Maude cleared her throat. "Is it that she *can't* speak, or that she *doesn't?*"

"What do you mean?"

"I mean... we don't know she *can't*. What if she's staying silent—for another reason?"

"By Jove," said Elizabeth. "I think you're onto something, Maude. What *if?* Maybe someone's keeping her silent." She drew the scrap of paper from her bag. "Well, maybe this address will help us. Do you know the place?"

Sándor glanced at it and frowned. "But this does not make sense. This address is for Harlem."

"Well," said Elizabeth, "maybe it'll make sense when we get there."

Alexander Schteyrn paced the narrow corridor, careful not to step on scattered ropes and theatrical jetsam, as he made his way toward the dressing rooms. The space was confined and dark, and the dust irritated his allergies. He sneezed into the crook of his arm, then lumbered solemnly toward a waiting door.

He knocked once, waited a moment, and then pushed the door open. He peered through the crack, but did not pass the threshold.

"Madame?" he said, then added in perfect French, "May I enter?"

In the vanity mirror he could see Violeta seated on her stool, her hair pinned up, her face a patchwork of half-applied makeup. She nodded, but just as Schteyrn entered the room, he saw that the opera singer's face was also streaked with dried tears. She continued to dab her cheeks with foundation, avoiding Schteyrn's eyes.

"You feel ready?" murmured Schteyrn.

She did not reply, only heaved a great sigh and continued with her work. Schteyrn bundled himself in the corner of the room, pressed against a rack of costumes, his body slouched over. He collapsed inward like an empty suit.

"Sometimes," he said, "when my wife was in the powder room, she would leave the door ajar. Just a little. Just enough to see her. We never spoke of it. But I think it was a game we played. I would lie on the bed, and I would watch her, through this thin crack. She pretended not to be noticed, and I pretended that she could not see me. Yet a woman always knows when she is being watched. Sometimes this is bad. A stranger on a train, some lascivious creature. Other times, it is beautiful—a suitor, a husband, she loves his attention, which she pretends not to acknowledge. I know what it means to have this. And I know what it means to lose it." His head fell forward, losing itself in a drapery of silver hair. "I loved my wife..."

Violeta's eyes shot open. She smashed her fist against the vanity, and the many objects jumped from the impact. A single curler rolled off the platform and bounced on the floor. Violeta's eyes smoldered with emotion. Her cheeks puffed out.

Her expression was that of a wounded animal, cornered and desperate, capable of anything.

"*I know!*" shrieked Schteyrn, but then he clapped a hand over his mouth and shut his eyes. "I know—of course I mean I *love* my wife. I shall always love her. But how do we know…" His fingers became talons, digging into his face and grappling the skin. "What torture this is! To smile, to charm them, to even *look* at them! All those people—they have no idea what awaits them! And why do we do this? Is it all for nothing?"

Violeta shook her head so violently that her cheeks flapped.

"But how do you know?" Schteyrn gasped. "How do we know anything?"

Violeta screwed up her face and smacked a hand against her heart. Then, for emphasis, she smacked her hand again. It thumped powerfully inside her sternum.

"You are stronger than I am," whispered Schteyrn. "You still have the courage to believe."

He withdrew from the wall and moved slovenly to the door. He leaned against it for a moment, then murmured, "I would do anything for her. Even this. But will it be worth the price? What if…"

Violeta looked away, toward her reflection in the mirror, and then went back to her work.

"Good luck tonight," said Schteyrn. "And God save us."

Schteyrn made his way back to his own dressing room, a small chamber filled with music stands and sheet music. He briefly touched the cuff of his tuxedo, which hung from a rack, and then collapsed into a chair. He needed this time, a final moment of peace, before—

Then he saw the envelope on his own vanity. The space was empty except for that one piece of folded paper, on which was scrawled, "Alexander."

He flipped open the tiny note. Then he balked. He shuddered and crumpled the paper in his fist. Suddenly seized with revulsion, he screamed. It was not an intelligible word, just a primal sound directed at the ceiling. Schteyrn threw the paper, hoping it would vanish into a corner, but instead it wafted lazily through the air, changing course several times before resting at his feet.

Nach die Weltuntergang, it read, *toten Sie Gott.*

After the apocalypse, kill God.

It seemed less like a street than a carnival: Women in broad hats laughed loudly in front of storefronts. Men in plaid suits gathered around a card-table, shouting and jeering as they watched a shell game unfold. Laborers pushed wheelbarrows down the sidewalks, newsies called the afternoon headlines, and outdoor grills smoked every meat imaginable. Everywhere Elizabeth looked, black men and women went about their daily business, in concentrations she had not seen in years. Here was the great epicenter of the city's Negro life, its peculiar butchers and barbershops, the brightly colored zoot suits that seemed to have sprung from magazines, the children piled on nearby steps as they watched girls skipping rope on the pavement, and the dormant signs shaped like musical instruments, which would light up after nightfall and draw crowds from all over the city. Elizabeth hadn't seen such benign chaos since the streets of Cairo, and some how this seemed more exotic.

"Are... are you sure we're allowed here?" whispered Maude, clutching her purse. "I mean... is it safe?"

"Oh, pshaw!" bellowed Sándor. "It is very safe in the daylight hours!"

"Oh?" Elizabeth rejoined. "Not that I disagree, Sándor, but are you a regular in Harlem?"

Sándor looked surprised. "But of course."

"Of course? Harlem doesn't seem like the usual hang-out for Hungarian counts."

"I come here for the jazz." Sándor couldn't hide his defensiveness. He tapped his cane twice and proceeded into the avenue, unconcerned about the slow-moving cabs or flux of foot-traffic. "This way."

Elizabeth rushed across the pavement to keep up, and she grabbed her cloche hat to make sure it didn't tumble off. "What are you talking about? When did you become a jazz man?"

"When I arrived in New York. It is the most infectious kind of music. Although I heard much of it in Paris." Sándor stopped at the curb and rotated in a soldierly way, facing Elizabeth. "You would know this if you had read my letters."

"Let's just say I have a backlog, shall we?"

The building was nondescript, a leviathan of patterned brick and high windows, many of them covered over with rotting boards. The structure had once been a factory or a warehouse, and much of its volume looked shuttered and vacant. But a weathered sign hung above the front door, hastily stenciled and barely legible: WASHINGTON ROOM & BOARD.

"Fancy that," grumbled Elizabeth. "An authentic Harlem flophouse. These opera singers know how to pick 'em."

A man leaned against the doorframe. His fedora was cocked forward, so that the rim covered his eyes. He wore a plain shirt tucked into his belt, the sleeves rolled up along his forearms. In one hand he held a matchstick, and he was snapping his fingers to try and strike the phosphorus tip.

Elizabeth, Maude, and Sándor stopped at the wide doorway and peered inside. The lobby was dimly lit, thanks a single light bulb that flickered above the battered tile floor.

"Y'all runaways?" said the man. He continued to rhythmically snap.

"Not exactly," said Elizabeth. "Misfits, maybe. Why do you ask?"

"That's most of what we got," said the man. "All them kids, running away? Well, this is where they all run *to*. So I guess I'm curious." He pocketed the match and gave them his full attention, crossing his sinewy arms. "If y'all ain't runaways, what's your business here?"

"We're looking for a room," said Elizabeth.

"Oh, we got plenty of rooms," said the man. "But I'll warn you—when the super sees them nice clothes you wearing, he'll charge you extra. You can bet on that."

"We're looking for a *specific* room."

"Oh? Which one is that?"

"Room 14."

The man stepped back and swung his arms wide. Then he smacked his hands and rubbed his palms together. His expression was hard to read, until he said, "Damn, I knew them cats was trouble."

"What cats? Who are you talking about?"

"Y'all ain't fuzz or nothing, right?"

"No," said Elizabeth. "Nothing like that."

"In that case, if I was you, I'd turn right around and go back to wherever you come from. Room 14 ain't a place for two dames and a buccaneer."

"I'd like nothing more," said Elizabeth. "But we have to see that room. Can you tell us about it?"

"I think I'd rather not," said the man. "Nothing personal. Just don't want to get tangled up, is all. But I'll tell you this: Any time a bunch of a white folk rent a room around here, it ain't because they like the view. It's because they up to something, something they don't want nobody knowing about. You catch my meaning?"

"Loud and clear," said Elizabeth.

"Well, good. Best of luck." He moved down the steps, back toward the street.

Sándor watched him disappear into the crowd. He said,

"You see? Very friendly place."

"I'll take your word for it," said Elizabeth, and they ventured into the darkness.

Their eyes adjusted slowly as they climbed a staircase covered in scraggly carpet. Strips of flypaper hung from the ceiling. Pieces of the balustrade had been broken away. When they reached the second floor, a long hallway awaited them, also barely lit. The passage was so deep and foreboding that even Elizabeth gulped loudly before taking her first tentative step. An eerie quiet pervaded the rooms, a sensation that any malevolent thing was now dormant and behind closed doors. Sealed within each room, Elizabeth imagined an opium den, a pair of starving fugitives, broken men and beaten wives, emaciated children begging their mothers to wake, so many mortal dramas that had clamored toward their final act.

The entrance to Room 14 had lost its numbers, but the grime and soot had burned an afterimage into the door, so that the missing digits were perfectly legible. Elizabeth raised a hand and rapped the cheap wood. They waited.

When no sound rustled from within, Elizabeth nodded to Sándor, who kicked his boot against the door, dislodging the deadbolt from the wall.

The room was small and smelled of mildew. A cot was propped against the wall, its bedding a mess of moldy sheets. In the corner, beneath the closed glass window, stood a hefty barber's chair. Adjacent to the chair was a simple workbench covered in tools.

Elizabeth scowled at the scene. She tasted acid in her throat. The furniture itself was old and primitive, but it was the sight of blood that repelled her: Dry blood was dripped on the floor, splattered on the chair, and sprayed against the yellowed walls. A bundle of towels lay on the floor, stained dark red from sopping up so much blood. The tools on the bench were dull and rusty, their jagged and serrated blades as sickening as any torture devices. The humblest scalpel looked threatening alongside the row of knives and saws, and the metal was so thoroughly tainted that it was hard to discern blood from corrosion.

"Dear God," said Elizabeth. "So this is where it happened. This is where they performed the surgery."

Maude looked away and bent over the mattress. Nausea boiled inside her. For a moment she flashed to the insane asylum, where the sight of liquid dismemberment was a daily toil. But then she looked down, at the edge of the mattress, and squealed: "Elizabeth!"

"What is it? Are you all right?"

"Look!"

Large sheets of vellum paper were piled on the corner of the bed, each covered in brown ink. The drawings resembled sketches more than schematics, like the imaginings of a Renaissance engineer. Elizabeth plucked up a sheet and held it to the light. Technically, the drawings were masterful, showing realistic shading and foreshortening. But the objects were impossible to identify. Some looked like scarabs, others like capsules enwrapped in overlapping tubes. Around these strange objects swirled a kind of writing—a wild calligraphy. Indeed, the scribbles looked more like a young child imitating writing than actual words.

"What could it be?" said Sándor.

"For once, I'm glad you're as confused as I am," said Elizabeth. "Any idea what language this is?"

"I've never seen anything like it."

"Maybe we could take it to the library," said Elizabeth. "We could cross-reference it with their primers."

"Or we could find a linguist at the university," offered Sándor.

"Whatever this gobbledygook is, there's bound to be an expert who can read it."

"*No!*"

Elizabeth and Sándor looked up from the drawings. They looked quizzically at Maude, who looked stricken with horror. The color had drained from her face; she was albinoid with shock.

"We *can't* read it," she said. "No one can."

"What do you mean? What are you saying?"

"Elizabeth," squeaked Maude. "Don't you see? They've put this thing—whatever it is—*into Constanse Violeta's throat.*"

Elizabeth and Sándor looked down again at the drawings. Suddenly it was clear: The tubes that enwrapped the object were muscular tissue. They were the sinews that composed the human neck. And the beetle-looking object now seemed mechanical, a metallic device constructed with human hands.

"My God, Maude—I think you're right," said Elizabeth.

"It's... it's some kind of *implant*," said Maude.

"To replace her vocal chords," concluded Elizabeth. "To change the nature of her voice."

"That's why she won't speak," Maude said. "She could, but she can't. Because..."

"...it's *a sound weapon.*"

The two women stared at each other in shock and astonishment. They were now reading each other's minds, each too frantic to complete a thought.

"That's why we can't read the language..." said Maude.

"Because it's written..."

"...in the secret language..."

"...and this is what he was planning..."

"...the whole time!"

"This is the work..."

And they shouted together: "...*of Dr. Vermilion!*"

Sándor raised his hands and cried, "Wait! What are you talking about?"

Elizabeth grasped his wrists, grinning hysterically. "It all makes sense, Sándor! Not long ago, we learned of a scientist named Dr. Vermilion. During the war, he was testing some kind of sound weapon—a weapon that could destroy a man using only sonic waves. And *this* must be why: He wants to plant the weapon inside human vocal chords!"

"But how could this be?" asked Sándor. "Is this not an incredible coincidence?"

"Perhaps," conceded Elizabeth. "But with Dr. Vermilion, you never know. It could all be part of a broader plan."

"But why Madame Violeta? She is not a soldier. She is an opera singer."

"An opera singer..." Elizabeth's eyes nearly burst from her skull. "*That's it!* That's been his plan all along! We have to go! *Now!*"

"But where are we going?"

"We have to get to the theater!" gasped Elizabeth. "Before it's too late!"

She turned toward the exit, ready to race from the room, to find a phone, to do *something*. But before she could reach the doorway, a dark shape entered that hollow space. Elizabeth registered the familiar click of a cocked gun. And then she heard the words, "That's far enough."

Constance Violeta stirred the mug of water and watched its steam escape into the air. The dressing room was empty, per her request. She raised the brine to her lips and sipped, then gargled intently before spitting it into a nearby bucket. Contrary to everything she had ever learned, the salt water eased her burning throat. Ever since the surgery, she had endured constant pain. The scar itself had healed, thank to that saintly doctor, but she still found herself running a finger along that hideous ridge. One day, she prayed, she would touch her neck and the scar would be gone, and all of this would be a terrible nightmare.

Despite the comforting quiet of her room, the theater trembled with activity. She could hear the muffled voices in the hallway, the trampling feet of stagehands, her fellow singers practicing their scales. She had wanted to speak with them, those enthusiastic youths. It had always been her favorite pastime, during rehearsals, to ask them about their lives. She had always detested those prima donnas who hid themselves from the chorus and supernumeraries. *Tout le monde a une histoîre*, her mother always said. She had taken this to heart.

No longer. Her forced silence meant the dying of her soul. To lose her voice was to sever her umbilicus to fellow human beings. The lonely days and nights tormented her. She was forbidden to go out or be social. When she first arrived in New York, all those months ago, she had taken strolls around the block, if only to keep herself sane. But each time a stranger would appear and ask a question. She couldn't understand what they were saying. They always furrowed their brows, disconcerted by her pained and speechless face. She could have dealt with that. They walked away, mumbling to themselves. She could have puzzled through a conversation in English; that would have pleased her. But to say nothing?

Constance looked at herself in the mirror: Her face was caked in silver makeup, and her bound black hair was crowned with a gold turban. Her shoulders were crossed over with a crimson cape and a garland of flowers.

Tonight, I am the God of Death, she thought. *Tonight I beckon the end of the world.*

But she shook away this morbid feeling. Instead she thought: *This is for Justine. Soon, you will see Justine again.*

Constance rose from her chair and pulled a cloak over herself. She covered her face with its hood, to obscure herself. She went through the door, into the backstage area, and dodged racing stagehands as she made her way to the wings.

She planted herself near the edge of the stage, a dark nook where no one would think to find her. She leaned against the brick wall and saw a sliver between the curtains. Through this tiny space, she could observe the audience arriving. This had always been her favorite pastime, sneaking to the frontier between stage and house, to view the amassing crowd. She had lived for this moment. She loved to watch it swell with bodies and noise. The audience became an organism unto itself. And just when it could grow no bigger, the lights dimmed, and the spectacle began.

"*Please*," Elizabeth begged. "Just let us go. What does it matter to you, anyway?"

"We've been over this," said Pozzo. "Just relax. What's two more hours?"

"In two hours, Pozzo, *it'll be too late.*"

In her heart, Elizabeth knew there was no point reasoning with them. There were three of them, stubbly men in dark jackets and pleated trousers, and each held a nickel-plated pistol. The two younger men perched by the window; one groped his suspenders and chewed a toothpick while the other pressed his gun to his own cheek, as if holding a telephone receiver.

Elizabeth and Maude sat on the bed, while Sándor sprawled in the barber's chair. They were trapped in the flophouse dorm room, and there was no way out. Even if they managed to knock down Pozzo and grab his gun, the two young goons would shoot them in the back. There was no going anywhere without Pozzo's permission.

Pozzo leaned against the wall in his turquoise suit. He was a baby-faced man of perhaps forty years. His sleepy eyes belied his rapid speech, as if he were wanly reciting a scripted conversation. He had stationed himself by the door, but it was clear from the way he adjusted the knot of his necktie that the hoodlum was bored. He kept shifting his weight from one penny-loafer to the other. His right arm dangled limply, as did his fat pistol.

To his credit, Pozzo had been something of a gentleman. He'd confiscated Sándor's cane, told them to sit down, and concisely explained the rules.

"My name is Pozzo," he'd said. "Here's the story—we keep you here till nine o'clock. After that, we let you go. Nobody gets hurt. You mess around, do something stupid, we kill you. *Capisce?*"

Two hours had passed since that conversation, most of it spent in silence, but now and again Elizabeth would plead once more.

"Listen, Pozzo," she said. "You seem like a reasonable man…"

"I *am* a reasonable man," interrupted Pozzo. "Which is why I'm not breaking your legs right now. I'm a peaceful guy. But I got orders. And one could argue that trying to negotiate with your captor is kind of like trying to escape. And you remember what we agreed about trying to escape? So maybe just shut your trap, wait a couple hours, and we'll walk away friends. How's *that* for reasonable?"

"You want I should shoot her, boss?" said the goon with the toothpick. "Just to get the message across?"

"What kind of message is that?" exclaimed Pozzo. "Bang, you're dead, now behave?"

"I mean shoot her in the arm, or something."

"That is sick and uncivilized," declared Pozzo. "Look at this room. Like there's a shortage of blood in here? Looks like someone threw a grenade in a tomato patch."

"I'm just saying," said the toothpick goon. "I could do it, if you want."

"Just wait till they *negotiate* again," advised Pozzo. "Then maybe I'll consider it." He turned to Maude. "These kids, always hungry for the violence. Makes an old man cry."

"You don't look very old," said Maude.

"Why *thank you*," he said, suddenly smiling up at the goons. "See that? *That's* civilized behavior. Do I believe her? No. Do I care? Also no. Just a nice thing to say and to hear."

Elizabeth said icily, "May I ask what he offered you?"

"What who offered who?" said Pozzo.

"Your boss."

"My boss is a voice on a telephone. He calls me, I get instructions, I get paid. In money. So that's what he offers me."

"Was it a lot of money? Because I'm pretty sure a lot of people are going to die for that money."

"Oh, yeah? Why do you think that?"

"Because something is about to happen," said Elizabeth, "that will hurt a lot of innocent people. And only we can stop them. The three of us, here, in this room. If you keep us till nine o'clock, *you* are helping kill those people. Do you understand?"

"Hey, boss," called the toothpick goon. "Can I shoot h—"

"*No*," shouted Pozzo. "You *cannot shoot the dame*. If you want to shoot the dame, you wait for *me* to volunteer that idea. You understand that, dog-face?" He shook his head and scoffed, then returned his attention to Elizabeth. "Listen, lady—I been watching this building, nonstop, for weeks. Somebody tells me, 'You see something funny, you give me a call.' He says, 'Anybody goes to Room 14, you give me a call.' Well, youse guys are something funny, and you sure as hell went to Room 14. So I give my boss a call, and he says, 'Keep 'em there. Don't hurt 'em if you don't have to. But if you *do* have to…'" Pozzo lifted his gun and aimed its muzzle at Sándor. He puffed his lips, imitating the blast. "You get me?"

"It is no use, Elizabeth," Sándor said languidly. "There is nothing we can do."

"I don't want to see those people die, Sándor," Elizabeth snarled. "I don't want to just *give up*."

Sándor chuckled. It was a low and cynical sound, as humorless as a cough.

"What could possibly be funny about this?" Elizabeth blurted.

"*You* don't want to give up," Sándor sang tunelessly.

"What's that supposed to mean?"

Sándor sat up in his barber's chair. His movement was so sudden that the two goons shifted positions, readying to pounce.

"I write you *every week*," he proclaimed. "For years, I have written to you. Hundreds of letters, bleeding my soul for you. And when do you reply? Never. I tell you I am moving to New York City. I will live *one state* away from you. I invite you to visit, anytime. When do you reply? Never. I write every thought, every feeling in my heart, and I send these letters, because I cannot stop myself, in spite of the silence that follows. And when do you reply? Once—by telegram, when you are already here. And why? So I can *help you*."

"I'm not the epistolary type, Sándor," snapped Elizabeth. "Maybe I ran out of stationery, did you consider that?"

"You are afraid to write me," Sándor sneered. "You want to be alone. Fine. But why deny what is true? *Why do you deny we were lovers?*"

Suddenly Sándor's face was a mask of pain. His cool demeanor melted, and the fiery, temperamental Sándor emerged once more. This was the man Elizabeth remembered, the feral creature of her youth, his moods changing as explosively as fireworks. She hated to see the anguish inscribed in his downturned lips, the fury burning in his one hazel eye—yet the sight of his passion de-aged her, sent her reeling back through the years, and she was no longer a thirty-year-old uncannologist from Pittsburgh, but rather a nineteen-year-old drifter in Spain, as free and foolish as any aimless girl. Her heart pounded like a tom-tom. Her temples burned with a strange exhilaration.

"We *weren't* lovers," Elizabeth struggled to say.

"Because we were *never in love*," Sándor spat.

"That's right," Elizabeth said, faltering. "It was *more* than love. Don't you see? Love is a paltry word. That's a word for sappy youths and movie starlets. *Love* you? That's a sad little syllable, compared to what I felt for you. Whatever all those people mean by love, I felt a thousand times more. You took a lost and wayward girl and gave her life—a full life, a life worth living." Elizabeth stopped, sniffing through emerging tears. "And then you threw it all away. You risked it all. You did *exactly what I told you not to do*. It cost you your eye. It cost you your dignity. And—it cost you *me*. What kind of life is that, wondering if you might die at any moment? If all that *love* could end in a flash?" Now she wiped away her tears, and her expression went stony cold. "So *you* write the goddamn letters. Frankly, this girl's spent."

The rage left Sándor's face. What remained was a sheen of remorse. He grasped the lowermost hair of his goatee and murmured, "I had to avenge my father. Elizabeth, I *had* to."

"Yes, well, we can't have everything we want."

The room was taciturn, now. There was no movement or sound, only the honking of cars in the street, the hum of a plane far overhead. The sunlight had faded through the window, leaving only a glum orange glow behind the gauzy curtains.

At last Pozzo leaned forward, pulled a cigar from his jacket pocket, and said, "I'll be honest—I have no idea what just happened."

Mr. Stacks wiped his monocle with a kerchief. He placed the

circle of glass back in his eye and with renewed clarity took stock of the people around him. Every one of them was familiar: bankers, inventors, lawyers, politicians, prominent journalists, a pair of generals, and the wives—so many wives—clustered together on the sidewalk, talking gaily about nothing.

As always, Mr. Stacks watched them, studied them, like a biologist scrutinizing his petri dishes. They went bearded and mustached and muttonchopped and clean-shaven. Spats were smartly fastened, black shoes were iridescently polished, cummerbunds were drawn around waists, boutonnières were pinned, cigarettes were planted in long holders, cigars were chopped and lit. The countenances were long, flat, round, ovular, husky, and gaunt; their eyes were bulged, sunken, cheery, drowsy, long-lashed, and blankly staring; even their noses and lips came in all sizes, hooked and bulbous, plum and thin, straight and red and pale and gaping and everything in between.

One thing they all had in common: *They were all alive*.

Mr. Stacks felt a tingle inside him, a sickening delight, as he ushered gentlemen and ladies inside. For that's what they were—*ladies* and *gentlemen*, the propertied, the untouchable, the *royalty* of New York. He saw a famous actress, a known playboy, a newspaper magnate, a rubber mogul, and a man who claimed to be a real maharaja, though everyone knew he was born in Yonkers.

He knew them all by name, not only because of the magazines, the financial pages, and the newsreels that imprinted their images everywhere, but because Mr. Stacks had stood here so many years. They had stepped on his foot, blown smoke in his face, ashed on his pant leg, offered pitying tips, demanded late seating, and drunkenly hollered into his ears. He had watched their excitement and disdain, listened to their insipid chinwag, helped them into private cars. The *thank you*s were few and far between, replaced by orders and pleas and threats and ultimatums. They all filed past him, as impersonally as they would pass a fire hydrant.

"I thought this Kalki fellow was some kind of god," yammered one.

"He is!" said another.

"Then why is he played by a woman? What gives?"

"The part's for a mezzosoprano."

"A mezzosoprano? Doesn't sound much like a god of destruction."

"A god of *estrogen*, maybe!"

"Say, you know about this guy Schteyrn?"

"Yeah, I hear his place is a mess."

"No kidding?"

"Yeah—it's a total *shty*."

The laughter that followed was the very sound that always wormed its way into Mr. Stacks' skull, writhing through his brain, suffocating rational thought. How many nights had he lain awake, thinking of their insults? *Hey, Mr. Stacks, you having twins?* Or: *You ever meet my friend Mr. Stacks? Turns out they stacked him sideways.* He had only smiled at this—the tortured smile of the servant who knows no other expression, who is told he must be grateful for the menial job he has, who must wait in the rain and sleet and boiling heat, only to open the door, say *welcome* and *farewell* to famous strangers, and know that any given brooch or pocket watch is worth more than his life. On the outside, Mr. Stacks was pleasant and harmless, the consummate doorman, nearly three hundred pounds of invisibility. *But inside.*

Within the lobby, the light dimmed several times.

"Ladies and gentlemen!" Mr. Stacks bellowed. "Please make way to your seats. The performance will begin shortly."

Their voices rose as they converged on the doorway, congesting the entrance with top hats, tails, bustles, feathers, and every style of ribbon and jewel. They pushed their way through, clapped shoulders, clasped hands, kissed cheeks, nodded and bowed and doffed hats in all the ways that gentlemen do, until they were at last swallowed completely into the playhouse's gullet.

"Gentlemen, may I escort you inside?" said Mr. Stacks to a final pair of cigar smokers.

One of the men balked. He was old and gray, hardly five feet tall. He jabbed his stogie at Mr. Stacks like a reproachful finger. "I will *not* be hurried, sir."

"Don't mind the doorman," said the other. "He's just doing his job."

The first man wiggled his mustache irritably. "If his job is to harass me, then maybe this theater should be downsized. And from the looks of you, that would be *quite* the reduction."

The second man couldn't help but snicker, and somehow this was worse than the insult itself: The man who had tried to defend Mr. Stacks also found humor in his abuse. Mr. Stacks' lip no longer quivered, as it had in years past. He no longer squinted back the tears, or hid behind a pillar to sniffle at their cruelty. He had long cultivated his dignity with a useless monocle, a tailored suit, and silk gloves from a Bowery pawnshop—the camouflage of a fat pauper among grandees— but it failed to protect his soul.

Then he remembered. What was about to happen. The fate of these very men. *The promise of revenge.* A giddiness welled up inside him, like bubbles rising through water. For the first time in memory, Mr. Stacks allowed himself to smile.

"Don't smoke it all," he said. "Or what else will you use to satisfy your wife?"

At first the cigar smoker didn't understand, but when the slur finally struck him, the old man wheezed with shock.

"What did you say—*boy?*"

Mr. Stacks felt himself brimming with rage and euphoria. He sauntered forward, toward the older man, fists clenched inside his gloves.

"I said you can *rot*, you worthless geezer."

Mr. Stacks flung out a hand and grabbed the old man's collar. He whirled him around and wrapped an arm around his spindly neck.

"Let go of me!" the old man squealed.

"He's gone mad!" cried his companion.

But Mr. Stacks ignored them. He grabbed the old man's wrist and pulled it backward. The old man screamed in horror as his cigar's cherry drove into his own eye. The scent of burning ocular flesh pervaded the air. He writhed and kicked, but his struggle was fruitless.

"You want your cigar?" growled Mr. Stacks. "You *finish it.*"

But the tobacco unraveled, and its cinders crumbled down the old man's chest. At least Mr. Stacks released, hurling the old man to the ground. His companion, who had only stood on the curb in dumbstruck disbelief, now rushed to the old man's aid.

"Walter?" he said. "Are you all right?"

"*Goddamn you!*" screamed the old man. "*I'm blind!*"

"You want some more?" snarled Mr. Stacks, looming over the two men like an impending tidal wave. "I'll take that other eye, too! How about *you*, buddy?"

The second man started to drag his companion away. "No, please," he said. "He's had enough!"

Together the two men backed away, beyond the glow of the streetlamp, until their black tuxedoes blended with the night.

Mr. Stacks' heart pounded inside his massive sternum. He turned toward the theater, feeling victorious, thrilled. He was ready. He would do what he had been ordered to do. He would have his revenge. He would make them pay, every last one of them.

"By way of conversation," said Pozzo, "why should a guy like you need a cane?"

Sándor raised an eyebrow. He sat up in the chair and wove his fingers together. "Pardon me?"

"I mean, you don't got a limp. No wooden leg, as far as I can tell. What's with the cane?"

Only Elizabeth could feel the sudden tension. She tried not to look at Sándor, but her eyes kept wandering in his direction. She saw his conspiratorial grin.

"It is useful," said Sándor.

"Useful how?" said Pozzo. "I mean, I don't get it."

"Let me show you," said Sándor, pushing himself out of the chair and standing up straight. The moment he did so, the two goons stood at attention, guns raised.

"You can show me from there," said Pozzo, adjusting his turquoise jacket.

"I can't," said Sándor. "But you will find it interesting. You may even hold onto it. Your men can stand behind me. In fact, I insist."

Pozzo looked incredulous. "No funny business?"

"No funny business."

"All right, why the hell not? As long as we're just sitting around." Pozzo stepped forward, groping the head of the cane.

"Now," said Sándor, "you must hold the cane in the middle. With both hands."

"Like this?" Pozzo grasped the cane and held it close to his body, as if choking on a baseball bat.

"Precisely. Now hold on closely." He turned slightly. The two goons were now standing directly behind him. Sándor briefly glanced at them, then turned back to Pozzo and said, "You see, this cane is very special. But you must hold on tight."

"It doesn't blow up or nothing, does it?" asked Pozzo, chuckling nervously.

"No, nothing of the kind. It is a very gentle cane."

Sándor leaned forward slowly, then reached out a hand.

"Boss, I don't know about this," said the toothpick goon. "I got a funny feeling."

"Very gentle," said Sándor soothingly, as he touched the head of the cane. It was a simple top made of wound leather straps, like the handle of a tennis racket. "You are holding tight?" said Sándor.

"Yeah, of course," said Pozzo. "Why?"

"Boss, I think we should — "

The movement was so fast that even Elizabeth couldn't process it. Sándor's thumb pressed down on a tiny button, which clicked softly. With that, a lever was released inside the cane, and Sándor yanked the handle outward. What emerged was a line of steel, which glinted in the dying light as it slashed through the air. When the sword emerged from its scabbard, Pozzo toppled backward, onto the floor. His gun clattered under the bed.

The two goons didn't have a chance. They were seized with tension, and before they could pull their triggers, Sándor whirled around and slashed one of them across the throat. The goon's toothpick dropped from his lips, his knees buckled, and he slumped to the floor, grabbing his throat as blood gushed between his fingers. The second goon watched helplessly, his reflexes too slow to prevent the blade from piercing through his chest and jutting out his back. His mouth gaped with disbelief, a look of terror crossing his face before his eyes rolled back, and he too collapsed to the floor.

Sándor revolved once more and advanced on Pozzo. The gangster was lying on his back, his arm flailing beneath the mattress in search of his gun. But the instant he felt the steel point jab into his neck, Pozzo raised his hands in the air, petrified.

"I have heard you are a reasonable man," heaved Sándor. "So I have a bargain for you. I let you live. You walk out of this place, and you leave New York." Sándor then went down on one knee, so he could speak directly into Pozzo's ear. "My name is Sándor, Count of Veszkovár. In my family, I am the sixteenth generation of swordfighters. I have killed twenty-seven men, before today. Now I have killed twenty-nine, although I would hardly call them *men*. If I see you in this city again, you will be number thirty. I will cut you into ribbons. I will show neither mercy nor regret. Do you understand?"

Pozzo only nodded into the floor, too afraid to open his eyes.

"Good," said Sándor. "I think it is time for us to be going."

Mr. Stacks watched the open entrance. The crowd had thinned inside the lobby. Some still loitered with glasses of wine, conversing leisurely, even as the lights dimmed once more, signaling imminent performance. But at least they were all inside. The last stragglers had vanished from the street.

Mr. Stacks took the handles of the doors and drew them closed. They sealed shut with a satisfying clink. Then he lumbered to the edge of the theater, and in the dark alleyway he found a nook in the brickwork. This was the place he had selected to hide the hemp ropes, which were still coiled in the shadows. He found the ropes easily and drew them into the light. He caressed the fibers with his thumb, feeling giddy as he sauntered back to the entrance. He unspooled the rope on the concrete, breathing faster as he found a frayed end and prepared to tie a knot.

Just then he heard a commotion behind him—clacking feet. Mr. Stacks turned toward the street, which was vacant and hazy. From the gathering mist emerged two feminine shapes, one petite and the other tall and voluptuous. Their hair bobbed as they ran, and the hems of their gowns flopped along their legs. They slowed when they saw the theater, and skipped to a halt.

"Oh!" wailed the redhead. "Don't tell us we're too late!"

"Miss..." Mr. Stacks felt the sheen of sweat on his face. He suddenly felt abashed. "Miss McDonnough," he stuttered. "How do you do?"

"Oh, Mr. Stacks," whined Ruby. "Please say you'll let us in!"

"But, Miss McDonnough, the doors are closed," he said automatically. "The show's about to start."

"But it hasn't started yet, has it?" said Tabatha. "Surely it's all right to sneak us in. We have our tickets and everything!

In Stacks' mind, the street became a vacuum, a place without time or temperature, surface or dimension. There was nothing here, only three people, a man and two young women. And they were all alive. Still alive. Still standing here. And they could keep living — if he just allowed them to. It was his decision, whether to let them live or die. He was the gatekeeper. With one word, he would decide their fate.

"Sorry, girls," he said, in a strained by kindly voice. "The door are closed. But I'll tell you a secret."

For a second they pouted, but the word "secret" enticed them. They leaned toward Mr. Stacks, ears turned.

"Tomorrow evening, there's a special performance. Top secret. It's just for the crème-de-la-crème. And because I like you, and because I know you'll enjoy it, I'll make sure you're admitted." Then he added, "As long as you're here on time."

"Oh, we will be!" Tabatha cried.

"See! This is what we get for taking the train!" scolded Ruby.

"It *was* a dumb idea," admitted Tabatha. "But that woman at our table made it sound so romantic! And didn't we have an adventure? Wasn't it swell, in its own way? You can't tell me it wasn't!"

"It *was* a wild time," said Ruby. "I'd even take the train

again, if I didn't have somewhere important to go."

"Why don't…" Mr. Stacks could barely catch his breath. "Why don't you girls get an ice cream? There's a soda fountain a few blocks down. It'll make you feel better." He dug into his pocket and pulled out some coins. "And because I feel so bad you missed the show, have one on me."

"Oh, you don't have to," said Tabatha. "But that's awfully nice of you, Mr. Stacks. My daddy is always saying so. 'That Mr. Stacks, he's a real gentleman. If he comes back in another life, I hope he gets a better deal.' That's what he says, exactly."

"Good night, Mr. Stacks!" called Ruby, and they scampered off, as carefree as children.

Mr. Stacks no longer felt the same thrill as he pulled the rope straight, then threaded it through the brass door handles. He searched for the same exhilaration, but tying each knot only filled him with foreboding. One minute, he had reveled in violence. Inflicting pain had excited him like nothing before in his life. Now he felt disgusted. The sight of those girls, their sweetness, had made it all seem so selfish.

And yet he kept tying his knots, until the handles were bound together as tightly as masts. He stepped back to survey his work. He pulled one of the handles, but it hardly moved. He pulled harder. Nothing. The doors would not budge. Mr. Stacks knew no particulars. The voice on the telephone had no told him what would happen inside. The voice had only promised vengeance. Their demise would be slow and terrible. And whatever happened, there would be no escape.

Mr. Stacks then remembered the final instruction. He reached into his pockets and pulled out two small objects. They were rubbery nibs, with only the circumference of a dime. He studied them for a moment, then stuck one in his ear. He pushed it hard into his aural grotto. Then he stuck the second plug in the other ear.

The street was empty. He could hear nothing. Now, all he

could do was wait.

The lights dimmed. Constance stifled a gasp. The crowd in the audience vanished from sight. A single spotlight pierced the darkness, right in the center of the orchestra pit. There, among the sea of musicians, stood an elder man with white muttonchops.

Alistair Bromley. The owner of the theater. The soft-spoken Englishman who had welcomed her when she arrived. It was *he* who would conduct the orchestra.

Applause flashed across the audience like wildfire. Hundreds of people rose to their feet, standing tall. Some had known that Bromley was once an accomplished conductor, but there had been no announcement. The audience cheered, hollered, called out: *"Hurrah! Bravo! Bless you, Mr. Bromley!"* His three bows only fed their excitement.

At last Bromley turned to the orchestra and tapped his music stand with his baton. A cacophony rose up as three-dozen players tested their instruments. Then Mr. Bromley raised his hands, and a powerful chord blew across the empty space.

The overture was low and rhythmic, a brooding mix of cello and drum. Then came tuneless blasts of the tuba, atonal thrumming of a harp, a tangled skein of syncopations that moved through one another with dizzying complexity. The sound was cold and savage—a war-call, a desperate threat. At last the violinists joined the fray, scissoring furiously at their strings, generating waves of fearsome melody. It was a sound both beautiful and sickening, like torrents of rain on a metal roof.

The curtain lifted. From behind it, the entire cast appeared. Nearly a hundred performers stood on risers, dressed in a multiplicity of costumes. Their skins were stained pale blue and flecked with gold paint; they wore chest plates, stolas, breast caps, and loincloths. They carried spears and shields and scimitars. They opened their mouths to sing.

It was all happening so fast—the overture was not a discrete piece, but rather it blended imperceptibly into the opening chorus. The voices seemed to fly in all directions at once. The blend of disparate tones was barely recognizable as harmony; it sounded more like a doleful moan, a funereal chant. The sound amplified, smoothed out, until it coalesced into a sinister wail.

Constance watched the audience. They winced. They shifted. They looked uncomfortable, as if uncertain what it was they were watching. One man shook his head in disbelief. A woman burst into tears. But the sound transfixed them with its malevolent beauty, its roar of vocalized despair.

And then, abruptly, the music ceased. The instruments stopped playing. The mouths of the chorus snapped shut. Everything was silent and still. The absence of sound left a void that seemingly nothing could fill.

Except for Constance.

It was time. She took the plugs in her hand and wedged them hastily into her ears—just as she had been instructed over the telephone. When they were securely fastened, she could hear nothing. She felt disoriented, mute, stumbling through the dark wings, deafened by the infernal plugs.

She felt the overhead lamps shining down on her. She sensed their peculiar heat on her skin. She sauntered downstage, her harem pants swishing with each stride. The lack of sound frightened her, but she could *see* everything. The audience rose again. Their hands clapped wildly together, their faces turned feverish with exultation. She could see them all, these living people. She watched their soundless ovation. She waited for it to subside, but they kept going. In the absence of noise, she felt the warm breeze of their movement. She could *feel* their praise.

Constance wanted them to go on and on. Every second they clapped, she could defer her aria a little longer. Maybe they would clap all night, preserving this joyful moment. She would never have to open her mouth, just stand there, communing with these beautiful strangers.

But gradually they settled down. They reseated themselves. She observed the quieting of the room, the entropic retreat. Now she felt the all-consuming silence, the expectance, the desire. She could delay no longer. The time had come.

Constance stood in the middle of the stage. She gulped down a breath, but she knew that wouldn't be enough. She blew it out, then inhaled as long as she could. Just as she had always trained to do. She lifted her chin. She extended her arms, like a raven taking flight. Her mouth dropped open.

She barely heard the sound that erupted. It was like being underwater and listening to a mechanical drone. It sounded distant and strange. But she could *sense* it, vibrating inside her tortured throat, like water gushing through a fire hose. The sound vomited out of her, emanating through the room. She realized her eyes were closed, so she opened them.

Constance watched the people in the audience. They covered their ears with their hands. They cringed in pain. They blenched with surprise. But she could feel the power building inside her. The voice rose in pitch, increased in volume. Her cheeks pulsated around the explosion of sound. Now people were doubling over, their mouths agape, their eyes clenched. People fell out of their seats. They crawled on the floor. They trembled and collapsed into fetal positions.

And then she saw it: A woman stood up, tall and skinny. Her face was ghostly white. Her eyes were large as golf balls. Her head cocked sideways, and blood dribbled from her ears, splattering the man next to her. She jolted, as if struck by a rock, and crumpled lifelessly into her seat.

211

Near her, a heavyset man screamed, the veins in his neck nearly bursting—and then it happened: His eyeball popped from its socket, dangling over his chest by gory strings.

Over and over Constance watched them, people who were clearly shrieking in agony, though they couldn't hear their own voices. Their eardrums spat blood, their bodies buckled beneath them. They tripped over each other, descended into piles of flailing limbs. Bodies toppled over the balconies, dropping like grain sacks into the chaos below. Men galloped to the lobby entrance and pushed with all their might. But the doors wouldn't budge; they only juddered mockingly in their frames. One by one, they felt their brains hemorrhage in their skulls, and they fell to the carpet, dead. Constance watched them, knowing it was her voice that was killing them, her own lungs that wrought their demise.

Tears blurred her vision, but they could not distort the face of Alistair Bromley, who stared at her in horror, palms pressed against his ears. He seemed to curse at her with his dying eyes, even as blood squirted through his fingers, his eyes went white, and he fell forward, impaling himself on a cymbal stand.

At last her breath ran out. The muted sound she heard diminished. Her neck muscles relaxed, now sore and tender. She fell to one knee. She acclimated to the total silence. She panted for air.

Constance reached to her ear with trembling fingers and withdrew a plug. Then she heard it: The screams and moans of the people still living, the ones her voice had failed to slay. She looked around and saw them—scattered individuals, crawling through the bog of corpses, weeping and crying for someone to save them. She swiveled around, and there lay the chorus, their cadavers flopped over the risers like so much discarded laundry.

She wanted to cry out, but she couldn't. To unleash her voice again was to sentence the survivors to certain death. She couldn't so much as whisper, such was the lethal power of her vocal chords.

Tonight, I am the God of Death, she thought. *Tonight I beckon the end of the world.*

"Step on it!" shouted Elizabeth as the taxi careened around another corner.

"I'll get a ticket!" hollered the driver.

"Bill me!" Elizabeth shot back.

The avenue looked familiar, but the rolling fog had confused Elizabeth's sense of direction. The overloaded taxi wove through the streets, narrowly missing a wagon, then nearly clipped a badly parked truck. Elizabeth was glad there wasn't much traffic at this hour, only clusters of pedestrians, who raced out of the way of their speeding cab.

Elizabeth crinkled her nose.

"Do you hear that?" she said aloud.

"You mean—dogs barking?" Maude said.

"Dogs barking?" asked Sándor incredulously from the front seat.

But then they all heard it. The sound came from all directions: Dogs barked and howled, whistled and whined. Even as wind blew through the open windows, they could hear the gathering choir of howls. It was as if the entire neighborhood had awakened every canine at once, and they had all gone to the windows of their apartments to bay at the sky.

"You hear a lot of dogs around here," slurred the driver dismissively. "I remember this one time—"

Something slammed against the windshield. The glass crackled, and a blotch of blood emerged at the point of impact. The women screamed as the driver swerved. The dark city blurred beyond the windows. Tires screeched, until they finally clunked to a stop.

"What in God's name was *that?*" shouted Elizabeth.

Before they could consult one another, Sándor threw open his door and bounded through a gray puddle. He looked up and around, examining the high brick walls of the tenement buildings, the triangular patterns of their fire escapes, but nothing seemed amiss. Then he looked down at the front of the car and knitted his brow in disgust.

A poodle was sprawled across the hood. Its paws twitched repulsively as its body allowed itself to die. The skull was crushed and its curly white fur was matted with blood. The scene was all the more ominous as the howls of distant dogs augmented across the night sky, sounding more tortured with every second. These were not hounds happily calling to the moon. They were suffering animals, expressing their agony.

"The sound weapon," Sándor exclaimed.

"Where?" said Elizabeth, struggling out of the car.

"Listen!"

Then they heard it: Beyond the yowling of the dogs, they could just discern a single human voice—yet not *precisely* human. The high F had a mechanical tone, like a train whistle, a tea kettle, a foghorn. Even at a great distance, they scowled at the irritating pitch. Elizabeth could taste mucus in her mouth, and she felt a radical desire to retch. She watched the others teeter dizzily, and her thoughts jumbled in her mind.

All at once, the sound died out. Some dogs continued to yawp, but far away.

"You can keep your money," said the driver, starting the car again. "Youse guys are too much for me!"

"Wait!" Elizabeth yelled, but the car was already wheeling around. Within seconds, the driver and his shattered windshield had vanished into the fog.

"Fine then," Elizabeth snorted. "Let's get a move on."

"What if they use the weapon again?" said Sándor.

"That's a risk we'll have to take." Elizabeth was already jogging down the pavement. "Come on, Sándor! I thought you had an appetite for danger!"

The theater stood only a few blocks away, but the setting had already changed. Dogs lay in the street, blood draining from their ears. Lamps buzzed over the theater's moniker, but otherwise the place was silent. As Elizabeth approached, she saw the ropes that bound the door handles together. Then she saw a man, obese and groaning, slumped against the wall. She recognized him immediately—the man with the monocle, who had tried to deny her entry. His eyepiece had fallen out. He hugged himself, shivering like an abandoned child.

"Are you all right?" Elizabeth said.

The man didn't respond to her voice, but when she came close enough, his head shot up, startled. He looked terrified of her presence.

"HELP ME!" he cried. "I CAN'T HEAR! I CAN'T HEAR!" He fell onto his side, and as Elizabeth considered his frantic eyes and trembling body, she realized he'd lost his senses. "THEY TRIED TO ESCAPE!" he wailed. "THEY TRIED TO GET OUT! I... I... I TOOK THE PLUGS OUT! I... I THOUGHT..."

Elizabeth grabbed the ropes. She examined them, agitated, trying to puzzle out their knots. But she could see they were too tight to untie. The humid air had moistened them, holding them fast. She whirled around, calling, "Sándor! I need your sword!"

Sándor sprinted toward her, ripping the blade from its sheath. He swung down, and its razor edge slashed effortlessly through the twisted fibers. Elizabeth yanked open the door and flew inside—but the moment she entered, she stumbled into a heavy mass on the floor and nearly fell head over heels.

Elizabeth shuddered, hopscotching between arms and legs. Her feet were clumsy as she stepped through the piles of carnage. Her shoe landed on ears and fingers, ankles and wrists. At last she found a clear space on the floor, and she moved through the lobby, toward the silent auditorium.

Corpses lay everywhere. The floor was a quilt of tuxedoes and gowns, the pallid faces twisted into expressions of horror. Broken survivors slithered through the heaps. Elizabeth heard bawling in the corners, rustling in the aisles, yet overall the room was as quiet as the morgue it had become.

Elizabeth trembled as she looked up to the stage. There, in the middle of the stage, crouched Constance Violeta, weeping softly. She was barely recognizable in her silver face-paint, her gold turban and sparkling dress.

"Violeta!" Elizabeth called.

The woman flinched, then looked up at Elizabeth. Her expression was desolate, like a condemned woman before her executioner. Elizabeth made herself smile as reassuringly as she could.

"Violeta, it's all right," she said. "I'm here to help you."

Violeta fell onto her back. She started to crabwalk away. She looked frightened, mortified. But Elizabeth continued her advance, stepping clumsily through the slaughtered masses.

"I know he took your child," cooed Elizabeth. "I know he made you do it—coming to New York, the surgery. *This*." She gestured to the carpet of bodies . "But it's all right. Anyone would have done the same. What wouldn't we do to save a child?"

Violeta sniffed, and then the tears poured out. Her body heaved with anguish.

"It's all right," said Elizabeth, reaching the orchestra pit. "I'm going to help you."

Despite the ringing in her ears, Elizabeth could hear a commotion in the wings. She glanced sideways, and then she saw it—a figure, stepping out of the darkness. He wore a tuxedo. His silver mop of hair blazed beneath the stage lights.

A small pistol dangled from his limp right hand.

"*Herr Schteyrn!*" cried Elizabeth. "*Stay right where you are!*"

Schteyrn's face was as ashen as the carcasses around them. He stopped and hung his head. After a long moment, he lifted the pistol—slowly, as he might raise a drawbridge. The gun was small and snub-nosed, yet he seemed barely able to elevate it.

"Alexander," said Elizabeth, quieter now. "You needn't do this. Whatever he said, whatever he promised you, it's not worth it."

"He..." Schteyrn swallowed croakily. "He took my wife."

"Your—*wife?*"

Schteyrn hadn't the vigor to nod, but Elizabeth knew it was true. He snuffled, then said, "No one even knew. We lived such a private life. We needed no one. No public. No admirers. Only us. Together. Alone." His lips curled tartly. "And then he took her. In the night. One moment, she was in the garden. The next moment, I could not find her anywhere. I searched the house, the grounds. I drove to town. She was nowhere. And then he called me—on the telephone. He said, *Tell no one.* He told me to compose an opera. An homage to the death of the world."

Tears rolled down his glistening cheeks. The gun barrel was aimed at nothing in particular, but it remained aloft, a deadly threat.

"And then this. After I agreed to everything. After I composed his filthy music. I met Frau Violeta, and realized that she, too, was a victim of this madmen. After I realized the truth—we have this horror in common. My wife, her daughter. And we could tell no one else. At least we shared this secret. At least we had each other." Schteyrn's lips vibrated with shifting emotion. "*Then* he sent me a note. One final instruction." He looked on Violeta with marble eyes and turned his head sideways. "To kill God—or rather, the woman who *plays* God."

"You don't have to!" said Elizabeth. "Think, Herr Schteyrn! I know the grief is killing you, but *think!* Didn't Dr. Vermilion make Madame Violeta the same promise? Didn't he promise to return her child in exchange for the surgery? For using the sound weapon? If she only massacres these people, just like she's done, shouldn't she get her baby back?"

Schteyrn frowned uncertainly. The pistol quivered in his grasp.

"Yet if you kill her," Elizabeth persisted, "doesn't that mean that Dr. Vermilion has betrayed her? Doesn't that mean she *won't* have her child back, despite his guarantee? Now listen…" Elizabeth spoke quieter now, almost a whisper. "What makes you think he'll keep his promise to you? He wants you to shoot Madame Violeta—not to kill God, but to make *you* responsible. Everyone will think you hatched this plot yourself! They'll think you killed your own wife and hid her body! Don't you see? He's trying to pin this whole charade on *you*. And if you do this, if you pull that trigger, no one will ever believe a word you say. They'll call you a lunatic, a mass murderer." Elizabeth reached out her hands. "But *I* know the truth. And I swear to you, Herr Schteyrn, if you just put down that gun, I will find your wife, and I will bring her back to you. And we'll make this monster pay for what he's done—to you, to all these people. We'll punish him a hundredfold. But first, you have to trust me."

Elizabeth watched something click in Schteyrn's mind. He seemed to rouse from a dream, to realize that he was awake, that he was here, in this theater. His eyes focused on the gun, which he turned in his hand, as if wondering what it was.

"Please," Elizabeth said. "There's only one way out of this."

Schteyrn nodded once. Then he shut his eyes, stood up straight, and drew the pistol to his head.

"You're right," he said.

The blast echoed through the hall.

There were times when Maude found herself sitting in one place for an hour or more, and she realized how much it vexed her. She had spent so much of her life doing precisely this — perched on a sofa, knees locked together, hands in her lap, waiting for something to happen. She didn't like this feeling of merely occupying space, here on the sofa of her stuffy Clutterbuck hotel room.

She wasn't alone: Santorini moved busily about the quarters, stopping before every horizontal surface to whisk it with a feather duster. He hummed to himself a nondescript tune, and every now and again he stopped to appraise himself in the mirror, suck in his belly, and frown in disappointment.

"I *have* to lay off the bourbon steak," carped Santorini. He briefly regarded Maude and sighed. "Waistlines are wasted on the skinny."

"How do you mean?" demanded Maude, suddenly ruffled.

Santorini put one arm akimbo, and the feather duster flared behind him like a peacock's tail. "Honey, I've seen olive oil less virginal than you."

Maude opened her mouth to protest, but no words would come, and by the time she could think of a retort, the front door clicked open and Elizabeth and Sándor entered the room.

Sándor looked as steadfast as ever — straight-backed, firm-jawed, his single benevolent eye glinting in the morning sunlight. But Elizabeth slouched with fatigue. She hobbled forward with all the elegance of an icebox, and when she finally paused to look at Maude, her eyes looked sleepy, her expression withdrawn.

"How is Madame Violeta?" asked Maude.

"She's recovering," said Elizabeth as she tossed her cloche hat on the piano bench and sprawled out in one of the high-backed chairs. "But she's in good spirits, considering. Looks like the doctors will remove the implant from her throat. She'll never talk again, let alone sing, but at least she won't be a danger to anyone. That seemed to be a relief to her." Elizabeth unlaced her boots and strained to pull them off, then added, "I think she's adjusting to the truth."

"The truth?"

"Well, Dr. Vermilion has no reason to hurt an infant. But I can't believe he'll give her back, either."

"You mean Violeta's daughter?"

"Exactly."

"He'll just—*keep* her?"

"Hard to say. But I wouldn't be surprised. He'll do anything for leverage, I'm sure."

Elizabeth dropped the second boot to the floor and yawned. Her body seemed to deflate into the fabric of the chair.

"Seems the doorman was in on it, too," mumbled Elizabeth.

"The doorman!" peeped Maude. "You mean the fellow with the monocle?"

"Just the one. Sounds like he was offered a good sum of money to rope up the doors. He claims he didn't know what would happen, but I think he had a good idea."

"How awful," said Maude.

"Well, a broken man is a hard thing to fix. And he looked pretty well busted."

They sat in silence for a moment. The room felt stuffy and impersonal. Maude was ready to leave this place. The French Room had never been her style, and she looked forward to fresh air, open skies, movement, momentum. Now that the excitement was over, she was ready for something new. She felt a sudden desire to climb mountains, ford rivers, fly in an airplane. She heard a voice inside her call out, *What are we waiting for?*

And then, as if by magic, Elizabeth piped up: "Say, Maude, how would you like to go to Europe?"

Maude nearly fell off the sofa. "To... *Europe?*"

Elizabeth glanced at Sándor and smirked. "I think there's an echo in the room."

"But—when?"

"How about a week from today?" said Elizabeth. "We'll book passage on a steamship. You've never been on a steamship, have you?"

"Why—*no!* Or any ship, for that matter!"

"Well, what do you say? Care to spend a few months gallivanting around the Old Country?"

"Well—*yes!* Of course! But is that all right?" She glanced at both of them. "I'm not intruding, am I?"

"Not at all," said Sándor. "I am not going with you. Not yet. I will meet you there. You see, Elizabeth and I have—" He searched for the right word.

"We have some business to attend to," finished Elizabeth.

"Does it..." Maude touched her earlobe nervously. "Does it have to do with your ring?"

Elizabeth flushed, and then she crossed her legs. "Well, Maude, since you ask, yes. Yes it does."

Sándor paled. He took a step toward her and murmured, "Elizabeth!"

"It's all right, I haven't told her anything." Then she smiled. "At least not yet."

ACKNOWLEDGEMENTS

Given my career as a journalist and playwright, this book is a wild departure for me. Like many a wild departure, it could not have been written — much less unveiled — without the enthusiastic support of friends and loved ones.

The release of this book finally gives me the chance to thank The Rahnd Table, my fiction-writing group in Pittsburgh, for all the nights of workshopping, reveling, bellyaching, gossiping, and telling risqué jokes. Particular thanks goes to Nathan Kukulski, my most trusted editor, the designer of this badass cover, and just a really awesome friend.

None of this would be possible without the love and support of our my wife Kylan, whose good advice is always making decent ideas so much better.